The Eleventh Joke

Also by Errol Bray

Berzoo
The Quarters
The Choir

non-fiction

Playbuilding
Are We Heroes?

The Eleventh Joke

a novel by

ERROL BRAY

rainshadow

ISBN: (paperback) ISBN: 978-1-7645843-1-9

Published by rainshadow, an imprint of Clouds of Magellan Press, Melbourne
www.cloudsofmagellanpress.net

Distributed in Australia by John Reed Books

Cover Design: Gordon Thompson

Only when an idea has been expressed in three versions
and laughed at once
can it be said truly to exist.

Drew Red, Eleventh

DREW

Bright red men fired arrows as our small plane swooped over the highland jungle. Barton, the pilot, was amazed at how high those arrows were flying and he pulled us away, up higher into the sky. I could see a clearing below but Barton had warned me before we took off from Moresby that he would not risk a landing. I was going to have to parachute in. Barton was from this region of the New Guinea forests and was very cautious of the place.

I was pleased to see the red men because we were at the exact location of the map co-ordinates I had been given. Their presence was a proof that the amazing notes and ramblings of the old prospector might hold some truth.

"Are you sure you want to do this?" Barton asked. His black, round, grinning face was more or less daring me. He wanted to see this crazy white journalist falling into that jungle. He probably had a bet on with the other pilots at the airfield as to my survival.

"I have no choice," I said.

Then I jumped.

I woke up three days later in a beautiful room that belonged in an elegant French mansion of several centuries ago. Except for the truly enormous TV set. My head was not all clear yet. The rescue by the tribespeople had been rather confusing, seen through a semi-conscious blur. Now this ornate room with painted angels floating about on its ceiling. When I opened my eyes a woman who was apparently nursing me ran from the room calling out something in a language that sounded remarkably like Norwegian. That was not a language I spoke but one that I recognised because one of my grandmothers was Norwegian.

I struggled to sit up in the sumptuous bed as a woman rushed to bring me several extra cushions. Another woman hurried in with a large breakfast tray which she placed on an ornate side-table and then across my legs when I had settled. She held some water to my lips and I drank. Neither woman was painted red. Both were very dark, shiny black and quite beautiful.

The breakfast was some sort of poached fish with poached eggs on thin, dry toast. A tall, thin, extraordinarily old, red man came into the room and also spoke in Norwegian. I shook my head and said carefully, "English. I only speak English."

"Dear me," the red man said, "you Australians might call your language English but one might as well say that a New Yorker or a Canadian or even a New Zealander speaks in English. It's not polo, old chap. Not polo at all."

"Do you mean not cricket? Is that …"

"Silly, silly, silly me," the red one chuckled. "I was so busy teasing you that I forgot how long it is since I spoke English. We tend to use a lot of Polish and Hungarian in the village. They like those for some reason. How foolish I've been. I've had them all nattering away at you in Norwegian because from your facial features, especially your eyebrows, you reminded me a great deal of Henrik Ibsen, the marvellous Norwegian playwright. Such a lovely man, although he could be cantankerous at times."

"I do have a Norwegian grandmother, so perhaps …"

"Of course. That's what it is."

"But if I must look like a playwright then I'd rather look like Shakespeare."

"And who wouldn't? Indeed."

The old red man was studying me closely. I tried some of the breakfast and it tasted awful. But before I had time to try a second mouthful it was whisked away and replaced by sausages with fried eggs and tomato, with thick, buttered toast. The pot of coffee was swapped for a big mug of tea.

"Please tell me why you are here, young man."

"I came to see you, sir."

He giggled and flashed his eyes at me. I was a little shocked that he was making something sexual out of that innocent statement.

"How exciting," he trilled. "I can't remember the last time a handsome young man – or a handsome young woman for that matter – jumped out of an aeroplane to be by my side. What a compliment."

"It's your stories. I want to hear your stories. I've read the old prospector's diaries."

"Ah. The diaries. Ah, yes. The stories. I must take a nap and then I'll see you for lunch. I'm old you know. I tire easily."

"I'm sorry. I hope I haven't said anything to offend you."

"How could a boy with such blue, blue, blue eyes offend anybody? *Au contraire, mon cher.*"

And with that he kissed me on the forehead and drifted out of the room. This was not really what I had expected.

BUTTERFLY JUICE

"We called it butterfly juice." The red face burst into laughter. The laughter went on and on until I feared that the face really would explode. "Butterflies are the nearest earthly equivalent creatures to the particular, gorgeous and indescribable animals from my own place that the juice actually comes from. We milk it from them. We don't have to kill them. Goodness me, no." The red one chuckled. "I would not be here to tell these tales if I had ever attempted to kill one. Naturally, there are a lot of chemical additives. Naturally." He burst into laughter again.

I was sitting in a drawing room that belonged in the same elegant French mansion as the bedroom did. My head was now almost clear but still buzzing from trying to reconcile the inside of this house with the jungle I had parachuted into. The coffee we sipped was excellent and was certainly helping my overwhelmed brain to get a grip on itself.

"Let me tell you some stories," my red companion said and laughed again, but gently this time. "These are stories from all over the North-West Segment. That was where I worked. It's roughly Europe and Britain and Russia now. Oh yes, and Ireland. The team sent me there a few times. I was fond of the Irish. But then, I'm sentimental. I became infamously sentimental. I became overly fond of lots of our little guinea pigs, our laboratory rats, our human monkeys."

In amongst the strangeness of this whole idea, my strange thought was to wonder if all the metaphors, examples and adjectives in the stories would be given in triplicate.

"I won't baffle you with language or overwhelming data. My memory is not always scientifically exact. They wouldn't let me keep a copy of the slates. But the basic stories will tell you what the project was all about. And maybe you'll even be able to guess the outcome. I'll tell it in simple, colloquial language. I'll be like a friend reading you stories from an old-fashioned book and updating the words as I go along to help you understand. There'd be no point telling you the Russian adventures in Russian or the Italian tales in 15th century Italian or the Elizabethan episodes in the English of that day."

Another triple, I told myself. I reached for my tape-recorder but hesitated.

"You can record if you wish. None of it will do you any good, except that you will know the truth and some people do enjoy being in that position. By telling you my stories I'm condemning you to a future of madness. You won't be mad, of course – unless your brain is much weaker than all your physical signs suggest; your hands especially are well-formed – but you will, should you choose to tell my stories, be treated like a crazy person, like a loon, like the mentally deranged."

Three, again!

"I'll keep the scientific jargon to a minimum." Perhaps my inept fumbling with the rudimentary tape-recorder had prompted this comment. "The fact is that unless you have a detailed knowledge of the sub-algebraic links between the numbers 11 and seven … Base 10 of course. I will use your own parameters, limited though they be. Suffice to say that everything I tell you will be absolutely true, no matter how strange. I might add in a joke here or there – we Red people love jokes – and I might get a point wrong inadvertently – a misremembered date, the wrong hair colouring, an incorrect name – but the tales are true in their substance."

"Why did you …?" I began to ask, but a Red hand was held aloft to stop me.

"Some stories first, then you can ask questions. You're going to be here for several weeks I would guess. The Port Moresby authorities like to retrieve the bodies of foolish white folk who try exploring these jungles. And won't they be delighted to find you alive and well? So we should make your stay entertaining for you. We'll tell it like a novel. That's what you'll do with this material I should think. Your forehead reminds me of Dickens; your ears are like Tolstoy's; your lips are like Proust's."

I smiled to myself as I realised that I was in for weeks of glorious name-dropping. Sitting before me – from what little I already knew – was the name-dropping champion of the entire universe. I wasn't sure how thrilled I was about having Proust-like lips. I always thought he would be a rather prissy and pouty sort of person.

"What happened to Ibsen?" I joked.

"Oh no, no. Now that I know you a little I can see the novelist template stamped all over you."

"I've never written a novel, but then I suppose I am still young."

"Yes, you are. Of course, at my age, everybody in the whole world is delightfully young. Now, Old Red will help you shape your very first novel. How exciting. Let's have a beginning, a middle and an end." I didn't have the heart to tell him that this wasn't the way most novels were written any more. "I like packages of threes. The beginning will be some of the historical stories and I expect they will tantalise you. The middle will be the explanation which will bother you, even if it doesn't surprise you. The end will depress you at first but soon you'll have third thoughts and realise how uplifting it all is and what a splendid joke it is. We called it the eleventh joke or joke 11 or we would just laugh eleven times."

Red did that. Ha-ha-ha-ha-ha-ha-ha-ha-ha-ha-ha. It was a very disturbing sound. The Red face quivered and some tears came and he covered his face for a few moments with a colourful cushion.

"The end was not merely the finish of the joke but also the end of me, Drew, Red creature from the Eleventh. My ending was also a joke. Of course, there will be another ending. There'll be your ending. You'll become a Cassandra, a prophet ridiculed, the rejected repository of a great truth. You'll know enough to re-write the history of the world – the whole world, not only the North-West Sector. [My transcripts are accurate. Sometimes he said "segment" and sometimes "sector". He claimed English was not precise enough to translate many Red words with the nuances they deserved.] But you won't be believed. It has happened to many people, of course. William Blake, Lewis Carroll – my lovely, reverend gentleman – and Vincent. Van Gogh, in case you were wondering. They were all such literal men. They insisted on telling and showing the exact, blunt, total truth. But who ever believed them? They are now revered, respected, made out to be geniuses for their brilliant imaginations, but never believed literally. And all three did so much want to be believed.

"But I think I should tickle your taste with a tale about my first meeting with your own personal favourite writer."

WILL

Will did not resist the needle. Drew, the Red man, pressed the fine point against Will's head, found the correct mapping position and thrust the needle deep into the brain. He held Will's head steady and firm, fearing a sudden, drunken twisting. They had all become very drunk, except Drew, whose drunkenness was always a performance. Now, he watched the large syringe slowly empty its green liquid into the brain. It had not been difficult to get Will drunk. His life was not exciting. He had married at 18 and no choice in that matter. Now there were three children. The twins were still being carried by Anne and would be delivered in about three months. There was the shop. Gloves! Indeed, not an exciting 1ife.

The syringe was half empty when Drew heard footsteps and then a soft but urgent tapping on the door. All of the others had passed out. Who would, or could, follow them to this attic where he had dragged Will?

"Mr Shakespeare? Are you awake?" the voice asked softly.

It was the tavern boy; blond, pretty, very effeminate and named Robert. The boy had watched Will all night, played games with him and touched him too often. Twice, Will had patted the boy's bottom and made teasing remarks. Clearly, Robert had read more into this than was meant. The boy had helped Drew carry Will up here so he knew Will was in the attic. Surely, he must have realised that Will would be incapable of any activity at all for many hours. Drew had not yet adjusted to an understanding of the obsessiveness of human male love and lust.

The door opened slowly. Drew panicked. Here he was pumping green liquid into Will Shakespeare's head. The boy would scream. Drew would be found with the weird instrument. He would be burnt at the stake as bewitched. Or was this the right century for that? Drew pulled the needle out of Will's head and threw it out the window. He didn't have a chance to register the exact amount of formula that had been pumped into the brain. No matter. A number of experiments had failed. Will Shakespeare would be another failure.

The syringe bounced down the thatched roof and fell over the edge, sticking into the rump of an old mare that was wearily dragging its owner and his cart home through the dark night. The horse was too old and tired to take much notice of this new ache and shook the object off after a while. The syringe was lost in long grass on the outskirts of the town. It would be dug up 383 years later by one Richard Billings who would use it to claim that flying saucers had once landed at Stratford-upon-Avon. He was eventually hospitalised. The horse, during the last years of its life, would become renowned as a circus freak that could tap out answers to complex questions with its hooves. It would be reputed to have spoken several sentences on one occasion.

"What do you want, boy?" Drew hissed.

"I'm sorry, sir. I didn't know you were still with Mr Shakespeare. I was worried for him, sir. He was so drunk."

"You thought he might be so drunk that you would be able to steal his purse."

"No, sir! Some might do that but not me. And not to Mr Shakespeare," Robert declared.

"How old are you, boy?"

"Fifteen."

"Don't be scared. I know why you came here but he's a married man. You won't succeed with him." Drew reminded himself that perhaps the formula would change that, if enough had been injected.

"The married ones are usually more willing, sir. Tavern boys don't have babies."

The lad was certainly brazen. Drew reached out a hand to him. There was no more work to be done tonight so he might as well enjoy himself. And the boy was so pretty.

"I have money in my purse," Drew said.

"You're a strange one, sir," Robert said. "I've never seen a man with such red hair before. Are you a foreigner?"

"My mother was Irish." It was the stock answer.

"I don't mind if you're Irish, sir. So long as you isn't French."

[The reader will note that occasionally the story teller remembered a quaintness of speech. However, he did not attempt any consistent, historical accuracy with speech mannerisms or phraseology. I often thought that was unfortunate, but at least we have the stories.]

Drew and Robert made love then slept. Robert was delighted that Drew was Irish. He had never met an Englishman who could give such pleasure. Will woke and saw the boy asleep in Drew's arms.

"You got a pretty one there, Drew," Will said, clutching his head. "My bloody brain is on fire. I feel like death. Last time I go drinking with you. Where's my pants?"

"You've got them on." Drew laughed heartily at this, much more heartily than the observation deserved.

Will struggled out of the bed. He put his boots on with great difficulty and found his coat on the chair. He lurched to the door. "Got to get to the shop. I'll have the sharp edge of her tongue today. Stay single, Drew. Marriage is hell."

Will Shakespeare stumbled down the stairs, cursing the pain in his head. Drew regretted the boy's interruption last night because Will had been the wild card in the experiment. Drew liked the risky ones. It made the research more interesting. What was the point of always using people like Socrates and Dante and Homer? [Oh, yes, there was a Homer. I have it from this descendant of an eyewitness.] These men were absolute certainties. This Shakespeare could have been a real test. Ordinary, not much learning, not much talent. But he did have a great deal of what was called common sense and he told a good story. However, without the full dose, there would be 1ittle effect on him. Perhaps Will Shakespeare would become the best glove-seller in Stratford, unbeatable at card games, and the local wit.

After a hearty burst of laughter, Old Red stretched like a cat and then started settling into his big armchair for a rest. He was watching me keenly to see my reactions to his story. I was impressed, naturally, but not yet convinced.

"That memory always brings to mind my favourite English word, genius. I think I need to relish that word for an hour or so. We have plenty of time. The truth is I'm getting old and I need more naps now. In the 16th and 17th centuries I hardly ever slept at all. Things were so exciting then. I'll tell you some more stories soon. Be patient, blue-eyed boy."

The heavy, Red lids closed and sleep seemed immediately to engulf the slim body. These short naps were to become part of the regular pattern of our meetings. After a few moments of staring, I left the French drawing room, which somehow was a grass and wooden hut in its outside appearance, and walked into the village. The people were going about their business – cooking, making weapons, gossiping, playing games, creating a new mask. The women were doing most of the work. The men talked and planned tomorrow's hunting. Except for the inside of the hut I had just left, the village was typical of villages all through the unspoilt mountains of the highlands. Well, there were two other differences. Many of the tribespeople had dyed themselves red and they all seemed to speak nine or ten European languages. They would switch from Hungarian to Spanish in mid-sentence if the subject matter required it. Or so I was told. Not speaking anything but English and a collection of yes, no, thank you, good morning, where-is-the-post-office words and phrases from several other languages meant I was an uneducated nincompoop amongst this bunch of near-naked savages.

I was here in this incredible village because I had seen a small, sad piece in a newspaper. It told how in 1983 a white prospector came staggering out of a mountain jungle in Papua New Guinea, perfectly healthy after months of being lost but definitely crazy. He babbled stories of creatures from another galaxy, tribes of red people speaking Hungarian and miraculous electronic equipment. Worst of all, he claimed that he had been watching Chinese TV, in full colour, on a five-metre-square television screen that was made from some silvery, liquid substance. All this in a region where the people were known to be living stone-age lives. The red people could be accepted but the TV story proved the man was crazy. And crazy people often see space creatures, don't they?

I was an eager young journalist, always on the lookout for weirdness. I found the prospector. I shamelessly plied him with alcohol which was then his only consolation in life. He entrusted me with his diaries which were scribbled notes, lacking any real detail except for lists of names of hundreds of long-dead, famous Europeans. The words slates, butterfly juice, genius, eleven and red appeared often. But there was something invaluable in the diaries that was very clearly noted, the geographic location of this supposed village of red Hungarians.

Although I now know that the basic facts of this man's tales were true, he was crazy. He had forgotten what our society does to people who have irregular experiences with TV sets and who meet beings from outer space. Not that Red Drew was exactly a "space creature", but the effect was much the same. When I too staggered out of that mountain jungle in 1987, I was sane enough to keep my mouth shut about, well, about everything. I was particularly careful to remain silent about the off-planet person I had met and its amazing tale of inter-genus meddling in Earth's history over the past 3,000 years – and even before that, if the history books of his people can be believed. As with Earth's history, just because an event seems to be incredibly stupid or highly unlikely does not mean it didn't happen. In fact, given the general trend in human history towards perversity, stubborn ignorance and self-centred pig-headedness, stupid and unlikely events are likely to be the norm.

I remained silent until I could compose a book to relate the new history of Western civilisation. And I particularly remained silent until I got the pre-arranged message which told me that Old Red had died: a small, brilliant, signed drawing by Monet of a butterfly, sketched in his garden at Giverny. Proof of a kind that my entire story is true. Where would someone like me ever get an original Monet? Only if some alien being despatched it to me from the jungles of New Guinea as he was dying. Doesn't that seem perfectly plausible?

Added to this, about a week later I received a letter from the Red one himself. It was his dying exhortation that I should tell the world the broad truth about human history. There was also a colour photograph included: Drew with Monet in the wondrous garden at

Giverny. Monet looks resplendent in a creamy-white suit and hat and snow-white beard. Drew also looks marvellous in a pearl-grey suit and a bowler hiding his red hair. I have the photo on my desk as I write.

The letter explained to me that Drew had the honour of having operated on Monet's eyes to cure him of his cataracts. Despite his limited medical knowledge, Drew was able to give Monet a few last years of clear sight. What a gift! The history books explain the eyesight business in other terms but Drew assures me the yellow tints and the special glasses were a cover-up he organised with Monet to disguise the off-world nature of the "miracle".

The painting graces my writing room still and the photo remains on the desk. The letter disintegrated. The cunning Old Red obviously did not want too many tangible proofs. He had warned me in the letter that I should remember that Tells, his word for us humans, liked our gods to act in mysterious, even perverse, ways. Human perversity is made in the image of our chosen gods. Or are our gods made in the image of human perversity? Old Red's warning suggested that people might believe a book – as happens with a number of human religions – over tangible proofs. So, I have to admit that all the items I have from Old Red could be easily explained away and should not be treated as icons of some new religion.

The recordings might have been made by actors. The Monet butterfly could be a forgery or maybe I found it in a little antique shop somewhere and concocted this tale around a lucky discovery. What about the photographs? Many still exist and have been published widely. It is not only my photo of Drew with Monet that is evidence. In the photos of him with Diaghilev and the Ballets Russes company or with Einstein or with Picasso, Rimbaud, Brecht,

Grimes, Churchill, Wilde, Jones, and the list goes on, Drew is identifiable once you know it is him. Or her as sometimes happened. But who could prove it? Every character can be traced to a personage of the time. The same is true for the paintings and drawings in which he appears, including very famous pictures by Rembrandt, Caravaggio and Goya, to name but three.

Despite the difficulties, I have faith that this book will make sense to many readers. Incidents can be traced back to historical facts that cannot be disputed and in many cases have never been explained. For example, Mozart's brief disappearance at the age of ten and his deformed skull. But I must not try to tumble the whole story out in one mad rush. My passion for the story and the truths it reveals has to be restrained. I will try to tell it how it was told to me, although re-ordered a little into an historical timeline when possible. There were occasions, however, when Drew would not be constrained by chronology and would combine comparative stories about twenty-five or so geniuses from several nations across four or more centuries into one session of historical narration.

Of course, I cannot write here everything I recorded, for that would take several volumes. I have chosen stories which will reveal the extent of the experiment and which I think will most interest general readers because they most interest me. Perhaps one day I will compile an encyclopaedia of the new history as told by Drew, Old Red. In any case I am hoping that readers will look at the included episodes with open minds and draw their own conclusions.

JOAN OF ARC, 1430 and 1431

The team were all shocked by the ghastly sight of the young girl burning at the stake. Yet her face continued to hold a look of ecstasy, long after she must have been dead from suffocation. Dail had set the timber himself to ensure that the smoke would kill her long before the flames could bite into her flesh. The entire team was there to support him through an ordeal that had never been faced by this group before: having to kill one of their own subjects.

Drew held Dail tight in his arms and clucked soothing noises into his ear. Dail sobbed, great heaving sobs of agony. The team were suitably disguised as English soldiers and were, of course, all able to speak with perfect accents. They stayed until the end. It was their duty. The experiment had killed Joan and they were obliged to pay the proper respect and suffer the pain of this terrible event. Most of them had been forced to kill people from time to time. There were so many people they encountered who deserved killing. But Joan was not one of these. She was a delusional innocent. Her only crime was in being a woman.

Towards the middle of the burning her hair suddenly burst into flames and the team looked and, as often was the habit of Red people, broke into laughter which they muffled for the sake of propriety in the midst of this crowd which suddenly was crying out that the girl was a holy saint. Some called out that she was an angel. The flames were wrapped around her whole body forming wings of fire and her head was framed by a ball of flames that looked like a halo. Inside the flames her face still retained its look of ecstatic joy.

Many in the crowd knelt and prayed. The Red team giggled away to themselves as the body of Joan disintegrated. They were pleased that the incident had included such a nice joke amongst its grim images.

"It was not the team's fault," Dail insisted at their meeting after the execution. "It was not the fault of the experiment. The only person to blame was me. I should have taken more care."

The facts were that Dail had been captivated by an intense and energetic boy playing in front of his house in a French village in 1423. Dail was amused and delighted by the boy's passion and by the way he spoke strongly and directly to his god about his ambition to drive the English from France. The boy did not intend to wait until he grew up but was going to lead an army as soon as he could convince the church that he had been summoned by God for this purpose. God had spoken to him and now he was speaking to God and all he was asking was to be given the strength to achieve the purpose. The kid was fearless. Dail adopted an ethereal appearance and spoke to the child. He said he was sent by God to inject the strength directly into the child's head. The boy bravely accepted the injection.

How was Dail to know that this boy was a girl named Joan? The child's hair was short cropped; she wore boy's clothing; she carried quite a large sword in the game where she fiercely attacked a tree. Dail was astounded to discover on the next visit in 1430 that the 'boy' he had injected who believed he was destined to beat the English armies had not only done so at the age of 13 but was also a girl.

If Joan lived and had a child the entire experiment would have been ruined. Women were supposed to be the control group. Joan had to die. The team betrayed her and led her into the hands of the English and the church dignitaries who, each for his own reasons, wanted her dead. Under the very unusual circumstances, the team returned in 1431, out of the seven year sequence, to ensure, finalise and carry out her destruction. They even stole her ashes from the scene of the burning, boxed them up in a lead container and Dail took them back to the Eleventh with him as a permanent reminder of the misfortune.

LEONARDO DA VINCI, 1472

"I first saw Leonardo at Verrocchio's workshop in Florence. It was my only visit with him. He was Karrel's project and had been given his dose 14 years earlier at six years of age. At the time of my visit he had just become a master at his trade. And he was the most beautiful man I had ever seen or have seen since. Karrel's adoring descriptions of him had barely done him justice."

Old Red had decided to begin his stories with Leonardo and the Renaissance, partly because my early questions about the whole genius creation scheme kept going back to Leonardo and Michelangelo and the Renaissance. If that was manufactured by an outside hand then what was human evolution and genius all about, I asked both myself and Old Red. Da Vinci was a personality who had always fascinated me. I admired this brilliant man's life and I was deeply disappointed to think that his complexity as a human being was a result of this green juice. It was very difficult for me to accept the idea that the human genius – well, the human male genius – was produced by an artificial substance and I still felt a sense of betrayal. No doubt Old Red was recognising the disappointment in me.

"Leonardo was quite exceptional from an early age," he told me, "and a genius by the time I met him. Don't forget that we almost always used the juice on men or boys who were clearly outstanding, special, extraordinary among their fellow Tells. We augmented. We didn't create genius. Well, not exactly. Well, perhaps we did sometimes. The augmentation was probably in multiples of 11 and in Leonardo's case was, I would guess, at least 99 times. I had gone to Florence to check on Botticelli whom I had treated seven years earlier. Leonardo was 20 then and already an exciting talent known throughout Florence. When he came into the room I was filled with delight. He was grand, handsome, gorgeous. He had three qualities that seemed to crop up often in our most outstanding subjects: he was left-handed; he was a bastard; and he was a sceptic. The dignity of his bearing, his intelligence, and his remarkable beauty led me astray. I was entranced by him and stayed in Florence much longer than I should have."

Red flashed me a naughty smile of pretended embarrassment and modestly covered his eyes with his long fingers.

"You had sex with Leonardo da Vinci? You slept with the most brilliant man in Western history?" I stopped because I began stuttering, trying to express the enormity of such an idea. Old Red just smiled at me and nodded his head, over and over.

"Oh yes. How could I not? Many, many times. Oh yes."

I hated him for relishing the memory so much. I reminded myself that this was, after all, 500 years ago, and Old Red would have looked a lot better then. In fact, according to a drawing he showed me that Leonardo had done of him, he was quite a magnificent specimen of manhood or Red-hood at the time.

"He had a hundred lovers before me," Red Drew snorted. "And he was born a homosexual. It wasn't our fault. Although, the juice did tend to exaggerate his appetites. My adventures with him were conservative and pleasant and just the two of us. Four years later he was arrested on sodomy charges along with an entire consortium of men." Drew laughed heartily. "A 15th century gang-bang. What a lovely joke. Fortunately, the Firenzies were not very concerned about such scrapes. They were more interested in keeping a great artist out of gaol, free to work, able to complete his commissions. So the evidence was botched up, paperwork lost, witnesses disappeared and, in the interests of justice and art, the charges were dismissed.

"Sadly, for me, my friend Karrel was so inspired by Leonardo that he applied to the team to run an experiment which Tells now call the Renaissance. This meant that Karrel got all those marvellous artists to play with. He almost had Italy to himself right up to the time of Caravaggio. Now there was a sodomy man for you. I had to kill him, you know."

"Hold on, hold on," I was getting flustered by all this. It was early days and I was not used to such throwaway lines. Well, of course he had to kill Caravaggio. Nasty job but someone had to do it. How could I get my brain around casual chat about murdering a great artist? "Please, Drew, just tell me one story at a time."

"Caravaggio was a total aberration. I had to look after him briefly in sixteen-ought-five. We had several liaisons, although he preferred boys. I don't know what Karrel was mixing in with the juice, but so many of the Italian subjects preferred boys. Maybe the juice reacted somehow with the famous Mediterranean diet. Onions, perhaps? Anyway I saved Caravaggio's life when he lost his temper and attacked four men in the street. Then I got him out when he was arrested for carrying a weapon. Then I helped him escape from Rome after he killed a man in a duel. He was a complete menace.

"It was sad that I had to kill him. And totally unprecedented. If you don't count Joan, that is. I was called back out of the cycle. I had to visit in 1610. Karrel's group was having a baby so it fell to me. I ran him through with my sword on that desolate beach at Versilia. The scandals and mayhem and chaos the man had been causing could not be allowed to go on for even another two years. The Pope had issued a pardon to try to calm things. The truth about Caravaggio's scandals are too sordid to speak of. His talent was not compensation enough for the wreckage. And when you think of some of our other disasters – well, you can imagine what a lunatic he was."

"No, I can't," I called out in frustration. "I can't imagine any of this. You must tell me."

"Leonardo! You have nagged me about him so now you will hear about him."

"You must finish the Caravaggio story. What was he doing that was so bad? Why did he have to die?"

"The story is of no credit at all to anybody involved, least of all me. Leave me a little dignity and a few secrets."

He had tears in his eyes. So, I accepted and we moved on to Leonardo again which I had an awful foreboding would become a story I did not want to hear. I already knew it, most of it, from the biographies, but from this witness-at-second-hand I knew it would all seem much worse. Drew's motif was: in our late 20th century we scorn and condemn pederasty and yet the obsessive pederast, Leonardo, remains a model of Renaissance man, admired as one of the great geniuses of all time. At least I was able to console myself a little by blaming the juice and by saying in my head that things were a bit different in those days. Attitudes then were not so enlightened. And, anyway, young people were expected to be adults at a much earlier age at that time. Many girls were married and having children by 13 or so. Children were expected to work from about eight years of age. But the list of silent excuses did not really help ease my unease.

"So Karrel was given Leonardo and these things I tell you come from his observations. He did so love Leonardo but even he was shocked when he visited in 1493 and found our gorgeous genius at about 40 years of age had taken up with a 10 year-old boy. Well, Salai was 12 then, but the affair had been going on for two years. Salai was supposedly a student, but Leonardo showered him with gifts and with indiscreet kisses, in public, and with fond pats on his nicely rounded bottom. Karrel showed me a sketch he had stolen that Leonardo did of Salai. And Karrel also made a mould of him. [A 'mould' was a superior type of hologram.] Very beautiful boy. But to take a 10 year-old lover! What a dirty old man!" Drew burst into fits of laughter. "How delightful! As you well know, Salai stayed with Leonardo almost to the end, nearly 30 years. I suppose a 70 year-old man with a 40 year-old lover does not sound so bad. What devotion Salai gave his master.

"Not quite so much devotion from Leonardo, I regret to say. His pederastic adventures were becoming dangerous and unpleasant. Salai was in his late 20s and Leonardo yearned for younger meat. I see my off-hand treatment of this man you revere so much is upsetting you. Learn some lessons from this, my friend. Even the most intelligent Tell is still an animal. No-one is as good as we think they are, and no-one is as bad. I could relate stories about saints that would make your toes curl. Sadly, all this is equally true of the Red race. We have always held ourselves in much greater respect than we deserve. This Tell experiment is proof of our disastrous talent in hiding mistakes, pretending we were always right, papering over the cracks.

"In 1507, Karrel found that Salai could no longer satisfy the artist's sexual appetite. Leonardo was lurking in parks and by the river, looking for little boys. What's worse, no work was being done. It was hard to get Leonardo to finish anything at the best of times. Karrel found a nice, aristocratic lad and induced in him a desire to learn the art of painting and the art of fornication. The lad was Francesco Melzi and he was 15, but small so he looked younger.

Young enough for Leonardo, who was then 55. Francesco was a great success. A boy with a lovely nature, and handsome, and sexy. He stayed with Leonardo until the death too and he helped save the revered artist from a sordid old age of chasing children around the streets. Salai and Francesco between them kept the master satisfied.

"But they were not able to keep him happy. He suffered many and long and deep periods of depression. Three great flaws in Leonardo's nature that were exaggerated by the juice: rampant pederasty; depression; and his inability to finish projects. No great artist ever left so much unfinished and undone. The juice enhanced his genius but it also enhanced his flaws. I have to admit it. We Reds could not control the side-effects. Why don't you tell me what we should have done?

"Without the juice Leonardo would have been a talented painter; a happy homosexual romping with fellows mostly of his own age; a bright man with a few ideas for inventions and some commissions for flattering portraits and nice holy pictures. None of his inventions or works of art would have stood apart from the mildly clever works of his time. There would have been no Renaissance. But with the juice we have a man of genius and passion who screws little boys. A man whose mind roams actively across the scientific spectrum. A master artist of almost unparalleled skill. An inventor who opens doors for others to follow. A tortured depressive who rarely finishes a commission. But also a man who gave the world the Mona Lisa, The Last Supper and The Virgin of the Rocks. What would you choose to do?"

"The question is loaded," I said. "And it's old-fashioned." I was being pompous now. "For centuries the status of the genius has been debated. In a just world no exceptions can be made to the laws. Leonardo should have been thrown in gaol to rot. The world would have survived without the Mona Lisa. It's just a smiling lady after all. Could we still admire the Mona Lisa if we found out that Leonardo murdered her or raped her? However, I have to say that in my society we grow up believing that genius is an enviable quality. Greatness is the aim of everyone. We forgive the great and the clever and the beautiful almost anything." I was getting into the habit of the threes. "But what would the tribal people here choose? The people you live amongst now. Would they accept pain and misery in return for fame and artistic achievement?"

"I'm sure that if I offered a life of illness and hunger to any man in this tribe but guaranteed him a place in the legends of his people, he would choose it."

"But what came first, the juice or the desire for greatness?" I asked.

"Well done! Now you are approaching the crux of it. Indeed! You make me wish I were a few hundred years younger. There is much I could teach you."

I blushed and looked away. "I'm learning a lot now. Surely there is more about Leonardo. Surely …"

"No, no, no. Be patient. I will tell you too much, I assure you. But Leonardo is finished. No point spinning more of Karrel's gossip. Much of it is sexual and disgusting and not to the point of our history lesson. Leonardo and his boys; Michelangelo and his teenagers; Raphael and his young men. I could tell you amazing tales about Michelangelo's David. I could tell you such gossip. But why? Thank goodness the boys of Italy were so gorgeous at that time. There's a learned thesis for you: how the backsides of Italian boys made the Renaissance possible." Drew laughed great bellowing rounds of gut-busting laughter. He laughed on and on. "But all this is cheap gossip, idle chat, unworthy footnotes to the greatest scandal in Tell history.

The creation of monsters. Prepare to be horrified before you leave here, my dear boy, for I will spare you nothing."

Old Red promptly fell asleep after this speech which had been delivered with verve and passion. I was a little peeved at the way he spoke about Leonardo. I knew that he was trying to demystify the whole idea of genius in my heart as well as my brain. And I knew the basic facts of Leonardo's life as human history recorded them. Surely the fact that the boys stayed with him for so long ...? No. I was making excuses. I was really saying that surely the fact that he painted the Mona Lisa should mean he could fuck and destroy anyone and anything he wanted to. Could I really be thinking that way? No. But there had been something gloating and dirty in Drew's tone of voice. Leonardo should not be spoken of in that tone. I felt a great man's memory had been sullied. I had to keep reminding myself that there were, in truth, no great men by their own right, only clever men made great by the butterfly juice.

I clung desperately to the thought of Jane Austen. Drew had explained to me that she was the proof that human beings could be great in their own right. Women had never been included in the juice experiments and they were, in fact, the only true humans, although he also hinted strongly that even humanity itself was some sort of Red trick. To ease some of the pain, my mind ran over the names of famous Anglo-European women: the Brontes; Sylvia Plath [although she was basically American, I still counted her]; Virginia Woolf; Florence Nightingale; Marie Curie; Pavlova; Dame Nellie Melba [of course, Australian, but still ...]; Isadora Duncan; Sara Bernhardt. There must have been so many more whose names did not leap into my male mind and many others whose histories had never been taught to me, whose histories had been kept secret by envious men, by men who actually knew that their own genius was due to intervention while that of women was natural. It was not a time when I could feel any pride in being a man.

KIT and WILL, 1591

Drew paid his penny and climbed the wooden tower of St Paul's. The view was quite spectacular, church steeples everywhere. London was his favourite North-West city. It was bustling and exciting and already a centre of international trade. The Royal Exchange building, a wonderful structure, could be seen across West Cheap, between Cornhill and Threadneedle Street. Drew was determined to retire for refreshments to some tavern, as soon as Marlowe arrived. He had been walking about London for hours and was tired. Meanwhile, he allowed himself to enjoy the view. He felt that he had been away such a long time, the seven year gaps were sometimes almost unbearable.

In just a few days Drew seemed to have infected half London with the green goo. His alarming ability to adopt Tell exaggeration and emotionalism was beginning to worry him almost as much as it was worrying his team. Not that Reds weren't prone to exaggeration and emotion – especially laughter – just like these Tells. But the quality and control of those attributes in Reds would never fall – or rise according to your point of view – to the level of the Tells. Except, Drew reminded himself dolefully, in his own case. The team had decided that London was ripe for a renaissance or a movement of some kind – a group experiment. Drew's job, this time, had been to spread the liquid in moderate amounts amongst a lot of promising young people.

He had selected some safe cases: the very unusual young chap, Inigo Jones; young, romantic John Donne; the very young and deliciously pink William Norden – great promise even at 14 – and his boy-mate Nathan Hatton, who was destined to change the history of science in Drew's fully-informed opinion; and finally young Ben Jonson, admittedly an apprentice brick-layer, but an educated and determined boy. Drew had persuaded Ben to quit his step-father and brick-laying in an intense conversation. Unfortunately, Ben signed up with the Dutch for the wars in Flanders the very day after his injection. Now Drew would have to wait until '98 to see if Ben could survive to achieve anything. His physical and mental signs indicated great promise.

At a garden party, Drew happened upon Henry Neville, a brilliant linguist, and did a spontaneous dosing, despite the fact that Neville was almost 30. There was a certain something about the man and Drew always enjoyed the wild card options. Drew had also made fleeting visits to Francis Bacon and Edmund Spenser, both of whom had been treated in '77. Dosage had been carefully controlled in their cases for guaranteed success. Bacon had been especially triumphant and was one of the slates that Drew was fond of banging on the table at meetings.

Marlowe was also one of Drew's favourites and quite a success in objective terms, if not in his personal activities. Drew had spent time checking sources to find out what Marlowe had done since his dose in '84. There was considerable theatrical success and a saucy play could be written about the cheeky rascal's private life. He was a spy, for mercy's sake! Drew had been relieved to learn about the fine plays – Doctor Faustus was greatly admired – so that he would have something to boast about when reporting on Marlowe to the team. The team worried when the formula produced aberrant behaviour and Marlowe's new propensity for drinking and brawling was not a plus for the experiment.

Marlowe had been rather charming and quite sexy seven years

ago. An exhausting three-day love affair had followed the injection of green liquid. Marlowe had fully and consciously participated in the injecting operation. This showed what a remarkable young person he was. Very few three-dimensional Tells in 1584 had the imagination and bravado to permit a stranger to pierce their brains with a sharp spike and pump a lot of green liquid inside while watching it all in a mirror. Marlowe had been such a one. Drew had rewarded him with a love-making spree – in male mode – that few three-dimensional men would ever be able to tolerate. Marlowe had insisted on mirrors for that event as well.

The memories made Drew feel a little lonely for a moment. In his own way he was as odd amongst the Reds as Marlowe was amongst the English. There was so much fun Drew had with his pretty monkeys that could never be recorded on the slates. Suddenly, he felt two warm, strong arms about him and Marlowe was there. They gave each other many embraces. Marlowe smiled deep into Drew's eyes.

"Hello, Red. Is London still beautiful for you? It's worth a penny to come up here, isn't it?"

"Yes. Cold, but worth a penny. It's seven years, Kit."

"You said it would be. Your note was a pleasant surprise."

"Why couldn't I come to your lodgings?"

"Not totally safe, Red. I've taken the liberty of reserving a bedroom for us at a tavern. And we'll dine there too. We can drink and talk and eat and … I do seem to remember a certain romantic ability on your part which was very pleasing."

"I look forward to it."

"I have something here for you to peruse as well. I know you will be able to tell me the real value of it." Marlowe patted the bag at his side.

"It's not spying, is it? I'm not keen to be caught up in spying."

"You find out everything, you red fox. No. This is not spying. This is a great play. But shortly you will meet a friend who is a spy – Robert Poley. I thought you might find that exciting. We'll dine together. He's an interesting man, a great traveller, like you. Where've you been this time?"

They talked as they walked through the cathedral and Marlowe led Drew into Cheapside to the tavern which was crowded and noisy. Marlowe had a semi-private cubicle reserved where they could eat but still watch the whole of the tavern's noisy life. Drew watched Marlowe's large, brown, sleepy eyes, set wide apart in his head, as they absorbed the scene greedily.

"You love all this energy, don't you?" Drew commented.

"I adore it. People are so wondrously evil and greedy. There's not a man here who wouldn't sell his soul for an ounce more gold than his own body weight."

"They are a lovely lot of monkeys." Drew smiled as he drank deeply. "But it's the special ones, like you Kit, who make my journeys worthwhile."

Marlowe held Drew's gaze. "Nothing in my wild, wild years has equalled your last visit, Red. Seven years of wildness, but nothing to equal you."

"The same isn't true for me but still I am looking forward to our night together." Drew had forgotten that he was supposed to lie, even though he knew that Marlowe was not lying.

Marlowe laughed very loud. Drew loved that laugh. "Still the same Red humour," Marlowe said.

Drew stopped drinking and stared across the room. At a table with several other men, sat the quiet and pleasant Will of Stratford-upon-Avon. What was the glove-seller doing in London? To travel from the Avon to the Thames was a major event for a man with a young family and for a man whose ambition had never stretched beyond the fields around his hometown. What a curiosity. Perhaps enough juice had got into his brain to stimulate something adventurous.

"What sort of tavern is this?" Drew asked. "There's someone over there I never expected to see in London. What people come here? Travellers?"

"It's for everybody of Cheapside. And theatre folk. Some companies meet here when they're away from Shoreditch. There's some at that table over there – Burbage, Henry Lanman, Field, Slye, others."

"That table?" Drew asked, pointing.

"Yes. The table you're staring at. Who is the person that entrances you?"

"It's not that. I'm surprised to see a glove-seller amongst actors. See that man? The one stroking his nose. He's the glove-seller."

"Him? What a beautiful joke. I knew he was a country yokel but not a glove-seller. Wait until I tell everybody that piece of information. A glove-seller!" Marlowe laughed a great deal.

"So you know him?"

"Of course. I know everybody, Red. He's Will Shakespeare. He's an actor of modest talent who is trying to be a playwright. So far he hasn't been able to break away from King Henry VI – three parts no less. His poetry is ordinary and his history is worse. No doubt he is sitting there trying to cajole Burbage into reading his latest nonsense. I have heard that he's written a story set in Italy, where Shakespeare has never been. So he finally found something to write about that he has even less knowledge of than the Houses of Lancaster and York."

"It sounds as if you're envious of him."

"He has talent – of a sort. Many people support him nowadays.

Before long he could be quite acceptable in our theatres."

"Eclipsing Marlowe?"

"No, my dear red friend. Look at this."

Marlowe took the manuscript from his bag and placed it lovingly beside Drew.

"Read some while we drink and wait for Poley. This is greatness. Will Rustic is writing comic Italians while I bring forth a parade of characters beyond the narrow confines of comedy and history. I enrich the historical with the imaginative. I am educated, Red, while Will is a dull man. I am excited by the breadth of the universe while Will looks forward to a walk in Fleet Street. I draw upon the inspiration of paradise and of hell while Will tills the fields of earth. The only envy I feel is that you're looking at him now instead of giving your time to me and to Prometheus."

"The play is called Prometheus?"

Marlowe nodded proudly and placed his hand on the manuscript. Drew placed a hand over Marlowe's and squeezed gently. "I'll read it, Kit. You know that I will. But give me a few minutes with Shakespeare. I need some information from him. I need to know about Stratford."

"Oh, Red. Please don't lie to me. You're so bad at it. How sad that I should lose you to that dullard."

Drew squeezed Marlowe's hands and looked deeply enough into those large eyes to let Marlowe know that nothing was lost, that the memories of their passion tonight would last Marlowe for another seven years. All this was communicated without any doubt. Marlowe smiled in his most beguiling way and finally looked away, satisfied.

"It's almost as if I can hear the voice of your mind whispering to me," Marlowe said. "I'm going to rewrite my character of Mephistopheles now that I've met you again. It's not your Irish blood that makes you red, it's the fires of hell."

"Hell. Ireland. What's the difference?" Drew joked and again Marlowe's laughter boomed out.

Drew went to Shakespeare's table and tapped him on the shoulder. Will looked up at the red-haired, red-faced man but there was no sign of recognition.

"It's me, Will. Drew. From Stratford. Remember?"

"Drew! So it is."

The others at the table paid no attention. They were engrossed in deep conversation which was being kept strictly amongst themselves as they leaned over the table, heads close. Will had been sitting a little outside the talk in any case.

"Let me buy you a drink," Drew insisted.

"I seem to remember that those very words created the most awful hangover I've ever had, Drew. Last time I saw you – what is it? six, seven years? – the last time, you got me so drunk that my head pounded for a week."

"Sounds like you miss that headache. Let's brew up another one."

"Not tonight. I'm an actor now, Drew. Would you ever have thought that? I can't get too drunk or I don't remember the lines the next day. These people are busy. Let's go to another table and talk."

"I've got a place. Over there. I'm with Kit Marlowe. You know him, I assume."

"Christopher Marlowe. Yes, indeed. His Tamburlaine was very impressive. His Doctor Faustus is a masterpiece. I'm becoming a playwright too. Maybe he could give me some help. Although, I must tell you, Drew, I'm astonished to say that I find myself surprisingly gifted in the theatre arts. That's … surprising. Isn't it?"

"Why should it be? You were always the best tale-teller in Stratford."

"And the best joke-teller."

"What else does a playwright need?"

Will held Drew's arm for a moment and they stood in the middle of the tavern as Will tried to find the words to explain the mystery. "There's a lot more, Drew. Sometimes the changes in my life seem too unreal to be accepted. I'm filled with poetry now. And with great stories. I hear a story and I know how much it will appeal to the crowds. I know what it is people want to see on the stage. I copy out stories and characters and poetic dialogue and I understand them all and embrace them with my soul. But even then I can see how to improve them in the final copying. And I know exactly how the stories must be told, how the words should be sounded, how to decorate the stage, how to include the music. I can see every minute of the stories and words up on the stage.

"In Stratford I told good stories but had no imagination like this, no idea about theatre. My new powers are like some holy miracle for I know how poor a thing I was a mere few years ago. Yet now I'm filled with genius and beauty. Do you understand me? No-one else knows it, Drew, but I've held myself back until now because the power frightened me. But I am about to unleash myself. Burbage has read some of the secret plays and he says I am a colossus. Don't you find all this strange, Drew? You know what I was. And here I am, seven years later, an actor and playwright of renown in London. Soon to be the first and foremost playwright and poet of London, first and foremost city of the civilised world."

"Life is an eerie beast, Will. Ride upon its back and stay firm in the saddle so it doesn't devour you."

"Yes, I will, Drew. I understand your advice. I wish I could understand the beast a little better."

"You will. You will. Believe me."

They continued to the table and Marlowe and Will greeted each other. Marlowe introduced them to Robert Poley who looked like a very unpleasant person and who immediately sank back into the dark corner of their booth. The others talked and Will showed himself to be the same pleasant company that had attracted Drew to him in Stratford-upon-Avon.

"What's being said between Burbage and Lanman?" Marlowe asked.

"They compare everything," Will answered. "They compare their theatres. They compare their audiences and the profits. They compare actors and poets. Then they congratulate each other for owning the best theatres in London."

"Burbage's theatre is superior," Marlowe said.

"I agree."

"Burbage's actors are superior," Marlowe said.

"That's not such an easy matter. Lanman employs us as well, now that the two are partners."

"And how much of the profit goes to Will Shakespeare?" Marlowe smiled.

"The wages of actors are poor, sir. Very poor."

"And the wages of poetry?"

"As you well know, sir, very poor indeed."

Will had adopted his most humble and mean voice and they all laughed at his performance.

"But I hear also that you have great skills in the organisation of theatre. Skills that rival Burbage and Lanman," Marlowe said.

"You hear a great deal."

"Perhaps those skills were acquired in your days of managing a glove shop," Marlowe teased.

Will looked sharply at Drew and Drew smiled innocently. Will clearly did not enjoy being reminded of his past life as a yokel. But Marlowe gave a token of new friendship by confessing, "My father made shoes, Will. But I am not one who believes in shouldering – or 'foot'-ing – my father's sins."

"Unfortunately, my father 'hand'-ed his on to me," Will joked.

Drew decided to push the reminder of Stratford along a little to see where it might lead. "So, Will, how is Anne? How are the children? Where do you all live here in London?"

"Anne and the children are in Stratford still, Drew. London's not for them."

"Any more children? There was only Susanna, although the twins were well on the way when I saw you last."

"That's the lot. Judith and Hamnet are the twins. I saw them not so many months ago."

"What is this, Drew?" Marlowe demanded. "We haven't met with you in years and our time is spent in talk of children and wives. Come, Will, this is London. Leave the rustic talk behind you."

It was now clear to Drew that Will was also embarrassed about his domestic situation. Marlowe's gibe brought a smile of relief to Will's lips. Poley leaned forward and his lips held a sneering smirk. "I hear that Burbage has employed a young boy of remarkable beauty and that this boy has been placed in your hands, Will, for his … er … training."

"That's so. The boys are mere apprentices. They need to be taught the skills of theatre."

"So, Will," Marlowe joined the fun, "you must teach these boys how to be good ladies, then?"

"That is the major skill they require," Will agreed, smiling to show he knew exactly where this was leading.

"I hear that your beautiful boy is also named Will and that he is quite a lady in the tiring-house as well as on the stage," Poley said.

"You have very big ears," Will laughed.

"And I hear that the beautiful Master Will will master his master Will whenever he will," Marlowe said.

"A pun, Kit, that's truer in content than I would like to confess."

"Yet you've confessed it," Poley gloated.

"In the face of so much general knowledge of the boy's affairs, what else can I do?"

"And is he truly beautiful?" Marlowe asked. "How beautiful?"

"More beautiful than Helen," Will smiled.

"As beautiful as a sonnet," Poley declared as he passed a sheet of paper to Marlowe. "I assume you don't mind that a fellow-poet reads your verse, Will. It is in general circulation after all."

"Nothing in London can be private," Will said. "I've learnt that in my few years here."

"You've learnt to write a charming sonnet as well. It's very lovely, Will. I never knew we could have so much in our spirits in common," Marlowe said, reaching out both hands to Will. They twined their fingers together and smiled with each other. Drew saw how much this gesture and this warmth was Marlowe's very breath and also saw how hard Will wanted it to be his, yet was aloof. His fingers and smile, even his heart, linked with Marlowe's to be comrades but perhaps the Stratford part of Shakespeare would always stand apart from London and its ways.

Will shared the meal with them. Poley proved to be more and more devious and unsettling as the evening drew on. Marlowe ate up Will with his eyes throughout the meal, for now Will had become a mystery to him. Earlier this evening the man was a mere rustic to the poet who had created Faustus, but now the rustic was an enigma. Will clearly admired Marlowe and was delighted that Drew had brought about the meeting, even if some of the conversation had revealed Will's weaknesses rather too openly for comfort.

Drew enjoyed the company of his two experiments. He still believed that Will had little genius, although the sonnet itself was wonderful and the change in Will's life was perplexing, but there could not have been enough liquid injected to bring about true brilliance. Marlowe had been injected with at least three times the quantity pumped into Will's head. Could it be that a smaller amount, perhaps based on brain size, was more effective? Could the team be wrong in its calculations? Could a major re-thinking of the experiment be in order? If Drew were to find on his next visit in '98 that Will Shakespeare was a greater poet than Kit Marlowe, then the joke could suddenly be less funny. Drew watched the two men exchanging gentle banter and concluded that Will – nice, good, gentle Will – could never eclipse the mercurial mind and wit of the fiery Marlowe.

Drew took away two souvenirs of the evening and memories of another Marlowe love scene. His big bag now contained the Shakespeare sonnet – not the original but a nice keepsake just the same – and the manuscript of the play, Prometheus, by Christopher Marlowe. The play was too good, too far beyond the plays of the time. Marlowe would write it again, Drew assumed, when he realised it was lost but he would not be able to recreate it totally. Drew knew from his studies that Tell attempts to imitate or re-create an original burning-bright creation were always doomed to be diminished efforts. A diminished Prometheus would be enough for the world and this original would be a fine addition to Drew's unique collection of North-West artefacts.

GALILEO, 1591

"What have you brought me?" the large man bellowed.

When Drew produced two rare volumes on hydrostatics which he had supposed would please Galileo, the Italian brushed them aside, gave Drew a hard push and started searching in Drew's bag.

"I mean by the way of food. Food is important. Books are nothing." He slapped Drew on the arm.

"Food makes you fat! Look at you," Drew chided and slapped Galileo's well padded thigh.

"Books make your brain fat. I've eaten too many books. I need to starve my brain for a while." With a slap to Drew's cheek.

"You were supposed to become the father of the modern philosophies and physics and mathematics and astronomy. But you look like a mother pregnant with quadruplets." Slap to the substantial Galilean paunch.

The slapping game became more robust and there were now a couple of slaps for every sentence uttered.

"And you look like your red face has been out in the sun too long. And your red brain too if you think one man can be father to so many difficult children."

"I hear you are trying very hard to be father to a whole host of children with a host of different mothers."

"Nonsense! Women mean nothing to me."

"Women yes, but sex? That seems to mean everything."

"My observations as a conductor of experiments is that it is all your fault. This green juice you gave me has made me fat and made me much too lustful. And also it did not work on my brain because I failed my university. The only reason I permitted your crazy experiment was in order to pass. But I didn't! Ha! You are a failure, red man."

Galileo gave Drew a slap on the forehead that almost felled him. He quickly helped Drew upright and they both laughed, realising their bantering and slapping game had gone too far. They sat and Galileo poured wine and Drew produced the bag of food he had hidden behind a bush. Galileo's eyes lit up and he spread the food on the table and they ate bread and goat's cheese with the wine as they discussed progress.

Despite failing his university examinations Galileo now – some said through bribery – had a job as professor of mathematics at Pisa, where he had recently become famous for dropping things off the Leaning Tower.

"I needed a practical proof for my stubborn students," Galileo said. "They kept saying why should we believe you instead of Aristotle who is one of the greatest of ancient philosophers? So I showed them why."

"Aristotle was a complete numbskull," Drew told him. "Well, that's what one of my forefathers told me anyway. Although my great-granddad was rather prejudiced against the Greeks so I'm not totally confident in his judgement."

"Perhaps I should throw you off the Leaning Tower to prove that Leonardo was wrong about man being able to fly," Galileo laughed uproariously at his rather feeble joke. This was his way, the weaker the joke, the stronger his laugh.

Drew did enjoy Galileo's company but he was only making a quick check this time to be sure that the juice had worked and that Galileo understood his place in the grand plan for new science in the

North-West Sector. It had been Fyll's idea that the team should establish a number of great scientists spread across the sector who could feed from one another's ideas and form an interactive science community. The distances and the moderately substantial time taken for ideas to spread at that point in history were seen as positives by the team. The collaboration would be slow and steady. There would be little chance to visit each other, so personality clashes and jealousies would be kept to an absolute minimum. This group would be avid, co-operative, non-competitive scholars, each caring for nothing but knowledge, truth and intellectual adventure. And Galileo was meant to lead the way. Once he had proven to the team that the scientific juice mix was fully effective, others would be chosen across what is now Europe to form this brotherhood of scientific minds. Fyll had injected Kepler in Germany too, in case the Galileo injection failed completely.

Drew's report on Galileo was going to be a very positive one. If love of food and lust for women were the only side-effects of the juice for him, Drew could see no huge problems in the way at all. Galileo was already proving what an innovative, wide-ranging and dynamic intelligence he had. Drew could not imagine any clouds on the horizon in this man's progress. He was beloved and befriended by all. His mind was already widely respected. And to top it all off he was a complete rogue who could not be easily fooled. The great North-West science network was going to be even bigger and better than the Renaissance.

RED TEAM FORUM, 1598

Drew now knew that the team had greatly underestimated the power of the formula. His original report on Shakespeare had dismissed any possibility of an important effect and the Shakespeare slate had been archived and not retrieved until now, 14 years later. It was clear that the juice had worked despite the unknown dosage. They needed to discover the exact measure of formula that Drew had pumped into that rustic brain to turn him into a genius.

"And not only a genius," Khrys reminded the team, "but a genius without most of the complicating side-effects others have suffered."

"A sane genius for a start," Dail said.

"Leonardo became so depressive. Every year he got worse. And very openly a pederast, which caused some problems," Khrys giggled at his own deliberate understatement.

"Michelangelo became privately outrageous, but it was still difficult to protect him sometimes. Thank God for the Pope." Karrel laughed uproariously at his own joke. He shook his long red hair. "We had some unforgettable nights together in my male mode. Michelangelo and I, of course, not the Pope."

They all laughed and Dail said, "You go far beyond the needs of real research, Karrel."

"You should hear the stories my family told me about Alexander," Karrel said.

"Why don't I get the Italians?" Drew moaned. "One visit with Leonardo and then nothing until I get landed with Galileo. And he's obsessed with science and food."

"Michelangelo was the very best of the Tells. A lovely broken-nosed, hunchback. So beautiful," Karrel said. "They're such cute monkeys."

At this point Fyll became indignant. "I know I have no authority to prevent such demeaning statements being made …"

"That's right. You haven't," Dail teased him.

"… but I do have the authority to make you discuss the experiments and your actions and to reconsider and re-evaluate and re-assess."

"Yes, you do," Karrel admitted despondently, bracing himself for the oncoming lecture.

For some half an hour Fyll expounded his arguments as to why the experiments should not proceed. The controls were not drawn up clearly; parameters remained vaguely defined; limitations had not been established. The results were unpredictable; the consequences could be catastrophic; the ongoing effects could change the race forever. There was no given right of superior races to experiment with inferior; any advantage to Europeans of an occasional Michelangelo or Galileo seemed ephemeral at most; the gains made by the experimenting groups were limited to some laughs and ill-advised sexual adventures as there was no intention of using the results in Red lives or society or dimension. The Europeans were being treated as toys, playthings, pets.

"But they're monkeys," Karrel shrugged. "Loveable, cute, adorable – but just monkeys."

"And they'll never know," Dail said. "Never even suspect that we've been here."

"Jesus Christ knew," Fyll reminded them.

"Things were crude in those days. They gave him seven times the proper dosage," Khrys said.

"No wonder he was able to walk on water," Drew said and they all laughed.

Khrys continued, "Fyll, you know that I take this research very seriously. There are important results possible. We can learn how to manipulate and balance and control a reasonably complex hive of living creatures. The results could be revolutionary for our own dimension."

"We know that we cannot control all factors. Examine just three cases: Jesus Christ; Joan of Arc; William Shakespeare," said Fyll as he dropped the slates on the table.

"That's unfair," Dail complained. "Just one mistake I made, and I'm reminded of it every time we come here. We always agreed that we could interfere in extreme cases."

Fyll laughed. "Quite extreme to mistake Joan for a boy."

"She was dressed like a boy. She played like a boy. She spoke like a boy. I don't believe in having sexual activity with every subject, as Drew does."

Drew laughed loudly. They all laughed, except Dail who said, "There may be diseases here that we haven't detected yet. The joke won't be funny then."

Drew spoke calmly. "The disease factor is a risk I choose to take."

"And a risk you force onto your honeycomb partners."

"Which they accept too. The Tells are such warm, gentle and cuddly creatures."

"I find them rough, crude and violent," Dail said.

"Because you don't try to love them," Drew explained.

"Could we return to our examples?" Fyll brought their attention back to the slates he had prepared.

"Forget Joan. That was a simple mistake. We agreed not to use the females. Their repressed social situations make realistic results improbable. No matter how great a genius we were able to create of a woman, she would be crushed by the aggressive, dominating, ruthless competitiveness of the males. The females also act as a comparative control. If any of them can break through intellectually it will be truly remarkable."

"Elizabeth – the English Queen – has done so."

"Her unusual social status happily coincided with an advanced mental capacity. That is unlikely to occur very often."

Dail broke in, "Joan's death was necessary. It was not done on a whim."

"Joan was your mistake and you corrected it," Drew now spoke calmly. "Will is mine and I must correct that. Not by destroying him but by studying him in depth to discover why he is our best one so far. What was the magic dose that created him? This could advance our experiments by centuries."

"He's the best, but he's by no means perfect. He hasn't had any children since you dosed him and his passion for boys seems thoroughly entrenched now."

"Oh no, it isn't!" Drew snorted a laugh. "He has met a dark lady and he makes love to her with very entrenched passion. He's a sweet and pleasant lover."

"With his stable of boys he would have rejected your dark lady if you hadn't used your fragrance."

"He does not have a stable. He is faithful to one boy. That in itself is remarkable. And, even more remarkable, I did not use any scent to capture him. He's very versatile in his sexual preferences. You know what the formula does to some of them. I'm hoping to bring him back to having children, wean him away from his lovely boy, remind him of the joys of loving women."

"He's certainly not going to have more children – children with the juice in them – while you keep him as your lover. Can't you let some Tells have a turn with him?"

"That's my plan," Drew assured him.

Fyll interrupted. "The progeny aspect of this experiment is not due to begin until the nineteenth century. Why has it become so important with this Shakespeare case?"

"He's such an advance. Brilliant; intensely perceptive; a talent for expression beyond most others."

"Christ had a talent for expression. In China the team have found astonishing intelligence. Dante was brilliant and expressive and perceptive. Why Shakespeare?"

Drew held up a hand. "I saw him walk into the Seventh dimension." There was a respectful silence. "The entry lasted a matter of 15 seconds and he returned. This is why he is special. I told Dail and sought his advice. I wanted to observe another entry before I made a full report to the team. Will began to tell me about it one night when I was his friend Drew and he was a little drunk in the tavern. But he only began and then he dismissed it as some momentary fever of the brain. He told me his imagination was too strong, that sometimes it frightened him. Then he laughed and said that an actor and poet should not complain of that."

There was a sigh of recognition around the table, recognition that a landmark event had occurred.

Drew continued, "From further observation I have become convinced that the alcohol he had in him when I gave him the injection was a major factor in his development. We should experiment with a range of formula dosages combined with high alcohol intake. It is important to duplicate the experiment and create another Shakespeare. Then we will be making real progress."

"He's the first to ever achieve entry," Dail said. "I suggest we should officially authorise and encourage progeny that can be injected while in the womb."

Fyll stood and spoke very seriously for some time. Now that one of these creatures had been able to walk – even if accidentally – into the Seventh dimension, long before they had expected such an intrusion, the team must see that there was a great deal more unknown data in the experiment than ever was expected. The human race was probably more complex, chemically, physically and intellectually, than had been discovered in early probes. Even at seven times the dosage Christ had not been able to walk into the Seventh dimension. He had been able to create so-called miracles but not enter the Seventh dimension. Now, a mere 15 centuries later, a male Tell with less than the usual dosage in him could walk into the Seventh. These creatures were not monkeys and the experiments should cease, not expand. At the very least, this new development should be reported to the Research Council. The team gave Fyll permission to confer with the Council and also to check with teams in the other segments to find if there were more reports of entries into the Seventh.

"This is an aberration," Karrel insisted. "Entry into the Seventh will never be a regular occurrence and any entry to Eleven must be several millennia away, if ever."

Fyll had been entering figures onto his calcu-plate and now said, "This entry by Shakespeare creates a ratio that will lead – on my rough calculations of all variables – to a human entry into the Eleventh by the North-West year 1900. Two hundred years later, there will be Tells popping their heads in and out of the Eleventh Dimension at an alarming rate. By the 24th century we could have several million Tells travelling in the Eleventh Dimension willy-nilly." They all laughed at the punning joke. "Unless we change the experiment we could find our dimension littered with humanity. You all know what an amazing propensity they have for exploration. We've never had to inject anyone to increase his exploring abilities."

The others were gloomy about this speech because they knew Fyll's excellent ability to calculate variables. They often treated his cautionary speeches with scepticism because they knew it had been his family group that had conducted the Christianity experiment that got completely out of control and was still a scourge on the North-West Segment. It was now a type of emotional disease which was threatening to spread, by way of the North-West explorers, to many other segments. It had been an opportunistic experiment arising from the mistake made in the dosage given to Jesus. Fyll was now warning against trying to capitalise on the Shakespeare mistake. He saw this as a parallel to the Jesus situation and feared that equally disastrous results could occur for the Tells. This Shakespeare could end up becoming a religion too.

Fyll had made another worrying calculation that showed that the males of the Tells might already be irrevocably changed if the serum had leaked within individual body systems and been passed to progeny. With the high number of group experiments they had done, there was a strong possibility of leakage. Fyll expressed his personal relief that the Research Council had sensibly decided to exclude the female Tells from the experiment. At least the women would retain the genuine characteristics of the human race; the real Tell race would reside only in them; women would be the only creatures left on Earth that could be called human. That is, if Fyll's calculations were correct and if all variables had been taken into account.

Drew spent the night with some of his honeycomb partners. He could not bear to return to Will tonight. The Red system of sexual matching was called honeycombing because, as in a honeycomb, each person touched and was lover to several others, all of whom also had several other lovers, the combination forming a huge honeycomb of relationships. In order to have children – which every Red person could do – the semen of several Reds had to combine to impregnate a body. Any Red trying to become pregnant had to give an enormous amount of energy, effort and planning to the campaign. No Red had ever been known to become pregnant by accident. The honeycomb sexuality of Reds was an essential factor in ensuring the survival of their race and the high quality of offspring in body, mind and spirit.

However, the Red mating system brought to earth by the Red teams had led to a level of promiscuity that had been rare on Earth previously. The marked increase in male promiscuity in the previous 2,500 years had been a worrying issue for the Research Council which had finally decided that, while it was regrettable that such a specific alteration had been made to the whole Tell race, it was an alteration that would lead to long-term preservation of the species and could therefore be forgiven. Drew had noticed during this project that Reds had two major flaws: everything was an enormous joke to them, relieved only occasionally by token moments of gloom; and Reds were always prepared to forgive themselves for anything they did wrong. The word wrong was not often used in Red conversation, in fact, and an admitted mistake could be a major emotional trauma for a Red. It could even be life threatening.

Drew and three of his partners slept soundly in each other's arms, safely touching, content in their closeness. Drew woke in fright several times with the image of Will's smiling face before him. This experiment now seemed tainted with high risk. Future Red working lives could become hundreds of tedious years of re-examination of the Tell experiment, until the idea of error had been erased. Red history spoke in hushed tones about the Original Tell Error – OTE – which had consumed the working lives of a thousand of their best scientists. All Reds lived in fear of being involved in such a debacle. But Will Shakespeare could hold the key to resolving the butterfly juice dilemma. Gentle Will; good Will; genius Will.

WILL and WILL, 1598

"Where were you?" Will demanded.

Drew, now in female mode as the 'Dark Lady', smiled and said nothing. She had learnt that a smile was more convincing than a lie.

"You torment me. I can't work. I can't sleep. I can't eat. I sit about all day longing for you. Why are you doing this to me?"

"I'm not doing anything wrong," Drew said. "I love you. Believe how much I love you."

Will sat with her and held his arms about her and stared into her dark eyes. He stroked her almost chocolate-coloured skin. He stroked the thick, blood-red hair.

"Your beauty is so wondrous, lady. You're not a creature of earth at all. You're an angel."

"Yes, I am. Sent from heaven to reward the greatest poet on earth." Drew held Will's face and gave him repeated kisses and then a lingering kiss. "That's for The Dream. It's my favourite."

"You said that Romeo and Juliet was your favourite."

"It used to be. But I can't bear that boy, that wretched creature who plays Juliet."

"Will."

"Yes, little Willie. He'll ruin you. I even hate him for having the same name as you."

"Don't be jealous. I love you almost as much as I love him," Will said. Drew moved away from him, exasperated that Will had also developed the Red inability to lie well. Will followed her and held her firmly around the waist. "Don't be jealous, lady," Will insisted.

"Do you truly love me?" Drew asked and stroked Will's beard.

"Yes. Truly. Why do you think I get so hurt when you go away without telling me? Why do I get into such tempers? Why am I so helpless when you're about me? And more helpless when you're not?"

Drew laughed and tossed her hair, teasing him. "It's all because I'm an angel."

"I wish it was that. But you're not an angel, you're a woman. Beautiful, desirable, woman. That's why I love you so. Merely a woman, but never a mere woman. Always my special lady."

"What will we do today to make my return specia1?"

"I have to go to the Curtain. Come with me."

"And watch that little beast put his hands all over you and smile at you and wiggle his little bottom – and his little willie – at you? No, thanks."

"Don't be vulgar. It's not becoming. Anyway, Will won't be there. I'm rehearsing a new play."

"You said you couldn't write a word without me."

"You were only away three days. Anyway this is a new play by Ben Jonson. I have a part in it."

"Ben Jonson? That's wonderful. So he is writing more and more. Tell me about him."

Will kissed her. "You chastise me for loving my boy but then you ask me about every rival poet in London."

"Will Shakespeare has no rivals in all the world. Besides, I don't love those other poets. I'm simply curious." She moved closer to Will. "Tell me."

"It's surprisingly good. Terrible title – Every Man In His Humour. I thought Ben would forego plays after his last effort. Too lewd by far. He was jailed for his trouble. He used to laugh at me over my tax problems with the court but he ended up in jail. Anyway this play will serve to give him a good reputation."

"And reputation is all."

"So it should be, especially for beautiful ladies."

"Tell me, Will, of Kit Marlowe's reputation. It was only two nights ago that I learned he is dead. So tragic."

"That happened five years ago."

"Everything is news to me. On my long travels I heard little of London. Kit was my favourite poet until I met you."

"Lies, all lies. You never met Kit Marlowe. And, even if you had, he never showed interest in a lady. At least I have only one boy. Kit was a renowned lecher. He was killed in a stupid brawl over a tavern bill, though some say he was killed for being a spy. But whichever, wherever, however, the truth is that Kit Marlowe is dead. And Will Shakespeare is very alive and very much in danger of being late to the theatre. Come with me."

"No. I'll wait here for you."

"Do you promise that?"

"Oh yes. If you will promise not to linger with your boy."

"I promise. I must go to the tavern after the rehearsal but I won't linger. He's not your enemy, lady. He understands my love for you. And it was Will who comforted me and stayed with me while you were gone for three long days. Three days and not a word. But Will stayed with me."

"What a good little boy he is."

Will laughed. "Sometimes I think you are truly evil as well as truly beautiful."

Drew kissed him. "Go to your Ben Jonson. Go and learn another poet's lines. I'll sleep and wait for you."

Will held her close and kissed her many times. Then, reluctantly, he left for his rehearsal.

This period with Will was proving to be the most difficult time Drew had ever spent in the North-West. The importance of Will to further development of the whole Tell project had compelled Drew to spend a month in London – broken only by the three-day team meeting – and there was now the prospect of a further month. This had meant passing some of her other clients to members of the team who had never met them before and Drew worried about this. She knew that Galileo would cope. The man was infinitely flexible and, in fact, he might not even notice that a different redhead was visiting him. But Drew was quite concerned about Cervantes whose temperament was erratic. Without wishing to generalise unscientifically, Drew had to admit to finding the Spanish an extremely emotional race. El Greco was not such a problem as his Spanishness was by adoption only. Still, Drew thought of his charges often and bothered Karrel with demands for the latest information. Karrel was a little too flippant about Drew's monkeys for Drew's liking and she was left with an intense sense of disquiet.

While in London Drew had been able to meet with all her 'Elizabethans', which was the label the team had placed on the London experiment. She was exhausted from constantly switching between male and female mode. She had met several times – in male mode – with Spenser who was almost destitute despite the help of his patron, the Earl of Leicester. Drew had bought the poor fellow a splendid coat and hat. Also in male mode, Drew had eaten with Ben Jonson several times and had read Every Man In His Humour a week before Will had even heard about it. Bacon was still ploughing forward ambitiously and had only been able to spare Drew a few minutes of his valuable time. The meeting with John Donne was disappointing as he spoke all the time about a new bureaucratic position he was taking up instead of about his poetry. It did make

Drew realise how difficult things were in Tell societies when a man was poor. Another reason why the juice would be wasted on women was the way women seemed to be deliberately kept in poverty by men, or at least well away from independent access to money. Inigo Jones was fine company and had a warm, sparkling wit. All in all, the Elizabethan Age was looking like a successful project.

Some of the glory of the age had been snatched by Drake and Raleigh who were explorers and adventurers and outside the project's realm. Drew found the Tell obsession with exploration and physical danger extremely tedious. She had, fortunately, returned to find Drake – the most tedious of them all – dead. And good riddance, she had muttered under her breath when Will told her the news. Raleigh persevered, unfortunately, spreading his disgusting tobacco smoke and smells everywhere. The man could not seem to get himself killed off no matter how hard he tried.

In the midst of Drew's reflections, the young man bustled into the house, calling for Will. Drew was surprised at the invasion. She walked into the dining room where the young man had slumped into a chair, his hat tossed onto the table. He certainly was extraordinarily beautiful, Drew thought, as she had thought on every occasion when she had seen young Will. As Juliet, the boy had been enchanting.

"He's not here," Drew said.

"What are you doing here?" the young man demanded.

"I live here."

"You do not! How dare you! Will would never allow it. He wouldn't do such a terrific thing to me!"

"You get very angry. You'll make yourself old before your time."

Young Will rushed to a mirror and inspected his face. "You're ridiculous. I'll never be old. Never! What age do you think I am?"

"Twenty."

"Will told you. You'd never have guessed otherwise."

"That's true. You look 14. You are remarkably beautiful."

The young man grinned. "Everybody says that."

"And everybody is correct."

"You're black. Why does he like you?"

"Perhaps because I'm exotic." Drew walked to the chair where the young man now sat. She stood close to him.

"You are exotic. That's true. I shouldn't be jealous. He'll get tired of you soon."

"Perhaps."

Drew stroked the young man's cheek. Young Will looked up at her. "My skin is beautiful because it's white. Don't you wish you were white?"

"Heaven forbid. What an ordinary colour it is. Although I must say that your skin is very, very white. That makes it rather interesting. Are you as white as this all over your body?"

"Of course."

"Your pubic hair must look wonderful against such milky skin."

The young man leapt to his feet and moved away. "That's disgusting. A lady shouldn't say such things."

"Golden blond pubic hairs on milky white skin," Drew whispered. "How delicious."

"Will has been telling you things about me. I'll never speak to him again."

"He was boasting about how beautiful you are."

"The fool! He's always raving about my pubic hair. He's ridiculous."

"He's a poet, boy. Have you read some of the things he's written about you?"

"Those damn sonnets have circulated around half of London. I'm just grateful that the words pubic hair don't lend themselves to poetic expression."

"You're an ungrateful boy."

"Please stop calling me a boy. I'm 20 years old and Will Shakespeare belongs to me."

The young man stood by the window, arrogant and beautiful. It seemed as if he had arranged himself deliberately to catch the afternoon light, which made his hair even more golden, his pale blue eyes even more blue and his white skin even more white. It was as if he wanted to show Drew why Will could never choose her in preference to this young, white, beautiful god. Drew knew she had to have the boy for herself, if only the once.

Drew walked to young Will and stood very close. She allowed her scent, the secret of Red power over Tell sexuality, to work on the boy. Drew stared into the soft, soft eyes that were shaded by long, golden lashes. Young Will could not look away from the dark, red eyes. Drew's rich-red skin, almost chocolate, shone in the sunlight. Drew's scent enveloped the boy. Young Will was captured. Drew leant to him and kissed him and held the kiss for a long, long, long time until the boy, who was short and quite small of body, swooned into Drew's arms.

Drew carried young Will to the bed and soon had stripped his clothes from him. The sight was entrancing and Drew saw why Shakespeare was so captivated. The body was pure white and aglow and trembling. The young man was submissive like a lovely dove or a white fawn or a soft rabbit. Drew ran her hands over the body and kissed him more as she wriggled out of her clothes. The young man placed his hands tentatively on her breasts.

"I've never done it with a woman," he said. "I've never wanted to before."

"So much the better for both of us. I love little virgin boys."

"I'm not a boy," he complained and lunged at her, kissing her throat and squeezing her breasts too tightly.

"I see why Shakespeare calls you little Willie," Drew said, fondling young Will's genitals and running her fingers through the famous pubic hair.

Young Will sat up abruptly and turned away from her. "You just wanted to humiliate me. He's told you what an inadequate lover I am and how I'm too small. He's told everyone in London about my little willie. It's frightful. I can't stand it. I want to go home."

Drew pulled the young body onto hers and crushed him against her. Young Will was amazed and pleased by her strength. She licked the white skin and kissed the pink lips and then wrapped herself completely around the small body of the quivering boy.

"Now listen, young Will. You're a beautiful young man. I'm a wicked lady who loves to make jokes. You mustn't be so sensitive. Little willies are gorgeous. The Greeks of classical times admired little ones above all else. Yours looks like a fat, white grub. Makes me want to eat it all up. And soon I will, young Will. Soon I will do for you every exciting thing you ever dreamed might happen with a woman."

"I never dreamed at all that I would ever be with a woman."

"Now the dream begins."

"You'll have to do it all. I'm hopeless."

"Listen to me. No-one who is adored by Will Shakespeare can be hopeless. Have you heard him talk about you? No. You only hear the cruel things that jealous people whisper to you." Her hands were caressing his body. "Read the lines he has written for you. Half London would give a fortune to have Shakespeare write of them as he writes of you."

"It's not true stuff. It's poetry."

"It is true." Drew kissed him and ran one hand flat and firm over the boy's back to his round bottom and squeezed each cheek before moving up the spine again to the neck and the golden curls. And while Drew stroked the soft body, she whispered into his ear two lines that Will had written for young Will. "Shall I compare thee to a summer's day? Thou art more lovely and more temperate." Young Will whimpered softly as his whole body responded in shuddering pleasure to the dark red fingers of this beautiful woman.

Drew whispered an entire sonnet to the boy, as she worked on his body. It was the one that begins, "Being your slave, what would I do but tend upon the hours and times of your desire?" It took Drew quite a long time, quite a few kisses and a lot of stroking and caressing before the poem was finished. Young Will's first orgasm came with the final couplet. They remained in the bed for two more hours. The last half hour was spent in silent bliss as they lay in each other's arms, milk-white skin against chocolate.

"Did I satisfy you?" young Will asked.

"Very well indeed. And did I satisfy you?"

"More fully than I ever thought a woman could. I never imagined such a thing would happen."

"Well, it has. And it can happen again. Tomorrow, for instance. And every day that Will is at the Curtain, rehearsing Jonson's play."

"Every day?"

"You're young. You can do it." Drew laughed.

"I still love Will. I don't want to lose his love …"

"You've been bedded by many men and never lost him. Surely an affair with one woman won't bother him."

"They all bother him. But he seems genuinely mad for my love. I don't suppose he'll abandon me because of this."

"What would it mean to you if he did abandon you?"

"Death. He's a handsome man and he makes me feel very good when he makes love to me. And, of course, I would die without Will's poetry. He's a magician of the theatre, you know. I don't think anyone – not even the Lord Chamberlain's Men – know yet how much he is great. And his work makes all of us seem great artists also. The company does not value him enough."

"Then I have a special task for you, young Will. It's a task you must do in my place. I value Shakespeare at his full worth, believe that, but I must go away."

"Not now! Not now when I've found a lady I can love."

"Be sensible. You know all about love. You know that this is mere novelty. In two weeks you'll be weary of me."

"Never."

Drew slapped the round, white bottom. "Sensible! I've got an important purpose for you to carry out. Shakespeare is the genius of this age. He needs your love and your protection, young Will. I am charging you to stay by his side so that you can report to me when I come to London again. You will tell me how you have helped him to create great tragedies and comedies and histories and even more sonnets. That's your charge. And if he should meet with another lady and want to love her, perhaps to have children, you must not prevent that but encourage him. The next age needs another child of Shakespeare. He will always return to your arms for he is truly mad, quite crazy, in fact obsessed for your love. Can I trust you to do all this for me and for Will?"

Young Will felt spellbound by the serious and penetrating tone of Drew's voice. He nodded his agreement very seriously and then licked the chocolate-skinned belly, marvelling once more at the lack of a navel.

"When will you come back?" he asked.

"In seven years. But we still have some weeks left. We'll have enough love and excitement and pleasure to bridge the years."

"Seven years? I might be dead."

"So long as men can breathe or eyes can see, So long lives this …" – she kissed Will's white breast – "… and this gives life to me."

They kissed again and then young Will dressed and went to meet Shakespeare in Cheapside.

It was the sixth day of their love affair when Shakespeare walked into his bedroom and saw the small, white boy lying in the arms of the chocolate lady. None of them spoke. There was a considerable silence. Shakespeare turned and walked from the room. They could hear him weeping. Young Will rushed naked to Shakespeare and tried to wrap his arms about the poet.

"No," Shakespeare said.

"I love you, Will," young Will said, desperately. "This dark lady is so exotic. She's the only woman I've ever been able to do anything with. But no-one could love me the way you've loved me and no-one could love you the way I do love you."

Shakespeare laughed dismissively at him. "Go back to her and leave me alone."

Young Will returned to the bedroom and dressed silently, in misery. Drew tried to cheer him with whispers and kisses and strokings but young Will sadly pushed her away. Drew understood that this had been their last day of love-making. It had been such a sweet experience and she would miss young Will. But it was time for her to leave London anyway. She had carried out all the tests possible on Shakespeare's various fluids and on his hair and on the scrapings of skin she had taken from him during their nights together.

"I understand that it's over," she said to the boy. "I'll never forget you, little Willie."

"Don't joke," the boy said and looked up at her, his blue eyes swimming with tears. "What if I have lost his love?"

"You haven't. I promise. Go to him now. Everything will be all right for you. Just remember your promise to look after him, forever." For seven years anyway, Drew said to herself, hoping she would have permission to carry out a full progeny experiment on Shakespeare next time. And perhaps there may even be a child to test, if her work with Shakespeare had been inspirational enough to urge him into the arms of other women. However, after making love with young Will and knowing what charms the boy possessed, she suspected that Shakespeare would rarely stray from the boy.

"I won't forget my promise." Young Will was dressed and he went to the door but then stopped. "I have loved you very truly and I don't think there will ever be another lady in my life. Thank you for your kindness. And I will love my Will properly from now on."

Young Will dashed back to the bed and kissed Drew quickly and stroked her blood-red hair one last time. Then he went to Shakespeare and sat by him, on the floor, like a puppy-dog, holding onto Shakespeare's leg and saying nothing. Shakespeare sat at the table, writing. His eyes brimmed with tears as he wrote. When Drew had dressed, she came out to them and stood with her hand on Shakespeare's shoulder.

The older Will had no will to resist the lady's touch. He continued carefully writing out a fair copy of a sonnet from a scribbled sheet. She read it out loud so that young Will would know how Shakespeare felt about the affair, about the purity of young Will's love and about laying blame.

"Two loves I have, of comfort and despair, Which like two spirits do suggest me still; The better angel is a man right fair, The worser spirit a woman colour'd ill."

Drew stopped reading. It was time to go. Young Will wept as he clung to the poet's leg and Shakespeare allowed one hand to fall on the golden hair as he continued to copy out the poem. Drew left them, carrying her large bag, but there were no souvenirs this time because she was eager to allow Will Shakespeare the fullest opportunity to dazzle his contemporaries with his fine genius. She was confident that in 1605 she would return to find that Will's fame had soared to prodigious heights. And she knew she would find young Will still by the poet's side.

"Wait a minute," I interrupted, unable to be silent for one moment longer. "Are you telling me that you were the dark lady of the sonnets? That was you?"

"Oh yes. He was puzzled by my colour so he called me the dark lady," Old Red said.

"You were the mistress then? You know, as in 'My mistress' eyes are nothing like the sun'?"

"Oh yes." Old Red was squirming with pleasure at the memory. It was a rather awful sight. "That one was his way of teasing me, saying I was really ordinary and saving up his praise till the end. He was such a clever person."

"Who's teasing now? Such a clever person!" I mocked his expression. "This is Shakespeare we're talking about."

"I know, old chap. Don't get so excited. He was a bit silly at times, mind you. With that sonnet for me, he wrote, 'If hairs be wires, blood-red wires grow on her head.' Can you believe it?"

"He wrote black wires. Black!"

"Only after I told him that blood-red sounded stupid and it didn't even scan. He wasn't a genius every moment, you know. I had a blazing argument with him about Henry V – he was copying that out while I was there in '98. He had roughed in the first big speech for the Chorus figure but then decided to leave him out. I was furious. We had a great fight about it. I told him how exciting it would be to say to the audience, look we're all here in this wooden theatre but you will believe that you're in France and that you're inside a battle and that you're in the presence of monarchs. Tell them it's all just a play and then use your powers to convince them they are present inside history itself, I told him. Shakespeare kissed me and told me I was his Muse of fire, red and blazing. Bit of a joke because, as you probably know, the speech starts like that, '0 for a Muse of fire, that would ascend the brightest heaven of invention!' So I managed to save one of his finest speeches. I've always been a big help to my lovely monkeys."

Again, I was a bit shocked at Shakespeare being called a monkey. And it was rather horrible to conjure up an image of Old Red kissing him. But then four hundred years ago the creature I called Old Red might have been a more attractive proposition. Despite the rather modern idiom and the astonishing nature of his stories, I believed him implicitly. I felt I was listening to actual history. I was fully convinced that it was all true.

THE VILLAGE, 1987

"How long do you people live?" I asked.

"About 1,800 of your years. I'll die somewhere near the year 2000. A decade or so means nothing to us. I don't know what my poor little pets here in the village will do when I'm gone. I think they quite adore me. I try not to call people monkeys any more. It seems to offend some people although you are such close cousins that I can't understand why. One man I worked with was especially offended. He would say how insulting it was but I'm sure my little habit planted some ideas in his head. His name was Charles Darwin."

"You enjoy teasing me," I scolded him. "That was the most blatant bit of name-dropping you've done since I got here. You set it up."

"It's hard not to name-drop, as you call it in such an ugly fashion, when most of the people I've ever mixed with were geniuses. I'm sure you'd quickly get bored if I told you about all our failures; all the nobodies we pumped green liquid into; all the apparent failures. Would you rather hear about Napoleon or about Jean-Paul Picard? Picard died trying to fly with wings made out of chicken feathers in 1773."

"So you created Napoleon too?"

"We had to. In fact that was the first of our rear-guard actions. We created the French Revolution – well, we created the people who started the revolution and who ran the republic. And then we had to try to correct the excesses. Napoleon was our answer. Not such a terrible answer but hardly precise in our assessment of the variables.

We missed so many variables in all our experiments. Even the people who were failures provided factors that we overlooked. They managed somehow, through some process that we never came to understand, to secrete the formula in their glands without it affecting them and then they passed it on to male progeny. Sometimes it even skipped a generation and came out in grandchildren. It was very disturbing when we discovered that. The experiment was out of our control. We fought for nearly two centuries to restore order. We underestimated the huge number of complexities and the inordinate effect that a slight factor could have on the whole experiment. That's another reason we called it butterfly juice, the butterfly experiment, the butterfly impact."

"The butterfly impact?"

"That's recent. That's a phrase used by weather-people when they are accused of not being able to predict the weather properly – just as we could not predict the results of our experiments. When a weather forecast is wrong, they say it must be the butterfly impact. If a butterfly flutters its wings in a jungle in Brazil, weather patterns can change all over the world. Such a small variable, but everything changes. And we Reds came here from the Eleventh Dimension and unleashed an entire army of mad butterflies into your simple, little world. We didn't know the butterflies well enough; we didn't know how capricious butterflies can be; we didn't know how many ways butterflies would find to fly."

Old Red fell asleep and my day with him was over. I would have to wait through a long night for the next episode.

It should be noted here that the episodes I am relating are as he told them. He usually spoke in the third person as a story-teller. Occasionally I have had to omit salacious descriptions of love making as in the story of Drew and young Will above. Old Red often got very excited when remembering his sex life and went into much too much detail. There are some things even history does not need to know.

At times, of course, I felt like Old Red was just mad. Most of the information could have been gleaned from a lifetime of heavy reading. The little secret things had a ring of authenticity but how could I ever check them? The high-tech equipment all about me was a stumbling block. The fact that it seemed to be working without any obvious access to an electricity supply was also hard to explain. More difficult still was his museum which was a large grass hut, protected by some sort of, well, force field is the only term I can think of. It was also climate controlled from some source which I could not detect or explain.

The museum held all the souvenirs he had taken during his work with the various geniuses. Now, I'm no art expert but the pictures by da Vinci, Goya, Caravaggio, van Gogh, Rembrandt, and so on, seemed pretty much genuine. There was a library of manuscripts from a wide range of writers and scientists and it included the Prometheus play and some Shakespeare fragments, a letter to Galileo from his sister asking for food, short pieces by Mozart and Beethoven, Nijinsky's dance notation scheme which was too advanced for its time or even for this time, and more and more paper and parchment. Any library in the world would kill for this stuff. His pet tribe had orders to put the museum to the torch when Old Red died. Only these stories survive his death which occurred in 1998.

I have the tapes, of course. He instructed me to destroy them but I would have to be really stupid to dispose of the only real evidence I have. Not that the tapes are conclusive evidence. I could easily have written the episodes and employed an actor to speak Old Red's lines.

Wouldn't have been hard to do. So I could never produce the tapes in my defence unless I wanted to be made a fool of. There's not a shred of physical evidence that cannot be explained away; only the plausibility or not of Drew's tales and revelations.

THE SHAKESPEARE WORKSHOP, 1605

"I have lied to you a little bit, just a smidge, a tad," Drew announced. "But it was a lie from the heart. And now I've decided that I must not try to protect any of my little monkeys, even my very favourites."

"You haven't exactly held back as far as I can remember. You told me the most dreadful things about da Vinci."

"You don't know what dreadful is, young man!"

"All right. Who have you been lying about?"

"Not exactly a lie, because I didn't even know about it until 1605. When I told you about Will Shakespeare I was telling the story as I believed it to be at the time. But then in 1605 I paid his lodgings a quick visit and there they were at it, some dozen or so men."

"At what? Some grand orgy, or … what?" I had become too accustomed to Drew including overly lurid descriptions of sexual activities in his stories of the famous, fabulous and brilliant.

"Writing. They were all writing. All writing the same play. It was the Scottish play, Macbeth, and they were standing about with papers in hand, reading out loud and every now and then one would stop and they would argue about a word or a line and change it – or not – and so it went. In the middle of a scene someone produced more sheets and speeches were added in.

"Well, it was perfectly clear immediately that Shakespeare was doing a lot of organising but not very much actual writing. Do you understand? The plays were out of Shakespeare, from Shakespeare's hand, by Shakespeare's theatre, but Shakespeare didn't write all that much of Shakespeare. At first, in my mind and in my reports, I kept trying to protect the myth of the great individual genius, but the truth is he mostly … supervised. He probably made the main decisions like which story they would purloin this time, what did the crowd want to see, which actors were most in favour. He does seem to have written a few of the sonnets – but then so did half a dozen others apparently. And he did write the prologue to Henry V as I said but that was after about four other chaps wrote the rest – one of them was the actor who played Henry – who used to demonstrate his sexual prowess by fucking the boy who played the young French princess twice during every show. Which reminds me of the Duke of Wellington who pleasured his mistress five times on the night before Waterloo. Wellington was our antidote to Napoleon and he did actually remain fairly normal and steady throughout his life, except for that prodigious sexual appetite of his." Drew chuckled at the memory.

"Do you have to digress quite so often and be so bloody tantalising with your digressions?" I complained. "The Duke of Wellington in the middle of a Shakespeare discussion? And do they always have to be about sex?"

"You must realise, dear boy, that the outrageous, extravagant and athletic sexual exploits of you Tell folk are of infinite fascination for we conservative Red people."

"I thought I would hear all sorts of uplifting, inspiring …" I almost went on to a third adjective but stopped myself. "I thought that hearing about all these great people might make me feel some pride in the human race, just as you feel pride in your Red race. But it's not working that way. I feel shame most of the time."

"That's probably because you don't have such an advanced sense of humour as I have. I know Tell history is shameful, but you surely must see that it's also very, very, very funny."

He burst out laughing and so did I. He was right: our history isn't just funny, it's ridiculous. That cleared the air a bit. He was also right about needing a sense of humour. And from that point on I vowed to always see the funny side of these tales. The vow was broken often, of course.

"But," I continued, after the laugh, "you did outright lie to me, you told me you saw Shakespeare writing things like sonnets and so on. Said you saw it with your own eyes."

"I did. Indeed I did. But he was actually copying out things that had been told to him, stories he'd heard, lines people had suggested and poems created by a whole variety of common folk in the taverns. That's why he seemed to create the work so quickly and without blot. My mistake was in thinking that when he was copying he was writing out a neat version of his own work. In fact, he was usually copying out something given to him by others for inclusion in the latest project. Will's great genius was his ear for the genius of others, his ear for great words. His other areas of brilliance were that he had a photographic memory. Before photography had been invented!" He interrupted himself with an enormous outburst of laughter then continued, "And he was a brilliant organiser and editor. He would gather up all those odd sheets of paper with scribbles on them and shuffle them together into great plays and poems. He was truly the voice of his age because he borrowed from everyone. Stories came straight from books he'd read including some of the classics or from stories told during the writing meetings. Lines and sometimes whole speeches came from actors and other writers. Yes, he did actually write some of it. I know he did. It wasn't hard. He and his team chose a nice simple iambic pentameter to write in so the style stayed consistent. There were specialist advisors in these meetings for the stuff about courts and military actions and Greek or French or other languages. And there were plenty of scholarly men around who needed to earn a few pence for writing up a scene here and there. Will would give it a once over, keep it unified, patch up any obvious artistic flaws then away they'd go with a reading of it. They'd correct things as they read it out loud and soon you had another Shakespeare masterpiece into rehearsal and ready to roll off the production line. It was said that in her later years even Queen Elizabeth dashed off a scene or two for him. He used to boast of it but who can believe a playwright and a poet? The thing is no-one really cared whose name went on the plays as long as money changed hands and the audiences rolled in. The juice enhanced another human male quality which can be admired: collaboration. Men are just marvellous at clubbing together in a good cause and especially if the cause puts money in their pockets.

"I should have realised, of course, that no one man could have written that quantity of material across such a diverse range of knowledge. The man was supposedly writing two plays per year for 15 years. All without even a typing machine. How could he achieve that output and keep up with his business deals, his love-life, his acting, managing the company, reading all the books he would have needed to read to know even half of the facts and customs and behaviours displayed in the plays, and a host of other matters? He couldn't. I wanted to believe he could because he was such a personable man and so normal and because I had become too human in my thinking by that time. We Reds, we live, create and love in hive colonies. We share all input and output, all knowledge, all emotions, all creativity. That's how we have become the wonderful race we now are. It was probably natural that the genius powers we would choose to pass onto a race of monkeys would include the power of co-operation, the achievement of the cohort, the strength of group work."

"I suppose it's not so bad," I conceded. "His genius was still amazing. Brilliant organisation, brilliant editing, great at getting it all on the stage."

"Yes! Exactly. And such a wonderful model for others to follow. I told Bert all about it 300 years later and he did the same thing, set up a writing workshop, stole stories and translations and so on."

"Bert?"

"Bertolt Brecht! Of course, one must not be surprised at the ignorance of some people when one considers the horrid system you people call education."

"Stop being so arrogant and such a show-off," I scolded him. "I know who Brecht is. But you're the only person I know who calls him Bert. Your conversation ranges across centuries and you expect me instantly to know which Bert out of several million who have existed that you have chosen to digress to."

Old Red bellowed with laughter and gave me a big, smothering hug. "I love it when you get so grumpy and high-falutin with me," he chortled. "And everyone, just everyone, called him Bert in his early days, before he got all arty, and superior and pretentious."

"I wasn't around in Bertolt Brecht's early days. So, anyway, Shakespeare was just a great theatrical entrepreneur? That's not so bad."

"Actually, it is. I have, yet again, glossed over the truth by holding back one tiny detail. I am so used to protecting the Shakespeare myth that I just can't help myself. You see the myth is not just about individual genius. No, no, no, it's much more than that. It's humanity's favourite bunch of myths all added together. From a humble, small town background with little education and precious little experience of the world, Goodchap Will became the most acclaimed and revered and performed playwright of all time in all

Tell history. We even do his plays in the Eleventh Dimension, you know."

"Do you?" As Drew opened his mouth to leap off into some other reminiscence, I shouted at him, "Don't digress! My poor, limited human brain can't cope with it. Can't you see I'm finding it hard enough to get my mind around the concept of the human race as one giant experiment."

"It was several giant experiments actually."

"Back to Shakespeare. Just tell me the worst. Get it over with."

"There were writing geniuses in the Shakespeare workshop. I just omitted to mention who was in the room. There's a whole list of them. Francis Beaumont and John Fletcher for a start. Part of our Elizabethan experiment. Good playwrights. Beaumont was barely 21 at the time and very handsome, noble, gorgeous legs. They were sitting there making amendments to what we now call a Shakespeare text. Funny, don't you think? And Ben Jonson. Ben Jonson was there. He was just as famous as Will himself at that time. He was up to his ears working on Volpone and kept talking about it, much to the chagrin of Thomas Middleton who was keen to get Macbeth up. Middleton had already written a version of Macbeth under a different title with an emphasis on the witches. During the meeting he sang a couple of his own songs which were immediately placed in the play. There was no pretence about it. They enjoyed getting together and creating these theatrical events. That was Will's strength, getting great people together, working happily side by side. There was apparently a bit of shouting sometimes but not much. And there was nothing at all wrong with this process, ethically, legally or artistically."

"You're right of course. Theatre is collaboration. We all know that. They probably all had shares in the company and just wanted to get the best possible show together."

"Yes. But they weren't just creating plays, they were creating an entity called Shakespeare. And unbeknownst to them they were creating something that would become bigger than the whole Elizabethan era itself. They were creating a colossus. It was very similar to the whole Jesus industry and the invention of Christianity. All a big PR triumph for their membership drive. But I digress."

He had quickly cut me off in mid-breath and gave a quick giggle at his pre-emption. Then he raised a fat eyebrow and held a dramatic pause.

"Over in the corner, I saw him. By the way there were several other known writers and actors in the room. It was a big rowdy group so you can't blame me for not spotting him sooner."

"Who did you see?"

"First of all, let me tell you who was there giving opinions though not actually writing anything down. Wriothesley. Yes. The Earl of Southampton. Shakespeare's patron. The patron of Shakespeare's theatre. I had just seen him some month or so before at his London home where he had arranged a performance of Love's Labour's Lost for the queen of the day, whichever one she was. None of the queens seemed remarkable after Elizabeth went. Not until Victoria really. Wriothesley had stood there in his grand ballroom and thanked Shakespeare for his wonderful play. While knowing all along that Will wasn't the actual writer. At the time this cohort of conspirators at Shakespeare's lodgings seemed an affront to me. I wanted individual geniuses not a gang called Shakespeare but an actual, single, one-man genius. It was quite distressing. Especially when you realise that at one time or another I had given quite a few of these men a dose of the juice."

I could not help laughing at the unintended ambiguity of that statement and when Drew realised the double entendre he laughed himself into exhaustion and had to adjourn our interview for that day, deliberately leaving me in excruciating suspense about the mystery man in the corner.

When we resumed next day I immediately declared that I knew who the mystery man was: John Donne, the only poet of the period who might be said to match Shakespeare especially in love poetry. Drew looked at me as if I had gone quite mad.

"Of course, a lovely man in his youth and indeed a great poet, although he stole his most famous line from me. Should I marry? he asked me and I told him, no man can be an island, entire of himself. And so he married secretly, got in all sorts of trouble and ended up in prison. That was the least of his crimes in my eyes, in fact it was a lovely expression of his passion and youth and charm. He was charming. And his lips actually were as red as they are in the famous portrait. 'Rubious' was how he himself described them I think. Or was that me? Anyway to cut a long digression short – and remember this digression is your fault, not mine – "

As he took breath I jumped in and said, "He seemed to be the only poet in all England who you didn't name in your list of people present at the Shakespeare workshop. It must've been a very big room."

"Well, it wasn't him and neither Will nor I would have permitted his presence because he had become a blasted lawyer. You might notice in all our great lists of brilliant people we injected that none of them were ever ever ever lawyers! Well, I speak dramatically and very possibly one or two might have slipped through but not on my watch."

"Okay, I give in," I gasped and then as calmly as possible asked, "Who was the mystery man at Shakespeare's writing group?"

"Sir Henry, of course. Close associate of the Earl. A relative of Shakespeare's mother. It's the late 20th century, surely everyone knows Henry by now. I stumbled on him in 1591 and gave him a jab o' the juice …" He furrowed his brow, pretending to search for the memory. "It was at one of those boring garden parties they so loved in those days. He and I did some rather humorous verbal sparring in about 14 different languages. Very clever chap. I caught him out on a Slovak dialect. Henry Neville. The tortured genius who put the genius into Shakespeare. Well, not entirely fair. Without the Will genius for collaboration, organisation and polishing, the plays would have been rather flat. The lines of the comedies owe a lot to Will, and to some of the actors, a very great deal in fact to some of the better actors. Henry was a bit weak in the comic department.

"Nat Field was there, a beautiful young actor of 18 glorious summers. He'd been working with the children's companies since he was quite small and he had an almost evil sense of humour. Armin was spicing the plays with his wry cynicism. But o what a muse of fire that man Henry Neville did possess. He was the great individual genius but he needed the others, especially Will. There could never have been a Shakespeare without Will, we have to face that fact. But the core creator was Henry, sitting in the corner, quietly churning out scene after scene from the basic story that Will had copied from some book or some tale teller. Sometimes an actor would stand over Henry's shoulder insisting that he get a bigger role this time. Those sheets were passed around the room and argued about and acted out in huge voices and gradually made their way back to Henry who re-wrote and gradually piled the play up in the far corner of the desk until there it was a gen-u-ine, hot out of the ink bottle, Shakespeare original. I thought everyone would know this by now. Goodness me.

Do you mean that we are still getting away with the one-great-man-towering-above-all-others myth? How fantastical!"

"How long did this process take?"

"Weeks and weeks. I had a chat to Henry about it. They met at Shakespeare's place only a couple of times a week for the collaboration party. And according to Henry it was as much of a booze-up as it was a creative exercise. All sorts of business was done at these meetings. Actors jostled and intrigued and begged for roles. Even merchants turned up from time to time to put in bids to feed the company or supply cloth for costumes. Musicians arrived and played as if in an audition. Unknown writers tried to flog their own work and listened in to learn from the masters. It was busy. And it wasn't any sort of conspiracy. It was a bunch of theatre professionals getting together to put on the best shows they could; please the audience; make more money. Just as you said yesterday.

"They would spend about four hours in the house then retire to a tavern for lunch. Henry didn't go to the tavern, of course. He was much too sober a man. He did a lot of the writing at his own modest apartments and he sweated over the plays. However, he admitted that he rather enjoyed the raucous atmosphere of the collaboration sessions. Made his blood pulse in his veins, he said. Made him feel he was really in the theatre. But while I was there, my boy, I witnessed Henry write the famous words, 'Tomorrow and tomorrow and tomorrow' … The rest is not so important. Don't you see? Don't you recognise the habit? A three time repetition! It's all through Shakespeare's plays. Historians claim it is because the actors must acknowledge the three sides of the theatre but you and I know better, don't we? It was the juice. The Red habit of speaking in threes. Absolute proof that the juice caused the genius that was named Shakespeare."

I was about to argue over the word absolute and thought that even the word proof was drawing a long bow. But it was an intriguing and amusing proposition. I could imagine standing up in a public lecture and telling everyone that "tomorrow and tomorrow and tomorrow" was the definitive clue to my belief that inter-dimensional creatures created human history.

"This grand Shakespeare collaboration deception," Drew went on, "suited Henry because he had to earn a living but could not afford to have his family name associated with the theatre. In fact, he rather needed to remain anonymous. He had spent a couple of years in the Tower, you know, for being part of some plot or other. There were so damn many plots at the time. Hard to keep track of. So it suited Henry to sit in his room and write and get paid fairly decently for his efforts. And, well, it is really only in the last couple of centuries that name and fame and glory have become so sought after. Probably the greatest man I ever dealt with – a brilliant mind but a tortured mind, a mind of titanic contradictions – was also the most shy of public acclaim and glory, the most secretive, the least known personality. Yet the moment he got a taste for it he became ravenous for fame, and in fact he deliberately encouraged false history and myth-making about himself."

By now even the least aware reader will guess that this build-up led immediately to Drew excusing himself for the night as he needed his sleep. I was left to a sleepless two or three hours of wondering who this particular great one could be. The "greatest man"? The "most secretive"? I spent an hour in the Drew museum, wandering amongst the astounding exhibits. Galileo's shopping list always amused me. But now that I knew some of the background stories to these exhibits many of them gave me a feeling of melancholy. One of the strangest was half a red apple with a few bites taken out of it.

It was kept in a clear box filled with some sort of gas or fluid that preserved its appearance. It had prodded my curiosity several times before and the label simply read, "Alan". I knew that in time Drew would get around to it. Whenever I was in the museum I rather felt that I wouldn't mind living in this place forever more. The stories and the wonderment seemed infinite.

I suppose by now you have realised that you are getting in this limited volume yet another interpretation for I have elected to recount only my favourite stories, with enough variety to make the extent of the interference in human history evident. There are enough tapes and tales to launch a thousand histories and research projects. Excuse me if my selection seems unsatisfying, but then again there are tales on tape that no-one would want to hear about their favourite historical characters. More lurid than those about da Vinci. True revelations about the mind-modes – a Drew word concoction – of Kafka or Hans Christian Anderson would leave any ordinary person with nightmares for life.

There was an unknown, handwritten Kafka story in Red's museum. One of the tribespeople translated it into English for me. He read it onto my tape recorder, translating fluently straight from the page. The story chilled me to the bone. Who can tell what power it had in the original? I became ill for several days. It was as if the words off the page had trickled poison into my ear. Red had to nurse me back to health with a special medicine made from plants gathered by the tribe. I erased the story from the tape then burnt the tape to ensure I never would have contact with that story again.

Drew was amused, of course. "I see I was right to purloin that manuscript. Milk toast minds are still not ready for the truth. I enjoy the word purloin." He said the word several times with great relish.

Brief summaries of some of Drew's stories would reveal that

Byron's infamies are only half known and that Racine, Voltaire and Samuel Johnson had secret lives to make the stoutest hearted blanch. An overview would reveal that genius does not automatically rule out any of the grossest vices known to humanity, including sadism, incest and even cannibalism. And with these couple of paragraphs about the worst of it I must move on to more of the central tales. In my head, I can hear Drew's voice chiding me for my habit of trying to tell too much, too quickly, and of raising expectations that cannot be fulfilled. I am not planning to use the Red information to damn or besmirch great reputations. In most cases the truth, or at least many of the facts related here, are available from human research.

However, the context has never been known before except by most of the subjects of the experiments and a few select others, including some kings, princes, presidents and one queen. And none of these people, especially the subjects, is likely to ever have revealed anything in writing. Can you imagine some genius – Gutenberg, for example – writing his biography and then finishing with a by-the-way note that all of this happened because someone from the Eleventh Dimension injected butterfly juice into his brain? Unlikely. Or the Ballets Russes circle admitting that some very friendly red-skinned person placed a block of green "sugar" in their samovar every seven years. Improbable. Or Arthur Rimbaud confessing that the green stuff he used to drink was not absinthe? Would T.E. Lawrence ever recount how he had developed 23 separate language centres in his brain due to a childhood encounter with a giant syringe? He was, apparently, a rather crazy person but not quite that crazy.

GALILEO, 1633

Drew paid a very sad visit to Galileo in late 1633. Not that Drew showed his sadness and Galileo himself was falsely hearty about his sentence and also about his indifferent health. The sentence was life imprisonment, although it was immediately commuted to one of permanent house arrest. Perhaps Galileo was not so false in feeling satisfied with the sentence because he could easily have been burned at the stake, as so many others were. He had no sense of having betrayed any principles as later history would sometimes interpret his recantation. He knew the truth would eventually be accepted and meanwhile he was alive and able to think and uncover more scientific truths and write more books.

Knowing how important the connection to his daughter was for Galileo, Drew had stopped by the convent where she resided as Sister Maria Celeste and collected a letter, three wheels of cheese, and a veritable pile of other foodstuffs to be transported to the Galileo household-cum-prison. Drew established a credible identity with Maria and loaded the goods onto a couple of mules – who were very disoriented by the trip Drew led them through the folded map – and delivered everything safely into Galileo's happy hands.

For some years the daughter had written devoted letters to her father and, despite her devotion also to the Church, she never doubted the greatness and purity of her father's commitment to truth in science. The daughter revealed in her letter that she had been permitted to read her father's sentence and was proposing to undertake daily readings of psalms as part of his penance. The sentence had first been published in Florence earlier that year by being read out publicly in every university within the sway of the Catholic Church. The evidence of Galileo's crime, his book Dialogue on the Two Chief World Systems, was ordered burned.

[Of course, there was a copy of the book in Drew's museum alongside a copy of Galileo's final book, Discourses Concerning Two New Sciences, which helped kick along Newton's investigations into the laws of universal gravitation, apparently.]

"Better the book than my poor old fat body itself being put to the torch," Galileo laughed. "I'm not a great believer in pain."

They were in the study and Galileo discreetly pulled aside a wooden panel, revealing a cache of leather bound volumes, some of which were the forbidden book. He handed Drew a copy.

"You're not a great believer in even the mildest of discomforts," Drew pronounced, keeping alive the innocent conversation as protection against any spying ears planted in the household by the Inquisition.

"But in all seriousness, old friend," Galileo said quietly as they sat close, "my recantation can only be a hiccough in the progress of scientific revelation. Does the Church truly think that I am the only one who sees these things or who might ever see these things? Sometimes I have been the first and sometimes I have pretended to be the first. But I have never pretended that I alone will have the natural truths of the universe revealed to me. We are all afloat in an infinite ocean and there are so many discoveries to be made. I still have some years to continue discovering. Even if a time comes when I cannot see, I will still be able to think and imagine and draw conclusions."

It was then that Drew noticed that, indeed, Galileo was on the path to blindness. The joy of conversation with the great man had distracted Drew from early recognition of the signs. There was the unnatural squinting, the closeness with which he held his daughter's letter to his eyes to read and a subtle build-up of damaging mucus on the eyeballs. Drew immediately, in his own thoughts, blamed this affliction on the butterfly juice. He convinced Galileo to lie still in a dark room for an hour and then permit an examination of his eyes. Drew's limited medical knowledge still allowed him the ability to prescribe some usage of vegetable extracts on a daily basis as a wash for the eyeballs. This would probably delay the onset of blindness but Drew did not know enough to provide a cure. He cursed again the ruling that forbade Red medical personnel from intervening in cases where side-effects had clearly arisen from use of the green juice. He had a great fondness for Galileo. The man did not deserve to die blind.

Drew added a postscript to the story. "Of course, as you know, Galileo did lose his eyesight before he died. I use the term 'did lose his eyesight' deliberately for no-one could ever, ever, ever say that Galileo was blind. His inner vision was always clear as a diamond. And his recantation was never cowardice. It was courage. He had the heart of a whale. He was one of the finest Red creations. And his daughter was one of the finest human creations. I am proud to have known them, proud to have been alive in their time. I wonder, my dear new friend, when you are about to die, how many great and famous and brilliant people of the 20th century will you be able to say that about?"

Drew went into one of his morose moods and I was left to ponder his question. Apart from the fact that I was hoping that I would survive for a fair few years into the 21st century, I got the message. And I really had no acceptable answer then. Still don't.

Later, Drew told me that Galileo's affliction led to Drew undertaking quite serious medical studies at home in the periods when he was not visiting our world. The knowledge he acquired, though still limited, enabled him later to carry out medical procedures on Tell geniuses that saved lives and alleviated discomforting disabilities for some of his charges. Frustratingly for him, many of the side-effects of the juice still lay far beyond his medical skills.

THE AMERICAS, 1600s and on

Drew on several occasions made off-hand, derisive comments about North America, especially its modern condition which he had been able to follow on TV more closely since his exile. If I had not been told many times that Reds did not indulge in negative human emotions such as jealousy, I would have said he was quite jealous of the NA team and its achievements. But the situation was much more complex than my uncomplicated mind had perceived. Just as Drew often spoke affectionately about the different cultural approach of the Asian teams so he admired the early work done by the NA team with the tribal groups in North America because it concentrated on the spiritual, mystical and ritual. The genius of the tribes, ironically called "Red Indians", lay in their rich inner lives and those injected with the juice were the shamans, healers and priests.

Drew, in fact, resented the intrusion of Europeans into the world of the Cayuga nation, the Pequots and the Creeks – to name but three. Only the most northern Inuit groups remained relatively unstained by the skins of the invasion – the pinky-white, milky-white, and pale-freckled-whitish; the olive-brown, tawny, mulatto; Euro spawn were multi-parented – until the 19th century. The NA team were furious at first about the Euro-invasion, blaming the North-West team in particular for allowing it to happen. They finally did have to concede that no Red strategies had ever been able to stop Tell men, and even some women, from endlessly exploring and travelling. Even the Red Indians were not immune from that persistent Tell trait.

The NA team tried several methods of repelling the invaders. There were three schemes in particular that they thought were bound to succeed. They infected the visitors with syphilis, hardly known at all in Europe at that time. They believed this would stop the Europeans trying to have sex with the natives. It did not. They thought the spread of the disease in Europe would compel European nations to ban travel to America. It did not. So then they gave the visitors tasty potatoes which inevitably made pinky-white people overly fat. In the usual perverse manner of Tells, Europeans proceeded to make potatoes a staple food in their diet. The team taught the visitors to use tobacco, in its most virulent form. This seemed a wonderful way, to the Reds, to repel any sensible person from living in the place because the weed was poisonous to human physical systems, smelt dreadfully and discoloured anywhere it touched people's bodies. However, in the most perverse action in all human history the Europeans adopted this poison as an essential ingredient of North-West civilisation.

The Red team and the Red Indians lost these battles and many other bloody battles and the pinky-white cancer swarmed all over the great lands of North America. Meanwhile, the same was happening in South America. For that invasion, the Reds had only anecdotal reports because they had decided to leave the southern hemisphere of Earth mostly untouched by their genius experiment – except for Southern Africa which had no protective barriers to limit interaction – as control societies to see how humans might have evolved left to live lives determined by the needs of their surroundings and of their inner selves. Not unexpectedly, the peoples of South America, Australia and the Pacific Islands all went the way of the early Red Indians, that is, towards spiritual and mystical development, not easily understood at all by Europeans.

The various Red teams met up every century or so to report on progress in their sectors which meant Drew did get some information about North America. But he explained to me that he lost interest in America once it was about Europeans and he had little detail to give me about American development. It seemed to many of the Reds, especially the teams from Asia, that Europeans in America represented the most exaggerated and unpleasant characteristics of the pinky-white strata of Tells. It was as if the most contrary, contradictory and perverse people from Europe rushed to make America home.

To the great shame of their own race, Drew admitted, Reds accepted slavery as simply a natural thing in Tell mentality until almost the 1940s. It seemed that every nation wanted some race within or without their nation to be in subjection to the dominant race. The ancient Greeks had done it and their civilisation always seemed to be extolled as the great model for democracy. Reds tended to think that the assorted Euro types and religious persons who fought against slavery were just nutters, loons and trouble-makers. And wasn't America the promised land and the new great model for democracy, equality and freedom? Yet their early economy was based largely on wholesale slavery of blacks and even through most of the century after its civil war – during which one Red team member was actually killed – the economy was based on the low wages paid to blacks and other minorities and women.

America was the great perversity, the very epitome of gross inequality, the big lie in a world longing for peace and justice and morality. But Drew was proud to announce to me that the American team had never bothered to inject any black people. This meant that black Americans were pretty much true humans too, as well as

American women. There was some leakage into black men from the intermingling of the races but essentially black Americans remained human. That also meant that one of the great art forms of the last few centuries – jazz music – was also a true expression of Tell genius and had nothing to do with butterfly juice or Red intervention.

All the brilliant jazz musicians – even the white ones – and the creation of jazz itself came from unjuiced people, though it was true they did seem to be juiced up on several other substances much of the time. This was not only because of the race thing. The green juice was not readily adapted to improvisational mentalities. Euro geniuses developed within established systems such as science, music, the arts, politics. To the very day they gave up the Tell experiment, Red minds could not grasp the meaning and intention of jazz. "But fortunately," Drew told me, "our souls respond to it." Jazz was one of the three great collaborative art forms that developed most effectively in America and then went on to conquer the world: jazz, music theatre and the cinema.

"Oh yes, I met Orson Welles one time. He was a great, great man. American in spirit, European in mentality and very Red in his sense of humour. He thought it was great fun to do the alien invasion broadcast, when he was pals with so many aliens of the Red kind. We all loved Orson. He was one of the most pleasant dinner companions I ever knew. Except for those smelly cigars of his. Though once he saw how distressed we were by them, he didn't smoke them when Reds were around. They showed a really excellent tribute to him on American TV. Of course, Americans only appreciate their geniuses once they are gone. Sad nation. Sad, sad. No wonder their main aim in life is the pursuit of happiness. Sadder still is that so few of them ever actually seem to catch it."

"Welles was another genius who didn't finish projects," I noted, using my pseudo-wise voice. "A bit like Leonardo."

"Don't remind me. Sometimes the similarities in the fatal flaws of our subjects are too depressing to ponder."

Speaking about the flaws exaggerated by the juice, more commonly called side-effects throughout the tapes rather than flaws, Drew had a little laugh about two other American subjects, both born in the early 19th century and both clearly homosexuals. Drew commented on the very different ways in which the American public and American history reacted to this quality in the two men. "With Walt Whitman, for example," Drew said, "his homoerotic poetry was seen as a marvellous evocation of the full depth and breadth of human physicality mingled with a giant American spirit. It is beautiful stuff his poetry, oh yes, I admire it enormously. It glorifies humanity. And jolly good show that the Americans – not always as sensitive as they might be – have always regarded him so highly. The sexuality stuff was just accepted – I suppose in the same way we have always accepted the Shakespeare workshop's sonnets.

"But Abe Lincoln's homosexuality was basically ignored by his contemporaries and by history. He married in his 30s and had children of course, as so many homosexuals have done since the original … well, since Reds imposed the homo gene. There is copious documentation of Lincoln's sexuality but somehow America finds it hard to have gay heroes. Gay artists are okay for them – and many artists there have been tagged with the title without having earned it on the field so to speak. The Lincoln thing – and I would guess any other man who has ever so much as admired another male form – will be vigorously promoted by the new world-wide tribe of rainbow persons. I'm not sure I quite approve of the gay brand being applied to the rumps of so many historical personages. This habit has become quite rampant since the 1960s. But then who am I to approve or not? What do you think, my journalistic friend? Do you approve of the way gay groups nowadays lay claim to almost every genius, movie star and model as one of their own?"

"It does get a bit excessive," I ventured. I knew by then that Drew wanted to have a debate with himself rather than hear my view. And sure enough he proceeded to put the case for historical outing of famous persons as gay.

"You can't really blame them, I suppose. From being roasted alive on dark ages barbecues to the indignities of aversion therapy they have had a difficult time throughout history. And the irony that Tell sexuality was intended to be mostly homosexual adds irony upon irony to the iniquitous treatment they have received. Only the Greeks came close to getting it right – especially the Athenians. Oh yes, the ancient Greeks got it fairly right too but I am talking now about Athens in the early 1800s. There was something of an epidemic of homo-eroticism, orgies and homo-romance. It was well documented at the time but some righteous persons – an entire religious sect in fact – devoted themselves to erasing homosexual taints from the recorded history and the contemporary literature. Thousands of marvellous manuscripts, photographs and art works were lost to the world in that purge."

Naturally, Drew had several examples of the Greek works of the 1800s in his museum, not to mention some breathtaking statues from ancient Greece, still with the paint preserved. When I asked how he carried all this stuff around with him he pointed out that this village had been his earthly holiday retreat for well over a thousand years. He also repeated his description of travelling via map-folding but, yet again, I did not entirely understand the concept.

NEWTON, 1654

At 12 Isaac was a humble lad. His father died when Isaac was three so he never really knew him. He had been raised by his grandmother when his mother remarried. At 11 his mother reclaimed him. He was never sure who loved him – never quite believed that anyone did. That made for a lonely life. It created a man whose greatest expectation was to be respected as nothing else seemed possible. All efforts were towards the pursuit of personal respect for his work, his integrity and his person. It made for a certain coldness of heart and demeanour.

His early schooling revealed nothing remarkable about the boy. However in his spare time he created some exceptional, working models of machines. Drew particularly enjoyed the windmill. It was while he was inspecting Isaac's windmill that Drew offered him the juice.

"Will it make me more clever?"

"Yes. Much, much more clever."

"Will my mother admire me? Will my teacher admire me?"

"They will," Drew assured him.

And so Isaac Newton, the cornerstone of all Western scientific progress, received the juice. It was intended that Newton would be the key figure in the 17th century European Circle of Science. [ECOS the Red team called it.] This was to be a group of great thinkers spread across Europe who would share their knowledge and build on each other's work and theories until all the scientific secrets of the world were revealed, clearly and unambiguously. Some 30 scientists would share the glory. The stepping stone was Galileo. The keystone, it was realised by the second injection, would be Newton. But all the stones were essential in keeping the archway to scientific truth strong and open.

An hour after receiving the injection, Drew saw Isaac standing by a stretch of water, studying a rock. He was admiring the rock: how it was so smooth, how a seam of crimson ran through its structure, how its shape was so pleasing. Isaac was too afraid to lift his gaze to the great ocean of ignorance surrounding him. He needed to concentrate on the rock which was something he might be able to understand one day. The ocean and even the universe of knowledge was making itself present to him but he was afraid that he could never know enough, never even know enough to earn respect let alone feel some personal satisfaction with his own achievements. And he was only 12.

Drew told him, "You're going to be my most special young man."

"Perhaps special," Isaac said, "but not yours. I will never belong to anyone."

"And he gave me the loneliest look you could imagine. I sometimes called him Ize, partly as a tease. It always made him blush a little. It was not only a shortening of Isaac but also, being pronounced like "eyes", reminded him of how intrigued I was by his remarkable eyes which never left you, looking at you, absorbing you. I think of Isaac as a poet, rather than a scientist. His mind was dreamy and filled with beauty and ideals. But there was also a ravenous appetite, wanting to know everything, absolutely everything."

I saw that Drew was holding a stone. I actually gasped when I saw it. I asked if that was the very stone Newton had held as a 12-year-old boy on that day of the first injection. Drew nodded and handed the object to me. It never occurred to me for one moment that this might be a fraud. The stone almost burnt my hand with the power of its history. I stared at it for minutes. I felt and absorbed every bit of that rock. There was a bright crimson vein in it, almost glowing. I wondered if this was how Newton first became obsessed with the colour. This was a preference of his noted by several biographers although Drew had so far said nothing of it.

Drew spoke in a rather melancholy tone now. "I had another almost identical encounter with a 15-year-old boy in 1927. He looked and smelt like a poet but was really a scientist. So young but already in love, deeply deeply in love. He wanted to create a machine that could hold the essence of a human being so that no love in the universe could ever be lost. His beloved had died. He saved his nation but his nation betrayed him and destroyed him. He was an enigma. And even in death he was a poet. Newton knew a vital maxim all his life which would have kept our later scientist safe: keep everything important about your work and about yourself totally secret. Our 20th century man kept war secrets to himself – perfectly reliable about that – but he couldn't understand that shutting his mouth about his own personal secrets might be even more important to his safety and security. Ah but I digress and I know how you despise digressions."

I tried to prise from him the name of this 20th century scientist but to no avail. Drew was wickedly teaching me a lesson about digressions: they could be interesting and even necessary and certainly exciting, even when they were three centuries out of place. Drew gave me an evil smile. I glared at him. It did no good. He was going to withhold further information from me until the proper sequence of historical time. That would teach me to complain about digressions.

"You have seen an apple in my collection. Perhaps I should also have kept the apple that hit Newton on the head initiating his discovery of gravity. But, of course, that event never happened. There was no Newtonian apple. Isaac was a myth-maker. So many of the stories about him were created by him and all of the positive ones were fostered and spread by him and his close supporters."

Before we finished the session, Drew took me on another diversion which was a little bit of a joke upon himself. He had been told in the 1870s of a novel that noted in its conclusion that the way the world became improved was by small "unhistoric acts". This was such a wonderful description of the co-operative projects the Red team had been trying to develop that Drew could only assume that this writer, George Eliot, was one of their injectees – or 'infectees' as Karrel jokingly called them. But Drew could not find a slate for him or any mention of this Middlemarch novel in their lists of work achieved by their subjects.

Intrigued, Drew set out to meet this chap. He first picked up a copy of the book and read it – an activity that appears to take a Red reader only a matter of ten minutes or so for a fairly long novel – and concluded that it was certainly in the larger realm of work that might be expected from a juice recipient. Imagine Drew's shock when George turned out to be Mary. Being poor liars, it had not occurred to the Red team that women might use male pseudonyms to get their work accepted by publishers and readers.

"She was not a very attractive woman. Not like Jane [Austen]," he sighed. "Of course, Virginia Woolf was not such a pretty sight either. Natural genius in women does not discriminate, as we Reds sometimes used to. Mother Nature endows genius on ugly and pretty alike. On many occasions my colleagues would say to me that they just could not bring themselves to inject someone because he was so damn ugly. That never stopped me, of course. Let's be honest and admit that Mozart and Beethoven were not exactly handsome, although Mozart's personality more than made up for it in his case. Michelangelo was a positive gargoyle, and so was Galileo. But Leonardo – he was the most beautiful man who ever lived I think. Karrel could not stop babbling on about him, and when I got to meet Leonardo I understood. Whenever I hear the word breathtaking I immediately think of Leonardo. Such a pity he never fathered a child.

"But I digress from my digression. The team just could not understand how a woman could articulate this accumulation principle that the team had spent centuries trying to develop. The whole cohort and co-operative idea was intended to ensure that the world would not pay much notice to the moderately intelligent men, to the talented ones, to the individual geniuses, but would talk more about the Renaissance rather than about Leonardo or Michelangelo, speak more about the Ballets Russes than about Nijinsky or Diaghilev, remark more about the Elizabethans than about Shakespeare, who ended up as the golden idol. It was almost as if you Tells needed the individual genius to set some sort of benchmark for human achievement. Eras of progress, group achievement, time spans of brilliance in one field or another did not seem to register. Humans need stars. They yearn for idols. They demand mortal gods. And we Reds have churned them out for you across three millennia now. I'm so glad it has ended."

With that Drew did one of his abrupt departures and I was left to ponder more than a normal human brain could deal with. So I too slept.

NEWTON, 1661

Because the ECOS project – European Circle of Science – was so large and complex, it was decided that all the geniuses involved would be injected with the juice three times at seven year intervals. The Reds were trying to build on the Shakespeare workshop and the Renaissance project and the Danish orchestra model. At the second injection stage Drew was not to know that Newton's temperament would be such a negative force in the circle. The lad was always so quiet, always seemed so humble, always seemed so much in need of the good opinion of others.

Meanwhile 1661 was also the year that the two Roberts were linked – Hooke and Boyle – both great scientists. Hooke wrote a rather self-serving publication dedicated to "explication" of Robert Boyle's experiments regarding various qualities of air. Hooke was almost emotionally destroyed by Newton eventually, whereas Newton and Boyle were to remain friendly, as much as Newton could ever be said to have been friendly with anyone. It should be noted that there was, as with almost everyone Newton ever knew, an unpleasant spat between Newton and Boyle later in life. However, the point of this information is to note that at a time when Newton was commencing his university studies, two great British scientists were already on the scene, although the word scientist was not really in general use then. The base for ECOS had been put in place and Newton was to be the crowning glory of European science, uniting all natural philosophers, chemists and physicists in group companionship and respect and in a shared love of knowledge and experiment. And so yet another Red triumph was to become something of a fiasco but this time because of human nature, not because of the juice.

In 1661, finally, despite his mother's objections, Isaac was off to university at Cambridge. What a horror-filled town that was. Narrow! Physically, emotionally, and morally, even in the university halls of learning. Thin, disgustingly dirty streets with tiny, mean houses. They looked like many of the people with their nasty, stooped over appearance. The town was dangerous by day and deadly by night. The arrogance of the students and university staff jostled irritatingly against the pig-headed resentment of the general populace. In one awful incident, a student walking through the town complained to his friend about the smell of a market-place. The friend laughed and held his nose tightly closed. They were seized by a group of market folk, apparently respectable merchants. The friend had his nose cut off on the spot and the complainer was forced to eat horse shit. No police action ensued.

Drew accompanied Newton to Cambridge, after giving him a booster shot of juice. In the town itself Drew was compelled to paralyse several townsfolk, temporarily, who tried to get their hands on the new student no doubt for nefarious purposes. Newton did not notice. He tended to look down at his shoes as he walked. This was quite a good idea in Cambridge town streets for avoiding the detritus and muck everywhere but could be dangerous if one wanted to avoid the criminals and immoral bystanders who swarmed all about.

It never occurred to Drew on this day that the brilliant young man by his side would hide himself away in the Cambridge university for the next 35 years. After meeting Newton's first room-mate – an unprepossessing nonentity called Francis Wilford who spat a lot and picked his nose frequently – Drew felt convinced that Isaac would not last a year in the place. As a subsizar Isaac would have to carry out demeaning chores in order to pay his way. Isaac's mother paid for the basics but, considering her level of real wealth at that time, it was clear she just did not want her son to be there and was determined that he would have to do things the hard way if he insisted on following through on his silly education binge. Given Isaac's desperate need for respect, Drew feared that the lad's status at the university – which was zero – combined with the lack of money and the unpleasant duties, such as cleaning the rooms of richer students, would drive Isaac back home and close the door on the development of his splendid, scientific mind.

Before leaving Isaac in that unfriendly environment Drew performed a small trick which he hoped would keep Isaac intrigued enough to persevere with his studies. He placed the stone, from their first meeting seven years before, on the table and told Isaac that one day he would be the one man in all the world who would understand every secret that this stone held. Then he made the crimson seam in the stone glow and hum. Isaac picked up the stone and said, "I will keep this by my side until what you have predicted comes true. Your magic tricks are excellent but I will discover the truth about this stone. I promise you that. I will never cease from seeking the truth."

The stone was on Newton's bedside table when he died 66 years later. Drew reclaimed it from Newton's effects in 1731 when he was in London to meet, and inject, Samuel Johnson. No-one else knew why the stone had always been there but they knew it was important and had preserved it.

NEWTON, 1668

Drew was astounded when he next visited Isaac's rooms at Cambridge. The young scientist was only 26 and already a recognised genius. He was only a year away from becoming the Lucasian Professor of Mathematics. This success was expected by Drew, though the speed of it was a surprise. It was the number of seemingly contrary personal issues in Isaac's life that intrigued Drew who was convinced that these were not the result of the juice but arose from Newton's natural personality, formed in his childhood, pre-juice. In fact, given a close study of Newton's childhood and personality the issues were not so contrary at all but might well have been predicted.

[In an aside from the tale, Drew commented that Sigmund Freud would have found Newton a fascinating study. Drew injected Freud in Paris when he was a neurologist, in 1885, and the injection played a major part in Freud's change of focus to psychopathology. Drew felt that Sigmund might well have been able to help Newton with the personality issues and quite serious psychological flaws in the tormented man. However, performing a 'cure' on Newton might also have destroyed him as a scientist and robbed the world of his brilliant insights.]

Isaac had solved his financial difficulties by becoming a very successful money lender to other students at Cambridge. His meticulous records in his personal notebooks showed the conduct of this business. Despite his intense religious beliefs, which no doubt made him familiar with the story of Jesus violently expelling the money lenders from the temple, Newton's personality was ideally suited to the occupation. He was careful, cold and calculating. Those same traits would, many years later, see him, without an inkling of mercy, send many a forger of coin to the gallows in London for public execution. Over a period of his first four years at Cambridge, Newton's money lending activities had made him financially independent. But he was not greedy for money or obsessed by wealth. He abandoned money lending as soon as his position was secure.

Unsurprisingly, he had made no friends at Cambridge except for his room-mate – not the original, nose-picking one, but a quiet and rather dignified man called John Wickins. They had been sharing for over five years and Wickins had also become Newton's laboratory assistant, entrusted with many secrets, some of them dangerous to both their lives. As with most everybody at the cloistered university, Newton and Wickins had survived the Great Plague unscathed and unscarred. Drew was delighted by this for the Red team had lost an enormous number of their subjects to the plague. Many a promising slate was discarded during the 1668 visit.

Drew found, as expected, that Newton was an unrelenting and indefatigable researcher. He worked 18 hours every day and often missed meals because he was so absorbed in his studies. Yet, he was also a terrible hypochondriac, a flaw encouraged by Wickins who seemed to dote on nursing Newton. Drew was not surprised, though disappointed, to find that Newton was in the habit of writing moralistic letters to various student acquaintances denouncing their sins. It has to be said, however, that he also did the same to himself, keeping notebooks setting out his own sins which amounted to a list of tiny misdemeanours such as scolding Wickins without proper cause and thinking too often of money, which hardly seems like a sin in a money lender.

There were three enormous secrets in Newton's life at the time and these continued as essential strands of his personality and work throughout his lifetime and were intriguing for historians after his death. Any one of these secrets, if revealed or investigated, could have condemned him to a very painful death. Wickins would have died along with him because he assisted in and knew of the activities. Thus Cambridge was a true sanctuary for Newton. There he could be relatively safe from unsympathetic, prying eyes. There his private lives could flourish without the public contempt, humiliation and punishment which would be certain to arise if any of the three secrets were to be revealed.

Two of the secrets were obvious from the vast quantity of evidence in Newton's papers. The third was almost entirely speculation even on the part of Drew, the Red mentor, who knew almost everything else about the man. The Newtonian tendency to secrecy delayed the publication of much of his work. He was convinced that broadcast of his ideas, experiments and scientific conclusions would result in their immediate theft leading to undeserved fame for other natural philosophers and to his own ruin and poverty. His jealous rages about the work of other scientists, almost always unfounded, were terrible to behold. Even Drew was startled by their ferocity.

Drew was with him when he received a copy of Mercator's newly published book on logarithms. Isaac had been working on the same subject for some years and fellows of the Royal Society had sent the book to try to prod Newton into publishing his own work. Newton flew into a fit of temper because he had, years before, resolved these matters but had chosen not to publish. Fortunately Mercator's configurations and conclusions were wrong so Newton could hardly accuse him of stealing. But Newton, like most mortals, male or female, knew no sense when gripped by jealousy. It was as if no-one else should be allowed to work in any area of mathematics, physics or any science where Newton chose to dabble.

Drew helped Isaac to rapidly frame a short treatise on the subject. Drew's work was mostly tidying up the mess of papers in the room so that the notes were in some sort of form that could be used in the treatise. As Red physics was rather different from the way earthbound sciences were developing, it can be said that there was no undue interference in Newton's thought processes. Unless we count the butterfly juice injections as being interference. The treatise was sent off to the Royal Society fellow but with strict instructions forbidding its publication. The work was not published in fact for almost 40 years. This strangeness in Newton was not produced by the alien injections, Drew concluded, but by the complex lattice of fears that permeated his whole being.

One of the principal fears involved Newton's experiments in alchemy. He was a devoted alchemist and for most of his life never ceased from investigating its mysteries. He always had a significant library of books on the subject and there is no doubt that his experiments in alchemy assisted him in his formulation of his principles of physics and mathematics, especially in his work on gravity. But to be an alchemist could mean severe punishment and even death. Worse, for Newton, it could lead to his other work being discredited. And so, he kept it all a secret.

Drew felt partly to blame for Isaac's obsession with alchemy, as opposed to his interest in the subject, because on his first visit to Cambridge in 1668, Drew played a little trick on Isaac. It occurred because Drew could not truly believe that someone with a mind as steely and icy as Newton's could be serious about alchemy with all its mumbo-jumbo quackery, superstition and sleight of hand trickery. So, as a joke, Drew pretended interest and picked up a piece of lead and turned it into gold. What he actually did was similar to any cheap magician's trick. He turned around and while turning popped the lead into the Seventh dimension and grabbed a similar sized bit of gold and ended up facing Isaac with that gold in his hand. Isaac was enthralled and now totally convinced that his experiments in alchemy could and would lead him to the discovery of the philosopher's stone and transmutation of metals.

Despite Drew telling him it was a trick, a prank and a joke, Newton preferred to believe the evidence of his own eyes. Lead had turned to gold. Those eyes had almost been blinded by Newton in previous experiments on optics. He had stared into the sun for inordinate lengths of time and then in another experiment had prodded his eyeball with a small dagger. In both circumstances it was Wickins who saved the day and saved Isaac's eyesight by firstly stopping him from carrying on the experiments and secondly by nursing him in a darkened room for some considerable time after his sun-gazing ventures.

The thing was, as the Red team realised when discussing Newton's slate, the man had no sense of humour and no passionate imagination. It was always the passionate ones who ventured into the Seventh and Eleventh Dimensions. Newton never got there. Calculation and intellect were his only passions. He found no humour in anything. It seemed he found no pleasure in anything much either. The alchemy trick fuelled Isaac's belief that transmutation of metals was possible and this led to a certain distortion in Newton's research and beliefs and consumed huge chunks of his time.

A further distortion and the second large secret was Isaac's religious beliefs. He was an Arian and, at risk of blasphemy, torture and execution, believed in dogmas that denied the divinity of Christ and the creed of the holy trinity. Again, Wickins knew of this illegal and blasphemous stance that Newton had adopted and kept the secret, despite his own religious beliefs being strictly orthodox and quite devout. However, in all things, it seemed that for Wickins there was no god higher or more glorious than Isaac Newton.

The third great secret which could have led to Newton's torture and execution was one that Drew and the Red team assumed from circumstantial evidence. Drew was prepared to admit that because Red people could barely conceive of a life lived without prolific sexual activity and relationships, it was hard for them to accept that Newton might have abstained from sex all his life. The closeness of Wickins and Newton in their everyday lives, every day for so many years, plus the care and tenderness with which Wickins regarded Newton, and Newton's trust in Wickins, putting his life in the man's hands, all added together seemed to suggest something more than mere friendship or collegiality existed between them.

Certainly it was clear that Newton had absolutely no interest whatsoever in women. Drew and the Red team, in Newton's early years, were prepared to concede that there was no actual evidence that Newton was a homosexual. However, the man's ability to keep secrets could certainly have enabled him to keep this third deadly issue, if it did exist, well and truly hidden. Drew jokingly told his team that while staying with Newton he could possibly have inspected the bed sheets for evidence but felt that sort of thing was beneath his dignity as a Red researcher and as a friend of Newton.

NEWTON, 1675

In early 1675 Drew met Newton in London to assist him with his appeal to the king. This was a complicated matter and Isaac had researched and prepared copious papers, listed dubious precedents and drawn up several thin arguments. Drew immediately saw that they would hold no weight with His Majesty because they were legalistic and based in complex interpretations of scripture. The matter had arisen because in order to take up his professorship at Cambridge Newton was required to take holy orders. He could not do this in all good conscience because of his Arian beliefs. Drew pointed out to him that he very well could do it in bad conscience if necessary because he had already signed papers in previous years at the university vowing to uphold the 39 articles of the Anglican Church and that was as much blasphemy against his Arianism as taking holy orders. Isaac would not be swayed. Nobody at Cambridge and none of his advisers thought there was the slightest chance of Charles granting his request. But Isaac was determined to try even at the risk of his secret about his religion being discovered.

His audience with the king only briefly touched on his petition. Newton handed his papers to King Charles and mumbled a sentence of request that his humble petition be considered and weighed and perhaps approved in the king's wisdom. Charles passed the papers to a nearby flunkey and announced grandly, reading from a sheet of paper, "We are pleased to grant this petitioner his full request that holders of the Lucasian Professorship at Cambridge, now and hereafter, be exempt from holy orders and proclaim that we will give all just encouragement to learned men who are and shall be elected to the said professorship." Newton was astounded for he had not asked for anything so sweeping and magnanimous. But Drew, in a private audience with the king, had.

His Majesty then steered Newton to a seat by a huge window through which sunlight poured and demanded to be told all the secrets of light that Newton had discovered. Their conversation lasted an hour, much to the chagrin of the flunkeys, and for most of the hour Drew joined them. He helped to keep Newton on the path of describing the great adventure of light, rather than trying to explain it scientifically. By the time they left, the king was won over completely by Newton's brilliance and remained his staunch supporter for life, which was to be a mere decade more in Charles's case.

Isaac thanked Drew for his intervention in this sensitive matter. He was well aware of the enormity of the favour bestowed upon him by the king and knew he was safe in at least one of his secrets for some time to come. On the journey back to Cambridge, Drew gave Newton the third injection of juice. This one, it was calculated by the Red team, would consolidate, amplify and stretch his powers. For once, the team seemed to get the variables correct and Newton went on to become one of the most acclaimed geniuses in all the Red slates. The third injection did not assist in mellowing his personality, particularly his fears and jealousies. The Red team always blamed these on his human nature.

At Cambridge, Drew found that Wickins and Isaac had moved to new rooms. These rooms had a wooden shed-like structure attached and the two men had turned it into a rather messy laboratory, filled with equipment such as furnaces, crucibles and tools and the various substances needed for Newton's alchemical studies. Drew again assisted by re-ordering, tidying and cataloguing Isaac's papers. Drew was very pleased by the scope and quality of Newton's work. He stole some of the papers because they seemed to him particularly dangerous. These were on alchemy and also a study about the prophecies of the Biblical figure, Daniel. Anyone else stumbling across these would have had enough evidence to have Isaac arrested.

Drew was touched on this visit by the warmth of the care Wickins gave to Newton, who seemed not to notice. As well as his duties of moving equipment around – he was quite a strong man for his stature – Wickins made meals and drinks for Isaac, cleaned the rooms and Isaac's clothes, and also tried to keep some order amongst the papers. Drew tried to speak to Wickins about the experiments being done in the laboratory, but Wickins professed to know nothing about them as they were beyond his understanding. He was a friend with whom all secrets were safe.

Drew did not stay long in Cambridge on that visit. There were always far too many people to see during the year he was in the North-West Segment and he did not always find Newton's personality charming.

Before Drew could retire at the end of narrating this episode, I insisted he tell me how he had convinced the king to grant such a favour to Newton. "Was the king one of your injectees? How could you gain a private audience so easily? Weren't you worried to have the king know that you, a foreigner, were wandering his realm? What trick did you use?"

"For a start, we never injected anyone in such a position of inherited power. Tell vanity about blood lines is so overwhelming that the juice becomes useless. Even the son of a knight is usually so puffed up with pride that our butterflies flutter in vain. I know how you enjoy my word play jokes! [I didn't especially but I used to politely groan at them, to acknowledge I had got it. To Drew this groaning appeared to be an accolade.] Being good alien ambassadors we make a point of calling on the highest power in the land. We explain our mission which is to encourage trade between our small province in the middle of Europe somewhere – we make one up – and this mighty nation we are visiting. The king or power figure is given a small unusual gift to intrigue him – it's almost always a him – plus a larger bag of gold than he would have expected. In the Seventh dimension gold is so plentiful that it has become something of a nuisance. In return we ask for a paper of safe passage within the realm, with the official seal affixed, and the opportunity to send in a bag of gold to obtain an audience at any time we wish."

In 1675, Ambassador Drew sent a bag of gold to King Charles requesting an audience which was swiftly granted. They met in a great hall of the palace and the king had several advisors with him, including at least three high clergy. Drew knew all the bowings and courtesies and ring-kissing ceremonies needed for the occasion. But he also knew that kings wanted these sorts of matters pushed through quickly so he came to the point at once.

"Your Majesty, my petition on behalf of my good friend Isaac Newton is made out of concern for your Majesty's personal safety."

There was a shuffle of feet and guards moving in circles looking for the danger and some overdressed buffoon who looked and sounded like a lawyer leapt to his feet and demanded, "Are you claiming that Newton plans to assassinate the king?"

Drew knew he had their intense attention.

"Nothing could be further from the truth," Drew proclaimed in full Red orator mode. "In fact it is Newton's consideration that His Majesty is putting himself in danger by requiring holders of the

Lucasian Professorship in Mathematics to take holy orders. Newton has a great mind and great respect for the principle that enshrines the king's power in the land. That is, of course, the principle of the divine right of anointed kings to rule. As we know, King Charles has the authority of almighty God to exercise majestic power in this great land."

Some sort of bishop rose impatiently and declared, "Yes, yes, we all know this. How does the professorship threaten the king's right?"

"By taking holy orders as part of his post, Newton considers that this is tantamount to giving his position the same authority of God almighty as is enjoyed by the king. Such a view would make it impossible to ever dismiss a rogue or scoundrel from this position. In fact, a rogue who held the position with evil intent could claim to be acting on high scientific rationale supported by the power of God in order to overthrow or defy all laws, established order and the monarchy itself."

There was a hastily whispered conference amongst the religious dignitaries. The king stood. Everyone stood. The king looked to the bishop-like figure who said, "It is a cogent case indeed, your Majesty. Lesser anomalies have led to insurrections elsewhere."

"And what, Mister Ambassador, does the wise young mathematician suggest we do?" the king asked.

"Newton, in his great wisdom, is prepared to forego the honour of holy orders so that no such questioning of the king's absolute authority can occur. A royal decree changing the conditions of the professorship might be useful in preventing any hint of heavenly approval of the art of mathematics and any idea of equality between that position and the monarchy itself."

"Consider it done," Charles declared.

Ambassador Drew was invited to a lunch of partridges and

potatoes, which he accepted with much pleasure. And so the safety of the king, and coincidentally of Isaac Newton, was secured by Red diplomacy.

TEDIOUS YEARS, 1682 to 1752

Drew called this period tedious because there was no-one who was passionate enough, in his estimation, to be deserving of the juice. The visits to Newton were mostly brief and coldly polite. There was a range of worthy-ish people who lived through the injection and achieved things. Swift was probably the most lively, but he had some irritating habits that Drew disliked so we were not to speak of him. Bach was certainly worthy though not a great conversationalist, and if there was one thing Drew loved and craved above all else it was conversation. Drew was not fond of organ music and thought there were too many twirls, whirls and curlicues in Bach's music. I chided Drew over this, saying that it was much like saying that Mozart wrote too many notes. However, for once, Drew's sense of humour abandoned him and he dismissed my comment and responded with a complaint about Bach's lack of moderation which, apparently, was proven by the fact that he ended up with 20 children. Drew's judgments, I had realised much earlier in our sessions, were not always strictly rational.

He was strangely ambivalent towards Samuel Johnson, David Garrick, Joshua Reynolds and Adam Smith who the rest of his team came to accept as great successes from this period. Oddly enough, his fondest memory of that time was of Jethro Tull, a name not familiar to me at all. Apparently, Tull was injected in 1689 at age 15 but, under parental pressure, went on to become a lawyer, a fact that made Drew feel like a complete failure. Like Will/Henry, Drew was dismissive of lawyers. But Tull finally followed his streak of genius and became a farmer.

"A farmer!?" I exclaimed and questioned at the same time. "What about your moaning about Wordsworth and the Romantics being nature-botherers?" He had touched on this matter in several of his diversions.

"There is a big difference between being a passive nature lover and an active farmer. Tull went out there and wrestled with the soil. He invented practical items to help raise crops, to feed people. Wordsworth and the band of Romantic poets just kept throwing their hands up in awe every time they saw a blasted daffodil, or a nightingale, or a tree. Any kind of tree. And then they wrote interminable poetry about all that. Tull invented a thing that planted seeds in rows, and he had his workers out there pounding the soil, getting oxygen and water into it. He built a horse hoe to help that system along. How can anyone not love a man who wrote a book called The New Horse Houghing Husbandry? William dewy-eyed Wordsworth never wrote anything half as useful as that book. I can tell you that."

Drew thumped the table and looked at me sternly and then we both fell on the floor in hysterical laughter.

NEWTON, 1682 and a half century more

Drew was astounded to find that there had been a fire a few years before in Newton's laboratory and many papers had been destroyed. Drew's concern was for the physical safety of Newton. The man wrote so many papers that half could be lost without anyone noticing. In fact, at the end of the '82 visit Drew took some more of the material with him including completed notebooks – especially those too revealing about his alchemy work – and copies of correspondence. [Later researchers of Newton's life have noted these missing papers, which is not ironclad proof that Drew took them but at least lends support to his story.] Drew helped Isaac to get some order into his papers again as some unfindable material needed to complete his Principia Mathematica was almost certainly buried in the pile. Drew read the manuscript and gave Newton assurances about its power and importance. Isaac was rather off-hand about this praise. The third injection had given him supreme confidence in his own correctness and he did not feel the need of anyone else's support or approval. He only ever sought surrender to his point of view.

Even with publication of the Principia Isaac was eccentric. The text was in Latin so that only scholars and intellectuals could read it. He refused to allow an English language version to be published until 40 years after the original publication, which he put off until 1687 anyway. Drew could not understand at all why the man was not excited and eager to publish every insight, every experimental result, every idea in his magnificent brain. Isaac's reluctance to publish and to participate freely in scientific debate with other European scientists killed off the Red team's hopes for ECOS and creating a European scientific community. Newton's ambition and greed and fury prevented any thought by others of collaboration or co-operation. He had bitter disagreements with so many – Hooke and Flamsteed and Leipzin for example – and many of his peers were terrified of him and simply avoided interaction with him. Drew was also to take that course over the next 40 years – not of terror but of avoidance.

Drew said exasperatedly, "I spent a half a century with that astounding man and he was wracked by internal, infernal, mental contradictions and deep fear. An emotional man who constructed a coldly mechanical model of the universe. A passionate man who fell in love with other men but abstained from physical contact – well, most of the time. No, it wasn't me. It was his room-mate, of course. I always assumed it was. Well, I wanted it to be true, I suppose. I wanted to believe that the poor chap had actually received some pleasure and human solace and warmth from his fellow creatures at some time in his life. He seemed to gain a degree of cold enjoyment from torturing and hanging forgers in his later years, but that can hardly compensate for the lack of a sex life and affection from one's fellows.

"With Isaac any actual pleasure he might feel about anything was drowned in fiery guilt. He was a logical scientist engrossed by mathematics and the love of proof and yet committed to his irrational experiments in alchemy. As I told you, that commitment came from my magic trick. You might as well think that Einstein's inspiration for relativity came from an optical illusion – well, to be truthful, it did. Karrel performed something with a rabbit and a watch. No, no, that was my beloved Dodgson. There was something with Einstein, some light-bending trick. Anyway the whole point is that, when you're writing your book, remember how easy it is to come to believe the things you desperately want to believe instead of believing the evidence.

"You will not be surprised to learn that I was responsible for the breaking up of the relationship between Isaac and Wickins. They parted company not long after that visit in late '82. It was the silliest thing. Isaac began talking about London and about society. He said that should he ever have to participate in society he did not believe he would be capable of it. The chat, the false politeness, and so on. The salon life, the coffee houses, the clubs, he dreaded the thought of them. He dreaded the very things that I so enjoyed about London. So I decided I should help him. And the help I chose to give him would liberate two birds with the one stone. [I did not dare to correct him when he was in full flight on such a self-centred story.] I thought I might shake Newton from his stodginess and give him a vital social skill at the same time. So I taught him to dance. I thought dancing and music would appeal to his mathematical mind and also give him pleasure.

"I did that Red illusion thing whereby my mere humming of a tune emerged to Tell ears as if a small ensemble were playing. I showed him the simple, mathematically-based steps of this dance and then I took Isaac Newton in my arms and swept him about the room. For one moment I thought I saw him actually smile. I'm sure he did."

At this point in his narration, Drew sprang from his chair and grabbed me in his arms, hummed, and whirled me about the room. It was true that I could hear an ensemble of instruments playing and that the warm clasp of this Red person was making my heart beat faster and that I could not help but smile. I think I even giggled in those few minutes. Then he dumped me back in my chair and slumped back into his and continued his tale.

"You can see that he should have been pleased. But just when Isaac seemed to be on the brink of enjoying himself, he, and a second later I, saw Wickins standing there. The poor man had a face full of amazement. He had been watching his revered room-mate in the arms of another man, cavorting about the room in what must have seemed to Wickins as wild abandonment. Even the unbounded devotion of Wickins for Newton could not forgive this scene. And Newton's sense of humiliation at being discovered in such a position could not permit his near 20-year intimacy with Wickins to continue.

"Their joint human pride shattered a friendship that had overcome the lunacy of alchemy experiments, the blasphemy of Arianism and, in all probability, the burning lust of carnal desires. But their friendship could not overcome the awful sight of two men dancing together, of two men clasped in each other's arms, and about to laugh. Fate itself could not allow Isaac Newton to indulge in pleasure. The two men began to argue irrationally in cold, harsh statements. I left the room. I was rather hoping that after bitter recriminations they would fall into each other's arms and beg each other's forgiveness and then tumble into bed and make crazy, passionate love, as happens in so many Tell stories. But, alas, they did not and after some weeks of cold co-habitation, Wickins left and the two great friends never spoke again. But, it must be added that to his credit, Wickins never said a bad or angry word about Newton and never revealed that there were any secrets in the great man's life, let alone gave any hint of what those secrets might be.

"Just when I had assumed that it was part of Tell nature to be co-operative, to learn from one another and to build on one another's knowledge and insights and imaginations, along came Isaac Newton and crushed my idea with his stubborn, isolationary self-centredness. He blatantly refused to co-operate with anyone and would not share to the ridiculous point where he wouldn't even publish his discoveries. Some say this was because other scientists, such as his arch-nemesis, Robert Hooke, had found errors in Newton's mathematics and had publicly pointed them out. It was more than that.

"Take the issue of the calculus wars. Newton spent 40 years in battle with Leibniz to prove that he, Newton, was the sole originator of the calculus method. Newton set out to destroy Leibniz and succeeded. He set up a committee of the Royal Society, of which he was President, to decide the case of who was the original inventor of calculus. The whole of Europe knew that Newton created it but he created it for himself. Then Leibniz invented a form that was useful for everyone and that system is still used today, world-wide. But Newton pursued poor Leibniz until he was squashed, forced to make a living writing histories of some obscure royal family. Something like that. Fyll, who was Leibniz's mentor, was ready to go to London and assassinate Newton, he was so incensed by the man's outrageous behaviour. The team stopped him, of course.

"But even after Leibniz's death, Newton continued to crush his bones, calling Leibniz a 'second inventor' who counted for nothing and having every reference to the man's name and work removed from the third edition of the Principia. For Newton, Leibniz was not allowed to exist even historically in the world of science that was now dominated by Newton. Single-handedly, Newton smashed any hope of a great European scientific renaissance. His coldness and cruelty blocked all hope of scientific intercourse. His fanatical disciples were just as cruel, and so the influence of his frigid personality lasted well beyond his death. Newton wanted to be the only person panning for gold in the river of knowledge, or at least the only person who was acknowledged as having found genuine gold. He wanted to be the whole river. There must only be the river of light and the river was Newton and even the light must be Newton.

"I had to stop visiting him. Alarmingly, I found myself starting to feel hatred for him. That is not an emotion known to Reds so you can imagine my shock when, investigating these new feelings in myself, I found that they were most accurately described as hatred. His later life was filled with self-aggrandisement, positions of power, cruel punishment of clippers and forgers when he was Warden of the Mint. He lived in London for the last 30 years of his overlong life and yet there is no record of his ever having danced. Perhaps by scaring away Wickins, I was responsible for his callousness. Without the moderating hand of a friend such as Wickins, the man was a monster.

"He did seem to have some years of passion for a rather ugly, Swiss boy called Fatio. I say boy because although about 30 when they met, he was more than 20 years younger than Isaac. With Fatio, who had pretensions to being a scientist, there were many flashes of emotion and what even resembled lust but still no evidence, acceptable to Tell historians, that they ever consummated the passion. But they did. I am sure of it. I saw it in Isaac's eyes on several occasions. Fatio boasted about it but no-one was brave enough to believe him. However, even on his death-bed, it suited Newton's creation of his own mythology to insist that he was a virgin. Perhaps the man's greatest genius lay in his complete devotion to creating his own image.

"I could never really warm to Newton, except for that moment of wonder when he was a boy, realising the marvels there were to be explored in the universe. So, after the '82 visit, I didn't bother much with him. I popped in briefly to simply say hello and jolly good show sort of thing so that I could report to the team. I doubt he was capable of knowing or feeling real friendship for anyone. Look at his total silence towards Wickins after their separation. And poor Hooke who he attacked like a wolf on its prey, attempting to destroy him, and making cruel remarks about his physical defects. Leibniz was pursued beyond the grave. Silly Fatio who made sexual contact with him was finally spurned coldly and completely.

"There was a moment, maybe even a full minute, when I was dancing with Isaac when I felt his body begin to melt into the music and he almost smiled and almost felt some human warmth in his veins. Something might have been possible. I could feel that he might be able to become a marvellous man as well as a marvellous scientist. But that moment was shattered by the entrance of Wickins. The person in the world who loved Newton most in his entire life. And his presence made Isaac snap back from the freedom of spirit he was approaching, snap back like a big, stretched rubber band, back into the iceberg that was Newton, the natural philosopher. The spirit never ventured out again."

NOT TALKING ABOUT 1759

Red temper tantrums erupted when it was time to discuss 1759. These were much worse than the silence over Caravaggio and several other little displays of annoyance that had occurred from time to time. This time it mostly seemed to be Drew in a temper with himself.

"We congratulated ourselves all through that dreadful year," he confessed. "Could not stop patting each other on the back. Thought we'd turned all the corners and were in the home straight. Perhaps my metaphors are becoming too Eleven-dimensional. Never mind. An awful year. Success had blessed us. We found both Blake and Mozart that year. William was only two years old and such a darling and Wolfgang was a complete little terror and three. And so brave, both of them, when I punctured their heads. We all knew we had found two of the greatest ever. Oh it was grand.

"And it was then that I gave Voltaire his marvellous line. Yes, I created that idea. I said to him that he was seeing the world at its peak of greatness, that he was living at a time when everything was perfectly aligned for unbounded prosperity and unbridled genius to bloom. This is the best of all possible worlds, I told Voltaire. And he used it in a marvellous satire which to this day torments me when I think of it."

"But what happened that was so terrible?" I asked.

"What happened was that the Red North-West team came to believe in its own arrogant assumptions. We actually and totally came to accept that we had, in fact, managed to create the best of all possible worlds here on this Earth. This was the year when Red arrogance was at its height. Is the phrase 'cock-a-hoop' still in use? We were cock-a-hoop. We thought we were the ant's pants and the bee's knees. And we were hopelessly misguided. The French Revolution was just a short spin down the road, just over the horizon, within arm's reach with its terrible, bloody guillotine. And Napoleon was pretty close too.

"In our deep ignorance bolstered by false assumptions about variables and lines towards the future, we came to believe that the world was perfect and that we had made it so. What big-headed fools we were."

And he burst into tears and that was the end of that day's work.

MOZART, 1766

Drew watched as Leopold Mozart left the hotel, alone. The servants had gone after lunch and, by now, young Wolfgang would be having his afternoon sleep. The strains of the tour and constant headaches brought the boy to the point of exhaustion each day. Drew had seen the performance on the previous night and had noted how Wolfgang was distressed throughout most of the program. Of course, being a performing dog for his father brought its own particular stress to bear on the brain, but Drew had also observed the medical condition that would soon kill the lad. He was now only 10 years old and Drew calculated that he would be dead by 15.

Nobody noticed as Drew climbed the stairs to the second floor. He had created a diversion by powdering a lady's tea with a herb that caused loud screams, a fainting fit and bright, joyous recovery after only two minutes. As payment for her discomfort, the lady would receive the blessed benefits of the herb which included sensual euphoria for at least a week. Drew rapped loudly on Mozart's door. After a third rapping, a young voice yelled through the closed door, "Who is that?"

"My name is Drew. Your father sent me to fetch you. He needs you."

"What for?"

"He didn't explain. He simply said to fetch you."

"I'm not a dog to be fetched." Drew pinched himself for allowing the dog thought to carry over.

"I'm sorry. He didn't actually say fetch. But he does need you."

Drew was pleased though that the boy had latched onto the dog idea.

"Why?"

"He didn't say."

"Then I'm not coming. This is the time for me to sleep."

"But you must come. He'll be angry."

"He'll be angry if I open the door to somebody who is clearly telling lies."

Drew had never learnt how to lie like a European. He also found it distasteful to try. However, he had learnt that almost all social intercourse, politics and commerce were based in lying. People could only understand each other if they lied. If you didn't lie, no-one knew how to respond to you. The taunt that young Mozart was making to him was not that he was lying but that he was lying badly. Drew decided to try again.

"I'm sorry. You're quite right. But I was lying so that I wouldn't spoil the surprise."

"What surprise?"

This was becoming ridiculous, having this drawn out conversation through a door with a 10-year-old genius. Drew wanted to tell the boy that he was the nice red-headed doctor who had given him the injection of green liquid when he was only three years old and that he needed more treatment.

"If I tell you, it won't be a surprise."

"Go away. I have to sleep."

"Your father wants to buy you a new coat. He wants you to try it on for size."

"I already have several coats."

"This one is really grand."

"Liar."

"I promise you, I'm not lying."

"Stop knocking on my door. I've got a headache."

Of course you have, Drew thought to himself. A headache caused by green liquid. Caused by the extra growth of your brain due to that green liquid. And if you'd only let me in, you silly boy, I'd be able to help you.

"Have you gone away?" Mozart asked.

The boy sounded so tired. Drew had a flash of inspiration. This was not an ordinary monkey he was talking to. This was young Mozart, already a musical genius, already an extraordinary mind. Drew would tell him the truth.

"I'm still here. I've come back to help you. When you were three years old you let me pump a tube of green liquid into your head. It's made your brain grow too big for your skull. If you let me in, I can help you."

Mozart opened the door.

"So it is you," Mozart said, looking at Drew's hair. He then kicked Drew hard in the shins. "You told me the green stuff wouldn't hurt me." Drew was hopping about holding his ankle. At least he was inside the room. Mozart slammed the door. "You said it would help me with my music. You liar." Mozart kicked Drew in the other leg and Drew sank to the floor, almost in tears. The shins are the weakest part, by far, of a Red's anatomy. Mozart kicked him a third time.

"Please stop," Drew begged. "I didn't lie. Aren't you a great musician?"

"Yes." Mozart sat dejectedly in a chair. "But my head is killing me. My father says it's just growing pains, but I know I'm dying from it."

"In a way your father's right. Your brain is growing too much. It's a very special brain. That's why I've come back to help you."

"You helped me when I was three years old and too silly to stop you. Now I know better."

"My colleagues and I didn't know then that our liquid would create such strong growth in a young brain. But it can be corrected."

"I've had headaches for nearly five years. Why didn't you come before?"

"I only get to these parts every seven years, I'm afraid. I am sorry that you've had such pain." And he was genuinely sorry. He didn't enjoy the sufferings of these poor, sad monkeys, not even a little bit.

"Where do you come from?" Mozart demanded. "How do I know I can trust you?"

"It's almost impossible for me to explain where I come from, but perhaps I can suggest the place to you from your own knowledge."

"Why can't you just tell me the truth?"

"Let me ask a question that might reveal the truth."

"All right. I love riddles and puzzles and tricks."

"Where does your music come from? Not your performance skills, not the music you know, not the music you've learnt, but where does your own music, the music you create, the music that is your gift – where does it come from?"

"I don't know. It's inside me. From God, I suppose. I don't really know."

"Yes, you do. Close your eyes and picture how you feel and what happens when the music comes."

Mozart closed his eyes. He wet his lips and scratched his forehead. He was so cute and loveable and helpless. Drew couldn't avoid loving him. He also noticed how badly the skull was bulging at the forehead. Reconstruction was desperately necessary.

"It comes from behind a door," Mozart said. "It's a huge door that never really closes. It's always a little bit ajar and notes spill out into my mind. When it swings open – and I never really know when that might happen – it reveals a vast gold and black and red room that is crammed to the ceiling with music. It's solid music, like heavy statues, that I could touch if I could get in there. In fact, there isn't any ceiling. The music is piled so thick and high, it looks like there's a ceiling but it's more music, going on forever. Some of the music tumbles out and bounces up and down in my mind until I write it down. If I don't write it down it bounces and bounces until it hurts."

"One day that door will stay open and never close and you'll live in that room."

"Could I? Do you promise? I'd give anything at all to be allowed to live in that wonderful room. Anything."

"Give me four days of your life and give me your trust and I'll give you the key to your music room."

"Is that where you live? In a music room? You said you'd explain."

"Imagine that you have walked right into that room and passed through the gold portion of the room. Imagine more doors. Imagine each door leading into a vaster, richer, brighter room each time. Imagine passing through eleven of these doors into eleven of those rooms and you have come to the world where I live. I live behind the eleventh door."

"Can anyone go there? Could I go there?"

"Very few people ever have the chance to peek into the glorious first room that is in their own brains, let alone have the door stay open a crack for them. Hardly anyone in history gets to walk about in that first room. You will. You'll be so very special, my boy, that people will idolise you forever."

"Forever?" Mozart had a look of deep disdain on his face.

"Several hundred years at least."

"That's more realistic. What do I have to do?"

Mozart packed a small portmanteau and dressed warmly. He

wrote a note for his father, as dictated by Drew, assuring him that he would return in a few days and not to worry. The boy insisted on adding, "I have to have my brain repaired. The headaches are too terrible." Drew knew that this would worry Herr Mozart but he also calculated that the man would think his son was going mad and would be kinder and more careful in future with the boy. Drew also calculated, correctly, that Herr Mozart would not report the disappearance to the authorities, fearing the boy would be placed in an insane asylum if anyone else read the note. So, history does not record the kidnapping of Mozart or his four-day disappearance in 1766. It does record a bout of fever that confined the boy to his hotel room for some days, necessitating cancellation of several performances.

Drew took Mozart to the house he had rented near the cathedral. A further diversion was necessary in the hotel foyer before they could exit without being noticed. Mozart held Drew's hand as they walked along, mostly keeping to laneways and back streets where young Mozart would not be recognised. At one point they were approached by an extremely unpleasant man, well-dressed and well-spoken, who wanted to know if the boy was for sale. Drew negotiated a good price, accepted the money and then, while shaking hands with the man, induced a massive heart seizure from which the man fell down dead. Drew and Mozart walked on.

"It seems to me that you actually murdered that man," Mozart said, after some minutes of silence.

"Quite right. We don't want men like him lurking about, do we? Humanity is better off without them."

"Murdering anyone is wrong."

"Not at all. Don't be fooled by the preachers who tell you that all human life is sacred. Goodness gracious, Wolfie, what a crazy idea.

Most humans are hardly better than monkeys. Hardly more useful either."

Mozart was surprised by these refreshing views, although he was quite fond of the few monkeys he had met. But he had often wondered what use and value many people were. Drew cautioned against eliminating quite reasonable lives on the grounds of snobbishness. No, the elimination of humans needed to have sound logic behind it. Between them they made a list, as they walked, of the people who should be eliminated and Mozart agreed that traffickers in children and slaves, even black ones, should be high on the list. Drew had finally convinced Mozart that black people were indeed people and often quite worthy ones. Mozart's prejudice against black people was largely based in ignorance as he assumed they all had something to do with chimney sweeping. His father had often threatened to make him into a chimney sweep if he didn't practise enough and had told him he would turn into a little black boy and die as the blackness crept into his body and ate him up. Drew wanted to include people who told scary stories to children on the list of dispensable humans but Mozart would not hear of it. He did, however, agree to include people who kept huge, savage dogs.

The room Drew had prepared for the operation was almost empty. There was a comfortable chair and a small table with strange shapes appearing under a very white cloth. The room was warm despite the outside weather and the fact that there was no fire. Another fact that bothered Mozart was that the room was full of music but there were no instruments or players there. Perhaps, he said aloud, people were playing very loudly in another room, but the sound seemed to be right there, with him, beside him. Drew could see that little Mozart had begun to concoct an explanation from all the evidence he was amassing. Mozart thought he knew exactly who Drew was. The murder in the back-streets, the redness, being able to know his innermost mind, the promises of fame. It was all adding up.

Drew took Mozart's coat and hat and portmanteau and placed them in a corner. He helped the boy out of his shirt and sat him in the chair. Mozart was shivering. Drew came from the table, holding a large razor-like object in his hand. Mozart let out a quiet, high-pitched scream. His shivering increased.

"Do you want the room to be warmer?" Drew asked.

"I'm not cold. I'm afraid of you."

"I understand. But it won't hurt one little bit. Don't worry."

"I know who you are," Mozart blurted out. "But no matter how much money you promise me or how much you torture me, I'll never sign your dreadful letter."

"Oops," Drew laughed. "There's a misunderstanding here. I don't want you to sign anything. This is all to protect your future, your music, your fame."

"I'll never renounce God. Even you cannot make me do that."

"Who is it that you think I am?"

"I won't say your dreadful name. But you're all red. You've come straight here from hell."

Drew laughed heartily.

"Are you going to murder me?" Mozart's voice trembled terribly.

"No! I am not Satan, little Wolfie. Don't be afraid of me."

"You're going to use that razor to make me bleed and then make me sign away my soul to you in my own blood in return for fame and riches. Well, I won't do it. I'll never sign!"

"I'm going to use this instrument to cut off your hair. I need to shave your head to get at your skull. I've got to loosen up your skull a bit, you see, so your brain will fit in. Your skull is already misshapen, there at the forehead. You know how it bothers you. And even with that bulge, your brain is still too big. But you won't feel anything because I'm going to use these special devices to cure you." Drew lifted the cloth and revealed a shiny helmet-like object and other devices.

"You're from the Inquisition! My father told me he'd report me to the Inquisition if I didn't obey him. Please don't torture me. I obey him almost all the time."

The boy was trembling terribly. Drew sat beside him and placed an arm around his naked shoulders. "Don't be afraid. I'll tell you the truth. I'm your guardian angel. God has been so pleased with you that He sent me to help you."

Mozart looked at him, suspiciously. "Guardian angel?"

"Yes. Look."

Drew walked up one wall and across the ceiling and down the other wall.

"Satan could do that," Mozart said.

"At least you have to admit that I'm not from the Inquisition."

"My father says they have strange powers."

"How can I ever convince you? You're afraid of so many things. Surely, if I wanted to kill you and torture you I would have done it by now? I wouldn't be standing about here arguing with a child, would I? You are only 10, you know."

"I'm not a child. I'm Mozart."

"Wonderful. Yes. You are Mozart, but nearly a dead Mozart. If I don't repair your head you'll be dead by 15."

"Why did you hurt my head in the first place? How can I trust you?"

Drew was becoming agitated and he walked about the room, making Mozart even more nervous. Drew himself was nervous, hoping his medical studies had been enough to ensure he could actually complete this operation successfully. But he knew he had to calm the boy, had to be kind to him. It was true that Wolfie's head was full of fear as well as full of music and Drew needed to be patient about that. So he sat on the floor in front of the boy and took some deep breaths and proceeded quietly and gently.

"The green liquid helped you to develop your great musical abilities. Without it you would probably be the equal of your father but nothing more. Would you be satisfied with that?"

"My father is a fine musician." Drew was looking hard at him so he continued, "But of course I would not be satisfied."

Drew explained further, "I'm only permitted to visit you every seven years. If I don't fix your brain now you will be dead before I come back."

Mozart smiled and said, "I didn't know guardian angels were so restricted."

"It's not such an easy job. And I have many people to visit when I do visit."

"Who?"

"Not people you would know."

"Tell me anyway. Do you inject all of them too?"

"Yes. Not every visit. There's another little boy, almost two years younger than you. I gave him the juice when he was only one year old and since then he's been able to see visions of heaven."

"Do you make mistakes with us all the time then?"

Drew was somewhat angry about this remark as it was much too close to the truth. "That's not a mistake. It's part of his nature. It will help him to become a great artist. He lives in London. See how far I have to travel on my visits."

"I've been to London. I know how far it is. But I assume you can fly. Anyway who is this boy?"

"You don't know him."

"Perhaps I'll hear his name one day when he is great and then I'll know you told the truth."

Drew took more deep breaths. He was starting to realise that this poor boy probably didn't have many conversations with anyone – well, not with anyone who would treat him sensibly. So Drew humoured him. "One day, if my calculations are correct, and they are, you will hear about an Englishman who paints huge canvasses of sweeping grandeur, landscapes glowing with life. He will be loved and admired by all. I have just come from seeing him again and already he draws beautifully. One day, Wolfie, you will hear the name of William Blake ringing throughout Europe."

"I'll listen for it. William Blake, landscape artist."

"With William and you, Wolfie, I will prove that the green juice is best given when the subject is very young. The real difficulty is finding which baby is a potential genius. I've staked my whole reputation as a guardian angel on you two boys."

"Will my name ring throughout Europe too? And will I be rich?"

"Yes to both questions. You will be very famous and your cheekbones, lips and chin reveal your ability to deal well with the practical aspects of life. Wealth will be yours for the asking."

"Good. I like money. Perhaps you'd better repair my head now. But don't make any mistakes."

Mozart stayed silent while Drew shaved his head. Drew gave him a mirror and they both struggled to hold their laughter in, but finally both burst into convulsions of giggles. When they regained control, Drew massaged the boy's head with ointment.

"My father won't laugh when he sees my bald head."

"You have plenty of lovely powdered wigs. No-one need ever know."

"I like it. I want to play at my next recital bald."

"Not a good idea. Now, let yourself fall asleep. I have to crack your skull open like an egg and keep this bone part here separated so it will grow more and leave more space for your brain. It won't hurt but you have to stay here some days and you'll have to wear this helmet." Drew placed the large, shiny helmet over Mozart's head, leaving his face uncovered. "Don't be afraid."

"I'm not afraid any more. I trust you."

Mozart held Drew's hand and squeezed it warmly. A large tear of delight ran down Drew's red face. But he also felt some sadness for he knew that his sentimentality made him unfit for this work. He cared too much; became too upset when subjects were hurt; became too depressed when experiments failed. Worse still, he was too intolerant of human ugliness and killed people occasionally. That was forbidden, although everyone in the team admitted to the occasional imposed termination. After all if you were trying to better the race by creating geniuses, why not also get rid of some rotten apples too? But he shook these thoughts away because he had to concentrate on saving little Wolfie's life.

Three days later, the helmet was taken off. Drew's hands shook as he did it. The skull had healed and the extra bone growth was strong. Drew beamed with pride at his own cleverness. The bulge in Mozart's forehead was a little more pronounced but there would be no more headaches and it was clear to Drew – later to be proved wrong, of course – that Mozart would live a very long life.

Mozart was rather sad to leave Drew. They filled in their time with some wonderful games and jokes and it was the most relaxing time the boy had ever had. Drew promised he would come back in seven years. They retraced their steps through the ugly lanes and went into the cathedral so that Mozart could say a prayer of thanks for the visit of his guardian angel. Then they returned to the hotel.

Leopold Mozart looked tired and ill when he opened the door, but his face lit up when he saw his son standing there, smiling broadly. Leopold took Wolfgang in his arms and many tears fell. But Leopold soon turned furiously to Drew and declared, "You'll have no money from me, my man. In fact, you'll find yourself in prison if you don't provide a swift explanation."

"Drew saved my life, father. My headaches are cured. Look." Wolfie removed his hat and proudly showed his bald head.

Leopold gasped and then roared, "You did this to my boy?"

Drew induced a temporary paralysis upon the older Mozart then told Wolfie to go to his room as he and Herr Mozart needed to have a chat.

"Thank you, guardian angel," Wolfgang said and they shook hands with great seriousness. "Come back in seven years. You'll be proud of me."

"I'm sure I will be. I am already proud of you."

"You're really an African wizard, aren't you? Tell me the truth."

"Africa is close to where I live. And, yes, I suppose I am what you might call a wizard."

"I thought so. In Paris I saw drawings of Africa. Goodbye."

When the boy had gone, Drew said to the father who was quite able to hear and understand, "Leopold, you are not a nice man. But you have been blessed with a very special son. It's my job to look after him. I am a sort of guardian angel. I must tell you that if you ever beat him again I will find you and kill you. Do you understand that? You can see how I can paralyse you with a mere touch. It would take little effort to rid the world of your arrogant, cruel presence totally. Be warned."

Drew walked away, leaving Leopold frozen in the narrow hallway, terrified but unable to move. Three minutes later Leopold regained his faculties and history records that he never again beat Wolfgang after 1766.

[Terrifying Leopold was not such a triumph for Drew as it might at first seem. Drew later discovered that Leopold was, from everyone's account, bar the young Wolfgang's, a kind and affectionate father. The beatings Wolfie referred to were usually verbal chastisements when Wolfie was at his most annoying and perhaps, very rarely, a gentle slap "that would hardly harm a gnat" according to a family friend. Drew took it all in good humour and chuckled about Wolfie's trickery as he told the codicil to the story.]

NOTES on VISITS from 1780 to 1794, with a 1787 MOZART VISIT plus REFLECTIONS

"Willy-wagtail Wordsworth at 10 years of age was even then a tedious little Mother Nature botherer, tree hugger and writer of tracts against the destruction of anything organic; flower, animal, insect, bird, bee or bush. The only reason he accepted the juice was because it was green. I told him it was pure sap from a flowering plant on my home planet which had teats on it like a cow, so the sap could be extracted painlessly and if, in fact, we did not milk it the plants would burst and die. He actually believed this fantastic story. But he was a little beast. Never liked him. Never liked his milk-sop poetry. He was not so self-righteous some years later when I caught him in Paris with his mistress and their illegitimate daughter. Ha! That was a sweet revenge.

"It was one of those you-should-have-seen-the-look-on-his-face moments. I was a perfect gentleman and took them to lunch in a lovely little place in Montmartre where several of my other mentorees were living at the time. Willy sent me a nice note thanking me for my discretion. It's in the museum. You'll find it."

Drew thought little Sammy Taylor Coleridge was a lovely kid. At eight he used to get high from sniffing the excessive cigar smoke in his uncle's drawing room. One day he explained to Drew very seriously, "I want my family to call me 'Tail' which is short for Taylor which is my middle name, but the long and short of it is that they will not. They say it would sound as if I were the family dog. I think it is very unfair. When I am writing poems there are many words that rhyme with Tail, such as snail and quail and bail and pale and prevail and mail and ail and hail and fail and sail and dale and gale and nail and whale and rail and ...."

"Stop! I follow your idea and I'm sure your parents have scarred you for life, but there are worse things they could do to you. I know little boys who are beaten by their parents every day."

"I'm quite sure I wouldn't like that. I don't even like it when I see someone beat a horse or hit a dog with a stick. Of course, I think hitting a cat might be quite a good thing to do if you could ever catch one."

The kid kept rambling on all through the injection. He just would not shut up. Drew told him that this must remain a secret and he said, "Of course. I'm eight years old. I know when something must be kept secret. I'm very reliable."

Drew laughed a lot at the memory of little Coleridge, "Such a damn chatterer but a lovely child. Who could have known he'd be the one to turn to opium?" Drew seemed to do very well with children. He side-tracked to his meeting with Beethoven when Ludwig was 10. "I liked him from the moment I set eyes on him and he liked me too. It was also nice to meet a young composer who did not insist on kicking me."

Drew enjoyed the company of Tell children, including the Romantic poets when they were "kiddies", except Wordsworth. He claimed the Romantics, a broad grouping of great English poets, as another planned achievement of his Red team. He was not all that fond of the older poets because he thought Karrel, who had ended up as supervisor of that particular congregation, had influenced them too much with his own overly sentimental approach to life, nature and poetry. Leigh Hunt and John Keats were two children Drew especially liked. He injected Hunt at 10 years old and Keats at six.

"Of course, Keats was done in 1801 but this time issue is such an odious restraint when we are dealing with history because I can't speak about Keats without Leigh or Leigh without John. There was a deep, deep purity about John that few other people seemed to possess even as children. In fact, I think he died a virgin. That's what Karrel said anyway. Very sad. Leigh was a decade older than John and had a terrible political influence on him. Poets don't need to be political. What were they all thinking? It was the fault of that damn French Revolution, of course. Many of the English were much too keen on those ideas. They weren't there watching the blood run in the gutters though, were they? John was a lovely boy. Even when he was 20 and I visited with Karrel he rushed to us and hugged us and kissed us on both cheeks. Such a warm boy. I sometimes wondered if we got the kisses because he thought we were French." That produced a huge laugh from Drew.

"1787 was not a good year for me. I'd been trying to have a child while I was home but … I've always been a restless creature. And conceiving is such a complicated process for us Reds. I'd been having an unpleasant time with one of my hive partners and even a slight falling out with one of them affects all the others and makes simultaneous fertilisation almost impossible. Can you imagine the difficulties? No, of course you can't. How could a human person ever know the hardships of conception? You promiscuous, prolific, fecund monkeys only have to co-join for two minutes and someone gets pregnant."

"Don't pick on the human race," I retorted. "Everything about us is the fault of you interfering, arrogant, terminally mistaken Reds, who think you have the right to go running around the … the …

solar system or universe or dimensional hyper-space or whatever it is you run around, doing anything you like to any other race of creatures you can get your hands on. And getting it wrong every time."

Drew stood and looked at me with an imperious air. My attempt at being smart and off-hand and profoundly critical was indeed rather pathetic. Then Drew fell on the floor in fits of laughter. My indignity could not hold up and soon I was bellowing with laughter too. It was a pretty foolish speech even though I believed it to be true at the time. By then also, I was completely caught up in using triples. After a few minutes we took some deep breaths and settled down and agreed that we both felt so much better. Drew poured ice-cold drinks which were delicious and made from some jungle fruit the tribespeople cultivated.

Then we got to work recording the trials and tribulations of 1787, ignoring the whole French turmoil, which would eventually become the biggest collaboration mess the Reds had ever been responsible for. "Someone clever called it the French Revolution. Should have called it the French Chaotic Bloodbath. Doesn't have the same ring of idealism as revolution I suppose." The whole thing pained him too much to recall it. He insisted that all the blame lay with Khrys and Karrel who were the chief team members involved, although he admitted that every one of the team put a finger in the pie, adding more mistakes to the mistakes. He declared that when reporting on the decades of the 1780s and 1790s he would not discuss with me anything French, especially if the names Danton, Marat or Robespierre were involved. Of course, he broke the rules himself occasionally, but all rules in our discussions were only meant to apply to me anyway.

"So, it's 1787 and I call on Beethoven in Bonn and he's not home. His teacher told him he must go to Vienna and meet and learn with a miraculous composer and harpsichordist who could inspire him and teach him to be great. He was sending him to Mozart. Can you picture those two together in the same room? Well, I suppose you can't."

"I know they met. It's history. Mozart was very impressed by him."

"Impressed? Are you joking? De-pressed is the word. There was no possibility that Mozart would ever teach Beethoven. Both of them were masochists, long before the word was invented, but not enough to tolerate each other's personalities. And as history records – Tell history, not Red history – there was no teaching involved. Anyway, I did not want to be near those two temperaments right then and it was clear from my brief call at the Beethoven home that things were unhappy there. His father was a hopeless alcoholic. What is it with Tells and alcohol?"

"Your fault!"

We both had a bit of a giggle.

"Anyway I popped down to … where was it? Spain! Somewhere in Spain to see Goya. That was quite pleasant. He had been doing these cartoons for tapestries. He painted them and the factory made them up. Very commercial arrangement. It didn't seem to me to be a worthy thing for a great artist to be involved in and I told him so. I never have learned to stop giving advice. It's almost invariably wrong. Madrid! I'm sure that's where we were. Goya made a lot of money out of those tapestries. They were enormously popular. And they were excellent pictures too.

"He was doing some magnificent portraits. Not as many commissions as he would have liked but, by and large, on the whole, as far as one could make out, everything was fine. I told him he was going to have a long life, which he did, and enjoy excellent health. Being a famous historian [that was a sarcastic remark] you will be aware that he went stone deaf later and suffered perpetual ringing in his ears, which almost drove him mad. And he developed an unhealthy interest in bulls. Just like his Spanish compatriot, Picasso. Although that was some years later."

"Picasso was a hundred years later. Can we please stay somewhere near the nominated date?"

Drew gave me an ice-cold look then another ice-cold drink and a warm smile. Then he told me the 1787 Mozart episode.

Drew knocked at the door of Mozart's apartment in Vienna. The piano was playing. The music was magnificent. Drew smiled proudly and waited. A few minutes later he knocked again. The piano played on. The music was entrancing. Ten minutes went by and Drew knocked yet again. The piano stopped. Then a voice roared through the door, "Go away! You're disturbing me."

"Wolfie, it's me, Drew, your Red friend."

"Don't call me that! Don't say anything. Just go away."

"Don't you remember me? I did the operation on your head when you were 10 years old? We had fun."

The door swung open and Mozart stood there, all five foot of him, in his nightshirt, smiling with his arms wide in welcome. Drew was surprised that he was so short and also rather ugly. They embraced.

"Drew, it is you. Twenty-one years have gone by and not a word, not a visit." Mozart led him through to his work room, where rather incongruously there was a billiard table quite near to the piano.

Mozart saw Drew's look and said, "The place is so small. Give me your coat. Constanze is with friends. Our baby is due very soon. So you must put up with my terrible manners as your host."

Mozart took Drew's coat and draped it carelessly over a chair. Then he turned and kicked Drew hard in the shins, remembering after so many years that Red people have a particular weakness in the shins. When Drew went down, Mozart kicked him in the other leg. Drew moaned in agony. Mozart took a billiard cue and held it at Drew's throat as if it were a sword.

"Twenty-one years and you come back disturbing my work and expecting a welcome after all the lies you told me. You said I'd be rich. Look at this place. Does this look rich to you? You said I'd be famous and loved and all I am is a failure. Liar!"

Mozart took the billiard balls off the table one at a time and dropped them on Drew's head. Drew begged for mercy. Of course, he could have overpowered the little man any time he wanted to but it did seem fair to let Wolfie take out his frustrations for a while. But after the sixth ball Drew had had enough and he caught the seventh and crushed it in his hand and showed Wolfie the small pieces.

"Oh," Mozart said. "I forgot you could do things like that. Let me help you up, old friend." He extended his hand and helped Drew to his feet but gave him one more shin kick for good measure. Drew growled but kept his temper and sat on a rather splendid chair.

"That's the last decent chair I have left to me," Mozart declared. "Things went well for a while and I started to believe in your predictions but soon I will have to borrow money to pay the rent. If it wasn't for the support of my friends in the Freemasons I would be in real trouble already. Is this how the greatest composer of the millennium is supposed to live? Isn't that what you said I was?"

"And you are, Wolfie! But the world is strange and genius is not always properly rewarded. However, I must say this is not such a terrible place. Not every composer can afford to have a billiard table of his very own. And there's plenty of room. In fact, this is a rather pleasant apartment. And surely you must get so much satisfaction from your ability. That piece you were playing was wonderful. What was that?"

"That was written by a child called Ludwig van Beethoven! Seventeen and he's already better than me."

Mozart threw another ball at Drew who caught it and crushed it. They both laughed wildly and then they hugged.

"I must stop throwing those things at you."

"Thank you. I would appreciate that."

"I don't have the money to replace them."

Mozart made some coffee as they talked.

"I suppose this Beethoven is one of your juice people," Mozart said. "I could see that you recognised his name."

"Yes, he is. But his music is very different from yours. I have high hopes for him. What do you think?"

"You didn't send him to me, did you? Is this another one of your tricks?"

"No. I didn't know he was coming to Vienna. I called at his house in Bonn and was told he was here and was planning to visit you."

"I was very busy. All I do now it seems is teach and teach. How else can a genius composer live? Rich! Hah!"

"A small mistake. Did Beethoven play for you?"

"I was only with him for a few minutes. There was little time to assess his skill." Drew raised his eyebrow and Mozart took a gulp of coffee. "His playing is superb. His composition is marvellous. It only took two minutes to know that. I'm sure you sent him just to show me what a miserable failure I am. Beethoven is the genius, not Mozart. And only 17."

"Wolfie, you were a genius at six."

"I was a wind-up toy circus freak. Beethoven will be greater than me."

"You are already the most brilliant composer the world will ever know."

"Ever?"

"Well, for several hundred years, let's say."

"That's what you said last time."

Mozart played some pieces from the new opera he was working on, Don Giovanni. Drew fell into raptures over the music, Wolfie's playing skills, and the whole concept of the opera. Drew flipped through the libretto as they spoke and was very impressed.

Mozart said, "It's almost ready but is Vienna ready?"

"This is good," Drew said of the libretto. "And the music is … so moving, Wolfie."

Drew gave Mozart a huge hug and Mozart, like all humans, melted in the Red arms and was revitalised by the warmth and love he felt from Drew.

"Is Lorenzo one of your experiments?" Mozart asked, pointing out the librettist's name on the front of the manuscript.

"Not as far as I know. He's good. Very good. But my juice people are geniuses." He was lying a little, of course, because he knew some were not. In fact, some went mad before they could achieve anything, some just never responded to the juice, and there were many who just went into shock and died when the juice hit their brains.

"Died?" I roared, interrupting the story. "You never said anything about them dying."

"Some just couldn't take it. No point talking about them because they never became anybody."

"That's not how Tells see it. Us humans, we value every life."

"Don't be ridiculous!" Drew laughed. "I have to say I was always upset when the failures were children and they dropped dead right there before me."

"Children!"

"Hundreds of children are dying all around the world every minute we speak. Don't be so high and mighty with me, Mr Tell. You don't need a grain of genius or even much intellect and talent to be able to feed the people on this planet and to keep them healthy and safe. You don't need any genius to learn to say no to war. You Tell creatures are killing off your children at a disgusting rate of knots because of your own greed and hatred and pride. We didn't put those character traits in the butterfly juice. Don't blame us for your natural flaws!" He was shouting. And for once he was not able to laugh.

I sat down, completely deflated. He was right. It wasn't human genius that kept people poor and hungry and sick. It was indeed greed and stupidity. I had gotten used to everything being the fault of the juice. I had lost my sense of human responsibility. The Red crimes against humanity were nowhere near as severe as our own crimes against ourselves. Drew called for tea and we sat silently until it was served. Then Drew continued with his 1787 Wolfie story.

Mozart told him, "Lorenzo and I did Figaro together. I enjoyed that. But it failed in Vienna. Prague loved it. Prague loves Mozart. But Vienna does not love Mozart."

"Vienna simply doesn't know Mozart well enough yet."

Drew convinced Wolfie to dress – the composer had the habit of working in his night attire until he needed to leave the apartment for a meal or a meeting – and take a lunch break. They went to Mozart's favourite tavern, where it was clear from the many friendly greetings he received that some of Vienna loved him. On the way, Drew bought him a bag of billiard balls, pens, paper and ink, new stockings and a shirt, gloves and stockings for Constanze, and several toys for the imminent baby. Then, Wolfie saw a coat that was "essential" and despite Drew saying no several times, when they walked out of the shop the coat was on Mozart's back. Wolfie was like a child himself over lunch with the toys arrayed on the table amongst the food and the tankards. Every now and then, Wolfie would get up and go to a mirror to admire his new coat. After two beers, Mozart was the best company in the world.

"And so," Drew sighed, "in your new history of the Western world I will go down as the man who bought Mozart a bag of billiard balls."

We laughed but there was now a darkness behind my laughter as I thought of the numbers who had died in this giant experiment. Was it okay to have a Mozart if 30 others injected at the same time died from reaction to the juice? How many dead people would be a satisfactory number for a Mozart? Three hundred? A thousand for an Einstein? Three thousand for a Michelangelo? Part of my mind was also sad because, despite the 'happy ending' to the 1787 visit, I knew Mozart had only four more years to live. Drew was making this history so present to me that I had lost all objectivity. Like Drew, I was starting to grow much too fond of these funny, little monkeys called human beings.

Napoleon was 25 in 1794 when Drew juiced him. Drew was inordinately proud of the many things Napoleon went on to achieve although he hastened to assure me that the butterfly juice created the statesman and emperor, the soldier and general was already there in his human nature. But that was all I got on Napoleon.

Barely enough to make one decent paragraph.

Drew diverted to another accidental meeting with Wordsworth in Paris – 26 years later. "There he was with his mistress on his arm. Annette something or other. Their illegitimate daughter called Anne – now an adult – was with them and in her arms she carried a baby. Goodness me, the old devil was a grandfather! How I laughed at him. And Willy-wagtail Wordsworth hated being laughed at. Very full of himself he was. No real humility. I made a passing comment about how admirably he behaved like a Frenchman when he was in France and how like an Englishman in England. We – Reds that is – have no concept of illegitimacy. How can any child be branded so inanely? It is their parents – especially the fathers who splash their seed about all over the place – who should be called illegitimate."

"What happened to Napoleon?" I demanded. "I thought you'd have lots of gossip and other stuff. He was one of the great figures in European history. And all I get is a few sentences."

"Stuff? You call my carefully crafted chronologies 'stuff'?" Drew snorted. "Anyway there's a thousand books about him. You know all you need to know. He was chubby and grumpy most of the time but he was not short. That's a myth. And it was Josephine who said the not tonight thing to him, not the other way around. Another myth. And she used to say not this morning and not today and not this week as well. After all, he was a Corsican, not a Frenchman."

My report on Napoleon therefore remains remarkably short, unlike the man himself, and I suppose finding out that truth was something worthwhile. The person who had sat in the Bonaparte tent and listened to him plan strategy with his generals and who had dined with the Bonaparte family and who had taken tea numerous times with Josephine had nothing else to report. I was beginning to suspect that Drew had no time and little respect for anyone other than artists. The scientists of whom he spoke with much affection were usually labelled as being more like poets than scientists.

[In a much later report, as a diversion, he did tell me that Napoleon had the strongest will and most forceful personality he had ever come across in Tells, with the possible exception of Florence Nightingale. When Napoleon spoke people obeyed and he was adored by the masses, especially by his soldiers. This just confirms what most of our own history books say anyway but it does come from an impeccable, first-hand source.]

GOYA and A MENTION OF SOME OTHERS, 1801

"This was a big year for the team. Karrel embarked on creating his Poets Ring which later became known as the Romantics. He did Byron, Shelley, Keats and little Johnny Clare all in the same year. From a lord to a peasant! You can see how very democratic we were. They were a lovely bunch of children, although at 13 Byron was quite the man. I always got on better with Tell children than with the stodgy, broken, empty souls that pass for adults on this world. How do you people lose your childishness so readily? The truly great ones never do, you know. Even Newton, filled with terror, remained a child in his relentless pursuit of knowledge. Napoleon planned his battles like a boy playing with toy soldiers. And that child-like quality was not preserved by the juice. My dear, dear Jane [Austen] had it and many other fine Tells who were never juiced were fine because they remained children in their spirits. Why can't you all be Peter Pans and never grow up? Wouldn't the world be wonderful?"

I interrupted him to say, "Could be incredibly chaotic and dangerous." He just looked at me with a wistful smile as if I had missed entirely the point he was making. And maybe I had.

"Poor Johnny Clare completely lost his mind in his 40s but I really do think that was not the fault of the juice. His writing fell out of fashion and he was forced to be a mere serf to earn enough to feed his family. The unfairness of earthly life often drives the sensitive to lunacy. And Clare was sensitive." Drew laughed at some unspoken memory.

"In 1801 I also visited Goya. I didn't want to because I felt so sorry for him. His deafness was worse than Beethoven's because of the terrible noises he had in his head most of the time. Although deafness to a painter is not as awful an affliction as for a composer. I assume."

Suddenly he stood triumphantly and grabbed my arm and dragged me into the museum to the library shelves.

"Proof!" he declared. "Speaking of the gallant Goya reminded me. Here is proof! Goya actually did an etching of me with the syringe. An existing picture – mind you, very satirical – of my adventures in the injecting game."

He had taken down a volume and was busily leafing through it. I said, "Some drawing hidden away in your archives is hardly proof for all the world to see."

"No, no, no. You don't understand." He showed me the cover of the book. It was Los caprichos, a collection of one of Goya's famous sets of etchings. This, indeed, was on sale in many local bookshops in a cheap soft cover reprint version. I had one in my own modest library back in Sydney. "Thousands of people the world over have seen this drawing of me and my syringe."

He triumphantly turned to plate 58, entitled, in English, "Swallow it, dog." Sure enough, there was a wild-eyed religious-looking person holding a huge syringe and aiming it at a cowering man begging for mercy. The man begging could have been Goya if you squinted a bit and looked at the picture in shadow.

"This is how Goya told our secret without telling it, so to speak," Drew explained excitedly. "There's a double meaning, as in so much of his work. A triple meaning if you count his associating the picture with words from a popular song of the time."

As I looked more closely at the etching, Drew sang the song, in

Spanish so I have no idea what it was about, and he also performed a slightly grotesque dance.

"To me, it looks like some crazy priest from the Spanish Inquisition threatening to torture someone, being egged on by a whole crowd of people. By the way, that hardly seems like a way to keep your mission secret." I was being deliberately sceptical and off-handed.

"That's what the normal public of his time would have seen," Drew said with a flourish of triumph. "Spanish Inquisition! And certainly that enema pump he's holding is a gross exaggeration of the instruments we Reds used – but the hidden messages are clear too. Although they are not pretty. Goya told me that the tall man standing at the back, his face mostly in shadow, was also me. And if you look closely you can see that's true."

Drew posed to give his face a similar masking and, by moonlight with the wind blowing in the right direction, I would have to say that the tall figure could, just possibly, if you squinted a bit, be Drew. The priest was also Drew, apparently, as Goya first met him, as a fervent servant of the juice, a priest of the needle, a ministrant of some holy communion wine which could cure all the ills of humanity. Well, Goya got that bit right.

The second message was the two faces of Goya himself. The kneeling man is Goya, face twisted in agony – beyond recognition? – at his past mistake in allowing himself to partake of the juice. The other Goya face looms above the laughers, almost like a death's head or a smarmy cardinal. But it is the present Goya – the 1790s Goya – grimly telling his earlier self that he was greedy and selfish and unprincipled when he accepted the juice and now he has his punishment through his terrible deafness. That deafness is represented by the entire picture: a punishment worse than the

Inquisition could administer, with his head filled with laughers and cynical voices and silent, looming presences.

[I was convinced at the time. But then, I am often too easily convinced. I do have second and third thoughts sometimes. A lot more third thoughts since I met the Red man, Drew. I'm not a journalist really, I'm a reporter. I see something and I write it down. Never mind the analysis, this is what I saw, take it or leave it. In the years spent preparing this material I came across a book about Goya written by another Australian, Robert Hughes. He deals with plate 58 in fine fashion, as he does all of Goya's work. And I hasten to add that neither Drew nor any other strange Red man appears in the brilliant account by Hughes of Goya's life and work. However, I am also compelled to say that Hughes does not deal at all with the two enigmatic figures in plate 58 which loom over the syringe scene. But there you have it. Proof, in Drew's eyes, or a possible mini-theory, in mine. But have a look at plate 58 for yourself. What do you think?]

WILLIAM BLAKE, 1808

"Oh, yes," Blake said, "I met Mozart and he was very strange. He said he regretted that he had never seen one of my large landscapes. He also said he wished he had become rich like I am. Where did he get such ideas? Very odd person."

"But with an excellent memory," Drew thought, "considering that I told him all that when he was 10."

"You've met him, of course?" William asked.

"Yes. Twice. And you're right. He was odd."

"He played a piece for me. Wonderfully beautiful."

It was 1808 and Drew sat on William Blake's bed in his humble house at 17 South Molton Street in London. There were not enough chairs in working order to seat three people and Drew felt it only polite to leave a chair free for Catherine, Blake's devoted wife. The surroundings were poor, mean, almost abject, but Drew felt relaxed. Blake was such warm company, almost like one of Drew's own people but with that human passion that Drew had come to admire, love and yearn for. The fact that Mozart had died some 17 years earlier did not bother either of them.

Drew knew that Blake had been able to wander freely in the Seventh and Eleventh Dimensions ever since he was four years old and had seen the face of Michelangelo peeking in at him. Being only four, William had reported that event as seeing the face of God, not an unreasonable mistake. Michelangelo always had a fetish for painting God in his own image. Then Blake adopted the habit of depicting God in Michelangelo's image too. Alas, in all things Blake was so far ahead of his age that he was condemned to a long life of misunderstanding and loneliness. Drew had asked William not to speak about his encounters with the dead but to no avail. Blake insisted on speaking out and so was thought mad by many of his peers.

Drew felt pity for this great man who was now chatting on excitedly about his exhibition to be held in the coming year. He told Drew that the catalogue itself would be unique and the exhibits would be his best work ever. He sincerely believed that the exhibition would establish his greatness as an artist. Drew held no such hope. He was aware of the unbridgeable gulf between William and his fellows of London town. How could ordinary mortals accept a man who regularly spoke with Milton, Voltaire, Jesus, Michelangelo, Shakespeare, Socrates and the Holy Ghost? This list names but a few who were cited in Blake's business correspondence. "Jesus has advised me not to accept this commission," William would write in all seriousness. In table conversation he spoke of his intercourse with the spirits of the great as if it should be an everyday occurrence for one and all as it was indeed for him. Even many of those who supported him assumed he was mad.

Blake's certainty that the earth was flat did not do him much good either, especially in the eyes of anyone with the slightest knowledge of science. But Blake was adamant. He knew from experience that the earth was flat because, of course, it was. The earth that he walked through, in and out of the Eleventh Dimension, was as flat as the proverbial pancake. It had to be so. It was the major factor in making travel possible to and from the Eleventh.

In Dimensions One to Three the world was a sphere but Blake was no more capable of limiting his thinking and physical being to three dimensions than he was of making money. Drew's reading of Blake's financial talents had been seriously flawed. He had made exactly the same mistakes with Mozart and Rembrandt. Fortunately for Drew's career very few of the team members in any of the sectors had been accurate in reading human physicality. None of them had effectively predicted, controlled or allowed for the variables. Often he and many of his team felt that the whole experiment was a blind guess, mere random chaos, a poorly told joke. Drew was at a low ebb. His last couple of visits had concentrated on group work: the French Revolution, the English romantic poets, the Balkan sculpture movement. This last had shown no positive results at all to date.

"I sometimes think Michelangelo is a little envious of me," Blake said. "He seems to think my likenesses of God are more accurate than his. I simply laugh at him when he starts with all that. I tell him that my images of God don't show him with a broken nose. That's a touch of vanity on Michelangelo's part. He has a broken nose so God has to have one too. The others laughed when I said that. No-one here laughs. A man at dinner – some weeks ago now – I'm not invited very often. I speak too openly and that's not admired. But on this occasion I was asked directly if Shakespeare resembled the famous engraving of him. I knew it was a trap to gain a laugh at my expense but what can I do? I had to answer and say that, yes, it was a quite fair likeness.

"Then I was asked how it was I could converse with Voltaire who is French. Firstly I told them that Voltaire and I do not converse, which surprised them. No, I told them, Voltaire and I simply shout at each other a great deal and declaim arguments back and forth. I do despise Voltaire. As to his language, I can only suppose that he speaks it in French and I hear it in English. After 30 years in the world of spirits, I should think he would have learnt such a simple trick. Once I'd started on Voltaire there was no rein on my enthusiasm and I held forth against war, abominable war, and against factories where bodies are crippled and minds shattered. I railed against the labour of children, the woe we bring to their tiny lives.

"I preached at my dinner companions to forsake the evaluation of everything by money. At this, they laughed and one touched the frayed cuffs of my thin coat, thinking to humiliate me. I looked at their gleaming faces, waiting for me to shrink from the insult, and I wanted to spew, knowing them so well. I told them that Jesus also wore a frayed and thin coat but they regarded that as audacious and almost blasphemous. They asked me why I didn't advance myself by painting works that customers might buy, thus pleasing the public and making my life richer. In terms of money was the clear meaning, not the richness of the soul. I replied that I painted because the Holy Spirit told me I must. Open talk about the Holy Spirit tends to kill conversation. I ate the dinner in silence then and came home alone. Even my few friends are embarrassed about the Holy Spirit.

"Imagination frightens all men. Newton was afraid of imagination. Especially Newton. But he was afraid of so many things in life. I'm not at all a friend of Newton. Another at the dinner became very serious with me and accusing. He said that I seemed to be so sure that my visions of these ghostly figures did occur in physical actuality. He thought I should be more humble and admit to doubt. I was shocked. Doubt, I queried him, doubt? How can I doubt what all my best senses tell me is so? 'If the Sun and Moon should doubt, They'd immediately go out.' Perhaps a little vain to quote my own poetry in my defence.

"But then I had to be truly silent because none in that room, in all London, could understand the pain of doubt that does rack me in parts of my being that seem hidden even from me. Doubt lodges there in the secret pockets of my soul and I cannot scratch it out. Is that so for you?"

"It has become so," Drew replied sadly.

"I felt sure you would know what I was trying to express."

"Oh yes, William. I am one of the very few people in all this world who knows what you are trying to express."

"I think that is so. Will you be in London next year for my exhibition?"

"I'm sorry but I won't be. I wish I could see it but I won't be in London again until 1815."

"Your seven year cycles are not unlike the rhythm periods of some giant insect. Sometimes I think you have the eyes of an insect, you know."

William looked deep into Drew's eyes and held them locked to his own for some minutes. Drew did not attempt to turn away.

"You're not human at all, are you?" William stated more than asked.

"No, I'm not."

"I thought so," William said and turned back to his work.

"How do you cope with it all, William? How can you have the patience? When no-one understands."

"There's Catherine."

"I suppose I never think of Catherine as a separate person from you. You two are so much one. She draws like you; she talks like you; she thinks like you."

"No," Blake corrected him, "she does not think like me but she accepts my mind. Some of my patrons and clients happily accept my engraving skills. Only you and Catherine happily accept my mind."

"Isn't that terrific for you?

Drew sometimes used the archaic version of words in his stories.

"Doesn't the isolation make you despair?"

"Oh no. In any moment of near despair I simply take a little walk."

Drew laughed heartily. "Of course."

"Then I have all the companionship any man could need. One cannot be lonely when there's Bacon and Milton and Socrates to gossip with. They're all great talkers."

"Good. I haven't done you so much harm in that case."

"You? Harm? Your visits delight me. I enjoy the seven year cycle. It's very gratifying that you spend some of your busy time with me."

Drew had begun to develop the horrific human quality of guilt. What had he done to this lovely man, this unique soul, William Blake? His guilt told him that his actions with the juice had condemned Blake to a life of loneliness, poverty and humiliation. His objective assessment was more positive. Blake could wander in the magic dimensions of Seven and Eleven; he could speak often and freely with the greatest figures and artists in earth's history; he could create poetry and art of blinding brilliance. It wasn't such a bad life.

"If you look in that top drawer," Blake said, "you will see two new works I have completed. They are my finest poems. The paintings for them are there too. I won't include them in the exhibition. I'll take my time engraving these. The world will be so surprised by them."

Drew spread the work on the bed and sat and read and re-read them and absorbed the pictures. This wonderful pleasure occupied some hours. The poems were titled, Barry Wood: A Poem and Book of Moonlight. They were of a beauty and intense revelation unlike anything written or painted to this time. Only the later work of the collaboration known as Shakespeare, came within range of this new work by Blake. Amazing, Drew thought, that this primitive race, so limited in so many ways, still only able to draw on a portion of their potential brain power, could in the past 200 years have progressed so far. Perhaps the team's work on improving the butterfly juice had been more successful than their wildest expectations. Or might there be something special and as yet unknown in the genetics and psyches of these monkeys?

To see the pictures for the Book of Moonlight was to hold actual moonbeams in one's hand. The world was not ready for this. Blake would surely be locked away. These books would be frightening proof to ordinary mortals that Blake was mad. Drew carefully slipped the manuscripts and pictures into his large bag. He banged the drawer as if replacing them there.

"Do you like them?" William asked.

"They are beyond genius," Drew said. "No-one else in this whole world can reveal such truth."

"Yes, I know. It's a wonderful burden. It gives me such joy to know the truth but I feel great pain when the truth is continually rejected."

"I think you're very sensible to lock this work away until your exhibition has been a success. Then the world may be ready." Drew had learnt to lie a little better since 1766.

"I'm pleased you have seen them and like them."

"I love them, William. I adore them. You're a great, great artist and poet."

"Thank you," William said with real humility. Tears ran down his cheeks. "It's not often that anyone says such things to me. Forgive my tears."

William placed his tools down carefully and embraced Drew. Catherine had been preparing inks in their small work room so that Drew and William could talk. William now got her and all three put on their coats and went out to eat. Drew was able to buy the poor man and his dedicated wife a feast of a meal. It was forbidden to give money to any subject but an occasional meal or other useful object was permissible. Rembrandt had been very grateful for a warm coat in a particularly bitter winter. Drew remembered several banquets shared with Galileo. A strong, white mare had solved Molière's transport problems at a difficult time. What a difference it might have made if Drew had been allowed to shower money on, for instance, Blake, Mozart and Rembrandt. Although Drew was aware that in all probability, given the in-variables with these three, Mozart would have just drunk even more expensive wine; Blake would have left the money in a pile somewhere for people to steal it; Rembrandt's inadequacy with money would have sent him bankrupt anyway. Interference had to be strictly limited. He knew that and he approved. But sometimes it did hurt him so to see his lovely monkeys struggle and suffer and go without.

The Blake poems and pictures which Drew acquired on this visit would be added to his impressive collection. The collection – even in 1808 – was quite extensive and each item was a superb example of the incredible development, growth and scope of the juice subjects. Drew's collection was also evidence which he hoped would eventually lead to the cancellation of the experiments. In his rooms he had the only copy – in Henry Neville's own hand – of the Shakespeare play *The Island of Time.* The group had remembered enough of it to create *The Tempest*, but that play, with all its greatness, was a pale shadow of the earlier drama. Drew planned that his child, not yet born, would release the collection of masterpieces into the world in five or six hundred years, when the people of the world would be ready emotionally and mentally for them. Some clever researcher would unearth them; probably several clever researchers.

The collection – only a third the size in 1808 of what it would become by the middle of the 20th century – included other plays. Goethe, Racine, Marlowe, Schmidt, Baxter, Molière, and a young Lord Byron all figured in the list of brilliant, unproduced plays purloined by Drew from their authors. Astounding pictures by Turner, Rubens, Rembrandt, Potts, Velázquez, El Greco, Raphael, da Vinci, and Botticelli graced the collection. There was an exquisite marble by Michelangelo which had been stolen in a clever raid on his studio involving eight strong men and two teams of horses. Fortunately, in 1521 Drew had also stolen a set of da Vinci's late drawings of a flying machine which would have flown if built and operated to exact specifications. Imagine the confusion for all Tell history if these drawings had fallen into the hands of a decent engineer. Drew's team had estimated, taking several thousand variables into account, that the human race would not normally invent flying machines until the 26th century.

Khrys had been dealing with da Vinci, who told him about the ideas in 1514 and that the plans were being drawn up. Drew had been given the emergency job in 1521, just two years after da Vinci's death, to examine his papers and remove the flying machine drawings. No Tell creature had realised what the plans represented at that time so no harm was done. Drew claimed the drawings for his own collection.

All the works in Drew's collection had the same qualities in common. Each was filled with light: emotional light, intellectual brilliance, and physical radiance. Each had the ability to almost blind with its sheer beauty. Each was revelatory to an extent beyond usual human capacity. But Drew strongly suspected that the time when humanity could accept and appreciate these works was racing towards the team more rapidly than had ever been thought possible.

Even in 1808 Drew knew that something was seriously amiss with the experiment and felt that it was exploding beyond their control.

Drew had come to love his gorgeous race of monkeys and did not want to leave them, did not want to abandon the experiment. He wanted to try, for another century or so at least, to bring the experiment back within the range of the original variables, calculated by some of the greatest Red minds in history, including one of his parents. But he was beginning to wonder if, perhaps, there was a greater complexity to human brains than had ever been allowed for. Certainly, the links between physical qualities and mental qualities were not as clear and precise as the Reds had observed in their earliest visits. There was strong evidence that human thought mechanisms were, amazing though it may seem, closely linked to their erratic emotions and lusts. It even seemed that strong and keen emotions actually enhanced the capacity for rational thought. From his own team's observations Drew had to admit that the original intricate tables of variables could no longer be relied upon.

Blake, Beethoven and Goya were the latest and most interesting examples of people whose creative and intellectual performances seemed to be enhanced rather than hindered by great hardship and physical incapacity. The continual ringing in Goya's ears would drive a normal monkey insane but Goya had risen above it, creating work beyond previous expectations. Drew's current favourite, Ludwig van Beethoven, was another experiment afflicted with deafness. Yet, despite the chaotic noises Ludwig had inside his head, he could create sounds of wondrous complexity, beauty and harmony. Drew was proud of him.

Over their dinner, Drew told the Blakes about Beethoven and they were delighted to hear of such genius. Catherine always assumed that all other genius was of a lesser quality than William's but was nevertheless pleased by Drew's story and deeply saddened to hear of Beethoven's awful deafness. William wept openly for the poor man. Drew then wept that he knew such people as William and Ludwig and had even helped to create them. Blake wept once more when they spoke of the isolation that Beethoven must feel.

"Drew, we must help this man," William said. "I myself know the pain of loneliness and of rejection. Why don't you bring Herr Beethoven to London and he can live with Catherine and me?" Catherine was nodding her head to this suggestion. "Catherine will never notice the added burden on herself because she is so loyal and generous. And then Beethoven will have an artistic companion and so will I. I'm sure we would understand each other and come to love each other."

Drew smiled and shook his head and William accepted the impossibility of what he was asking. Drew's smile broadened as he thought of the humble Blake house trying to contain the spirits and temperaments of Blake and Beethoven living together. How he wished he could be permitted to carry out such an experiment. What a chapter that would be in the Red report.

Drew did not walk back all the way with William and Catherine. The thought of going into the poor little abode again was distressing for him, seeing the shabby furniture, seeing the clothes lying on the sewing basket waiting for Catherine to mend the mends in the elbows of the shirts and the knees of the pants. So Drew embraced Catherine and then William, a long embrace for him, and they thanked him yet again for a fine meal and they all exchanged fond farewells.

JANE AUSTEN, 1815

Colonel Andrew Rosewood – for such was the name adopted by Drew the Red for his Jane Austen adventure – was very much admired in the Austen household for his impeccable manners and fine speech. His complexion was puzzled over, although rarely would anyone make comment upon it directly, and even then the remarks would be confined to concern about his health. This occasion was his first visit to the Austen home at Chawton Cottage. Some seven years had elapsed since his previous stay when the family was at Godmersham Park. Rosewood, rather boldly, seated himself by Miss Austen and talked agreeably of his travels, of new books and music, and of the pleasures of staying home. Jane was an attractive woman, rather tall and slender, her step light but firm, and her entire appearance one of animation and warmth. She had soft blue eyes and, although not conventionally handsome, her face had a peculiar charm all its own.

Jane and Rosewood conversed with so much energy and delight as to draw the attention of Lady Elizabeth and Mr Darnay who were also visiting. These two exchanged a knowing glance, or perhaps it was merely an exchange of hope, for Jane was still unmarried. Suddenly, Rosewood stood and made the following declaration, almost as if acting out the words.

"I am a single man in possession of a good fortune and therefore, according to the best advice available, I must be in want of a wife."

Jane laughed vibrantly at Mr Rosewood's daring reference to the opening of her latest novel, Pride and Prejudice, and gasped a little that he should know it so well and be so aware of its authorship.

"My goodness, Mr Rosewood," she said, "how can you be so tiresome as to talk of my simple, little book when your head is filled with your recent journeys. It is some seven years since we have had the pleasure of a visit from you and all you can think to speak of is my poor writing."

Rosewood's reference to her book was also a reminder to Jane of the games played at their first meeting in 1808. On that occasion they listened to the piano and then some light-hearted banter arose about marriage. In a reversal of what was to come in her book, Jane chided and teased Colonel Rosewood about the accomplishments a man needed to be a good husband, rather than accepting the direction of the conversation which was towards the ways in which a woman might attain the accomplishments required for a worthy wife.

"Surely a man's ability to recognise the accomplishments of a woman so well that he requests the honour of her hand is the only accomplishment a man needs," Rosewood said in an exaggeratedly mock serious tone.

"If that is a man's sole level of accomplishment," Jane said with equally mock serious surprise, "then you are saying, sir, that the only reason a woman would ever marry is simply because she has been asked. Should she not look for other agreeable qualities in her prospective husband? Does love figure nowhere in such matters? I consider everybody as having a right to marry once in their lives for love, if they can. But then I must also ask, what might be good reasons for a woman to love a man?"

"You set me to an examination, Miss Austen," Rosewood smiled. "Am I to consider myself a prospect in your eyes? Might my answers achieve a score that could elevate me to the rank of suitor?"

"As an examiner I must be impartial and so I trust you will accept the judgement as beyond personality and merely for academic purposes. If you fail, you fail on merit and not because of the examiner's temperament."

"You speak as if failing were the only option."

"In my experience in assessing the accomplishments of men, I'm afraid that is so," Jane said with an impish smile.

"If the verdict is already in, I will keep my evidence secret, for it may be useful another day, with another lady."

Others in the party who had been enjoying the exchange laughed at this finale and Jane politely applauded Rosewood's mock bow. A little later, in the garden as they strolled, Jane returned to her theme.

"I don't believe secret keeping is an accomplishment a woman would seek in a husband."

"I am not keeping my secrets, merely reserving them for the proper moment. I must confess from report of you I had not expected to find such an improperly flirtatious woman inside Miss Austen's very proper dress. I think paler shades might enhance your beauty more advantageously."

"I am well aware of my standard of beauty and cannot concede that a different colour dress would be enough to improve the lot that nature forgot to dispose upon me. But as many have said of me, my wit and tenderness will be enough for the man who can value them. Do you value such traits in a woman, Colonel?"

"Is flirtatiousness an appropriate accomplishment for a wife?"

"I think so. Would the romance and playfulness in our marriage be ended the moment we walked out from the church?"

"Our marriage?"

"I speak as an imaginative person who is able to imagine the unimaginable."

"I can never marry you, Miss Austen, or any other lady, because my needs are not those that a wife would accept. I cannot be tamed. I cannot be opened for inspection. I cannot be honest. I cannot reserve myself to one woman only."

"I could never marry you, Colonel Rosewood, even if asked. I see that you have no accomplishments that could satisfy me except perhaps one that has been teasing at me since I met you. But we will speak of that after I have admonished you."

Rosewood was astounded by the wicked smile playing on Jane's lips as she said those words. This was beyond flirting. Miss Austen was making a sexual proposition to him. The impropriety was unexpected but most enjoyable.

Jane continued, "I see, Colonel Rosewood, that you have no accomplishments of the heart or the spirit. I see no consistency of care or affection in your make up. You are a man for games. Everything and everyone is a passing hobby to you. You are an amateur seducer who could never be a professional husband. You could never be trusted to hold complete ownership of a lady's delicate heart."

Yet, that very afternoon, in the garden, Jane Austen did give Rosewood her heart as well as her body. Her lightness of mood and the sparkle in her eyes was remarked on in the drawing room after tea. No-one had ever seen Jane more happy and many hopes were raised that Colonel Rosewood, who was clearly the cause of her elevation, would become a suitor. It was also clear to everyone that he would be accepted.

Now it was 1815 and Rosewood had not become a suitor. However the glow in Jane's face and her good humour in his company showed that she felt no bitterness. Everybody, except perhaps her brother

Henry, settled back to enjoy the witty banter between the two protagonists.

"If your writing is poor," Rosewood said, "then only your pen can be to blame. Let me mend it for you. I am a remarkable good mender of pens."

"Thank you – but I always mend my own."

"You might remember that I was privileged to read some chapters on my last rendezvous with your family and your house and yourself. I am astonished to find the book was not published until only two years ago. Why was there so great a delay for so great a work of literature?"

"You speak too kindly, Colonel."

"And, if I might so boldly say it, Miss Austen, you are too modest and sadly you are rather too formal. Can we not adopt immediately the friendship, indeed intimacy, which we previously enjoyed?"

Jane blushed until even her throat was red with guilty excitement. Rosewood brushed her arm with his hand. Jane's breath caught and she coughed slightly. Lady Elizabeth hurried to her side in fright that she might be ill. Jane reassured her and insisted that all she required was a stroll in the garden and her temperature would right itself. Colonel Rosewood offered to accompany her and to carry her shawl in case of a sudden chill wind.

Her brother Henry watched as the couple stepped out into the garden. He smiled happily to himself. The happiness was tinged with a mite of fear that Rosewood should again prove unworthy of his sister, could even hurt her heart deeply again as he had done once before. Henry was remembering how distressed Jane had been when Colonel Rosewood so abruptly left her in 1808 during his visit at Godmersham Park. The excuse was an urgent note requiring Rosewood's attendance at the studio in Paris of a young Frenchman,

M. Daguerre, who was on the brink of miraculous discoveries in the art of capturing images by use of light itself rather than with the use of brush or pencil. There were chemicals involved and it seemed that the Colonel was something of an international authority on this matter. Jane declined into melancholy when Redwood was not heard from. She did not write for months on end. She ate less than a bird's weight per day. Her only solace was the garden and the polite letters to and from her friends and family.

In January 1809, in the middle of a bitter winter, Henry went to Paris to search for Rosewood. There was concern that, as an Englishman, Rosewood might have suffered some terrible fate at the hands of the French. Although the French were currently at war against the Spanish and Portuguese, no Englishman was truly safe in France. Henry bravely placed himself in danger on behalf of his sister's happiness and peace of mind. But he found no definite trace of Rosewood. Daguerre confirmed that a ruddy-faced man had visited him and fitted the description Henry gave of Rosewood's physique, bearing and clothing, including a rather singular overcoat he was wont to wear at times of snow. But Daguerre's caller was an old acquaintance known to him as André. This man had only two weeks previously rendered him some assistance with an experiment. But Daguerre knew the man André as a provincial Frenchman of high education. Certainly his French was perfect and without foreign taint.

[One of Daguerre's photographic plates from this period was of Henry Austen's distinguished profile. Daguerre used to insist that every visitor to his rooms be recorded photographically. In Daguerre's records, and in most history books, the picture is still labelled incorrectly, but there is no doubting the authentic portrait of Henry Austen.]

Henry had been quite disturbed by the information he had discovered about Mr Rosewood. It was clear the man travelled under at least two names, although this might simply have been sensible caution in the Paris of 1809. Now, in 1815, Henry prayed silently that no more disappearances by Mr Rosewood would blight his lovely sister's life. None of them were to know that she had a mere two years of life left to her and that Henry would swear to kill Rosewood if ever they met again. He sincerely believed that scoundrel of a man to all intents and purposes murdered his sister by yet again, in 1815, leaving her suddenly in an agitated state of mind.

Rosewood made love to Jane in the garden, as he had done seven years earlier in the vast park at Godmersham. It was the most intimate and physical expression of affection any man and woman could share. Jane responded with delight and a full surrender of her whole self; soul, mind and body. Rosewood held the moment of climax and ecstasy as if time had stopped and Jane's body and emotions were happily held in this pulse of excitement for many minutes as Rosewood whispered to her the truth of her magnificent place in the history of womanhood. Not the whole truth, of course, but enough so that this rare genius, one unsullied by the green juice, would feel satisfied that she had not laboured in vain at her writing. It was said of her that from the time of Rosewood's visit, when it was clear that the two were enamoured of each other, Jane lived too intensely within herself and in relation to her genius. Henry was convinced that she declined and died from a broken heart, betrayed for a second time by the cowardly deceiver, Colonel Rosewood.

Drew chose deliberately to tell the Austen story in a tribute to Jane's own style, even to the point, I discovered later when transcribing the tapes, of using whole sentences from her published works. During his 1815 visit, Drew as Rosewood was able to test Jane's physical signs and her blood to be scientifically certain that none of the butterfly juice had contaminated her system. He wanted to be sure none had leaked from male forebears into her DNA. And indeed none had. She was the real article, a human genius. At last, a genuine human genius who could be admired and held up as a model.

For the Red team the irritating issue was that no-one could explain how the Jane Austen variation had happened. Despite intense research into her forbears, her education, her friendships, her diet, her habits and one of her diaries which Drew had stolen, none of the team could concoct even a wild theory on how an untainted human being had become a genius. Another disturbing thing they discovered in this burst of research was that there were a lot, a virtual horde, a vast gang of clever human beings, males and females, who were not on anyone's lists of receivers of the juice. Previously, each Red had assumed that anyone fairly inventive and intelligent had been exposed to a drop or two of the juice somewhere by someone in the team. Their records and methods were not exactly scientific in the modern human meaning of the word. It should also be noted that the team – all the teams in fact – had taken to putting the juice into drinks at all-male dinner parties and gatherings. They had all noted that this diluted dose did not achieve genius but they thought it had stepped up the general level of human intelligence. They now knew they were wrong. If the level of cleverness was due to the drink then there would be green traces in blood, tissue and MVA [the Red version of DNA but using untranslatable words].

It was not only the research into Jane Austen's background that revealed this truth. Karrel had done an autopsy on a very clever young Frenchman he met at a gala ball. The other team members were slightly aghast, although they laughed heartily of course, when they found out Karrel had actually killed the man for the sole purpose of holding the autopsy. The whole affair was a scandal because Karrel had been forced to leave the body in the kitchen of his apartment and, when discovered, it was assumed some type of maniac had murdered and mutilated the man. It was in all the French newspapers and scandal sheets. Anyway, the real upshot was that not a single molecule or even atom of green juice could be found in the body of the young, witty man who had provoked interest by being a brilliant conversationalist, an expert on a rare type of worm found in the Burgundy wine region, and a homosexual. Karrel had foolishly assumed the green juice had caused or allowed all those traits.

The team tut-tutted his naivety and noted their regret at the mistaken execution of a hapless earthling, especially one who was so pretty. They all laughed heartily when Karrel included that note. Fyll rather dryly commented that a good many Frenchmen, especially Parisians, would have to die if wit and prettiness became criteria for a wave of autopsies. Sadly, as Tells are notoriously imitative monkeys, there was a spate of 15 similar killings in Paris, copy-catting Karrel's essential termination of the man. All the bodies were found mutilated in kitchens; all were reputed to be homosexual men; all were pretty. No-one was ever arrested. Several racy novels were written about the murders.

BEETHOVEN, 1822

"Good morning, Louis."

These words stopped Beethoven in his tracks which was not an easy thing to do once the master was thoroughly into his stride. He whirled about, raising his stick as if preparing to do battle. He was flustered and astounded and bewildered. The great man had been deaf for many years and yet he clearly heard the voice saying good morning to him. Drew immediately realised that his little joke had distressed the maestro and he quickly said, telepathically again, "My voice is appearing in your head, maestro, not in your ears. It is your friend Drew. It has been many years but you might remember that you and I could converse with our minds."

Beethoven threw his arms about the waist of the much taller Drew and wept. For a moment he had thought a miracle was happening and the tears of disappointment were understandable. The tears soon turned to cries of joy at seeing this old friend for Beethoven held fond memories of long walks and long talks together. Drew had been looking forward to renewing his acquaintance with Beethoven, for he was one of the most special of the special Tells on Drew's slates.

Drew had chatted with Goethe about Louis and had to agree with Goethe's estimation that Beethoven was an "utterly untamed personality". Those were Goethe's exact words, also recorded in his letters. But Drew did not agree with him that this was "unfortunate". The Red nature was to admire, even idolise, such temperaments. Perhaps, Drew had often thought, this was why the juice seemed so frequently to send its subjects into that wild state remarked upon with disapproval by tamer Tells and, by legend, to become intimately associated with the very idea of the genius. Drew had not been surprised, given Goethe's solemn outlook on life, that he had not only commented on Beethoven's attitude of finding the world "detestable" but had also agreed with it.

Fortunately Drew had purloined the only copy of Goethe's Job, the Victor for his collection of masterpieces for which the world was not yet ready. That play had the potential, Drew felt, of inducing mass hysteria, mass depression and mass suicide. Goethe had always been committed to the cult of human individualism and this play showed the victim of God as the ultimate individual who wins despite his torments, despite virtual torture by God. The utter despairing bleakness was unusual for Goethe but then from his first novel about the love-struck Werther onwards Gee had always held the rather oriental view that suicide was a perfectly acceptable solution to individual problems, no matter if there were a god or a God or gods or not.

Some seven years before surprising Beethoven on this morning walk, Drew and Louis had enjoyed deep and jovial conversations, unhampered by having to write everything down in conversation books. The intellect of Beethoven had allowed him to accept and participate readily in the telepathic process without undue questioning of the source of Drew's talent. The ease of mind this method of intercourse provided for Beethoven was tremendous in its capacity and was noted by all his friends, although they never knew the secret. When Drew was at table with his friend Louis, everybody saw the lift in the composer's spirits and the relish with which he joined in conversations, almost seeming to hear people. Indeed he did hear because Drew was able to transmit to him quite rapidly all the important statements from around the table, leaving aside those that were silly or grossly sycophantic.

On this 1822 visit there was a famous dinner at one of the inns frequented by Beethoven in Vienna where the young Schubert turned up with Rossini in tow. Both had been clients of Drew, but at early ages and they failed to recognise him. At this dinner it was possible to watch Rossini falling into a fanatical trance over Beethoven's brilliance. It was very like a passionate love at first sight affair. Rossini, as was true for Schubert, had always admired the music but now meeting the composer in the full flight of his most merry mood, at a time when Drew's presence enabled him to unleash the full force of his marvellous intellect and imagination in a group conversation, Rossini tumbled into adoration. That evening was spoken about in Vienna for many years and over time more than 500 people were given to boasting that they were actually there at the famous dinner with Beethoven, Schubert and Rossini where the conversation flowed like rich, red, matured wine.

Drew stayed some days with Beethoven and found himself caught up in helping him move house. This was another Beethoven characteristic. He hated landlords and servants and changed both regularly. It was said he had new servants every six weeks and new lodgings every six months. The amount of shouting and ill-temper going on during the move, from both master and servants, and with sharp yappings on the fringes of activity from the bitter landlord, drove Drew away for some hours. In that time he went shopping.

Drew had noticed that Beethoven's clothes, although perfectly serviceable and clean, were somewhat frayed and perhaps not entirely up to date in fashion. It was permitted that Reds could purchase minor items for the comfort of their mentorees so Drew replaced much of the maestro's wardrobe. He bribed one of the servants to assist in this and Beethoven never noticed that his best blue frock-coat suddenly looked like new and that he had acquired the latest fashions in trousers, stockings and shoes.

On his shopping adventure Drew assembled a collection of shirts, coats, trousers, boots, an excellent hat, ascots and handkerchiefs, socks, night shirts, underpants, undershirts, suspenders, and nightcaps. Many of these items were inventoried at the time of Beethoven's death, some five years later, giving the impression that the composer was a stylish dresser rather than the poverty stricken figure of legend, the unkempt, dirty, wild man of Vienna. In fact, Beethoven was a demon for washing himself and Drew had many a good laugh at the ceremony of the Beethoven ablutions. The maestro would tip large jugs of water over himself as he sang loudly and with his spare hand conducted some great, invisible orchestra.

The death of Beethoven was a greater blow to Drew than to Vienna or the world because Drew knew some of the work that was lost. At dinner in his rooms, in 1822, Beethoven confided in Drew his plans for three great symphonies. The world knows and loves the ninth which was the only one the maestro finished. Drew was delighted and thought it so appropriate that the most amazing, moving and intense symphony of the three was to be the eleventh. The glorious ninth and the awe-inspiring tenth were merely stepping stones to the eleventh. Drew felt Louis had bridged the gap between the Red Eleventh Dimension and Tell sensibility.

Here was a piece of sublime music that Tell consciousness and understanding could grow to understand and love. And yet, Beethoven had never ventured into the Eleventh or even Seventh Dimensions. Drew told him about those 'places' and offered to introduce him to them, but Beethoven declined. He said, telepathically, that he found the streets of Vienna and the woods of

Oberdöbling filled with such profound mysteries and such infinite fascinations that he could see no purpose in venturing further until his soul had absorbed all that his earthly surroundings offered. "I am a simple man," he said.

Drew loved the man's simplicity, wildness and talent. He was proud of having taken part in the creation of such a genius, while also ashamed of the infliction of deafness upon him by the juice. The rest of Drew's team were inclined to think that the deafness was a sublime joke, as if some god had said, "Here's a good one. Let's make the greatest composer in the world deaf!" Louis played his Missa Solemnis in D for Drew and Drew wept at its beauty. He was pleased that weeping at beauty was as common a Red trait as laughing at almost everything else. He always enjoyed a good cry. And Beethoven wept along with him because through his telepathic powers Drew had been able to allow Beethoven to hear the music, for the last time in his life.

Drew accompanied Beethoven to his beloved Oberdöbling for a few days in the summer. They travelled in a rented carriage provided by Drew and at the end of the visit Drew left a large packet of Beethoven's favourite coffee beans for him. Apart from the maestro's powerful intellect and greatness of soul, Drew found that he most liked him for his quaint habits and personal traits: the weeping, the washing ceremony, the way he counted out the 60 beans for his coffee, the raucous laughter, the out of tune howling, the invisible orchestra that accompanied him everywhere, his love of trees.

Beethoven not only loved the beauty, touch and smell of trees but also felt at home in their company. Once, on one of their long rambles in Oberdöbling, Drew noticed Beethoven had fallen behind, which was very unusual for such a tremendous walker. Drew looked about and was alarmed to see the great man slumped against a distant tree. Fearing some sort of heart attack or seizure, Drew rushed back only to find that Louis had his arm about the tree and was chatting to it as if they were old friends. And, indeed, they were. This was his favourite resting tree. It had a curve in its trunk that seemed tailored to take the composer's leaning, resting body. Beethoven thanked the tree for its comfort and support and the two men continued their walk.

"I like to stop and talk with this one, every chance I can. It is such a comfortable and wise friend," Louis said.

"Do you give your tree friends names?" Drew asked. "Or do they perhaps already have names?"

"Good gracious, no! A name is a limitation. How can one limit a tree? It is intimate with the earth and the sky. It is life, art, beauty. Each tree is a masterpiece. Ah no, we people only name things so that we can encompass them and trick ourselves into believing that we know a person or a thing. Every being or object is diminished once we name it. Even Beethoven is diminished by being called Beethoven. Am I not more than whatever ideas or images might spring into a person's mind when they hear the word Beethoven?"

"Surely there is a great wealth of ideas in the name Beethoven? For many it carries the same volume and breadth as the word music."

"But Drew, you know that much as I live for music there is more to my soul and my mind than the word music can define. Will it ever be said of me, when the word Beethoven is tossed in the air, that I was an intimate friend of trees, that trees loved me and that my heart was always humbled by their simple greatness and truth? I would enjoy such thoughts about me."

In that love of trees, Drew felt a great closeness to Beethoven. There were no trees in Red dimensions. A large part of Drew's joy on each return to Earth was the thrill of seeing and communing with trees again. It was a marvellous saving grace of humanity, Drew felt, that so many of them did love trees. Drew was more inclined to kill Tells who harmed trees than any other kind of miscreant. And he had done so on 27 occasions.

At the end of his Beethoven story, Drew heaved a tremendous sigh. "I miss that wild man," he said wistfully. But I was not going to let him off the hook just because he had a great sentimentality for Beethoven. I asked him how he was able to visit, talk with and be seen with such a famous man so often, and yet there were no public or private records of his being there. He patiently explained that ventures such as the carriage trip were undertaken in various false names he used, all with supporting identity documents. The principal records concerning Beethoven's life were the many conversation books and, of course, Drew did not appear in these as all their communication was by telepathy. There were several of the conversation books in Drew's little museum, for sentimental value.

"And why, dear boyo," he said in the lilting Irish brogue he sometimes adopted to tease me, "would people be taking any notice of a quiet, respectable man such as meself when they were in the presence of Beethoven? Anyone writing about his adventures or his dinners or his movings in and out of lodgings concentrates on the Ludwig personality, the Louis idiosyncrasies and Beethoven's famous friends. No-one has ever really noticed the red-headed strangers who move amongst human beings with needles and green juice. It's not in your nature. In Tell history fame and celebrity are all and Red people are here as researchers only, not to participate in your societies. Although, as you know, my vanity has allowed me to be included in several rather famous paintings and even a raft or two of photographs. But always as a bystander, not a protagonist."

"And yet," I said with some amusement, "if your stories are true, you and your Red friends are the main protagonists in the entire history of the human race."

"Ever so sadly, I admit that you are right, boyo. Quite right. And we Reds have been so infinitely wrong in all that we have done."

"Creating a Beethoven can't be a total mistake," I said to soothe his anguish. But I was no longer sure if I believed that. Drew saw the doubt and gave me a big Red smile.

OTHER VISITS, 1822 and 1829

Apparently a lot of people felt Lord Byron was one perpetual mistake, although most settled for simply saying that he was mad. Drew felt a certain madness had pervaded the entire Romantic gang of English poets. Their drug use did not help matters but by then Drew and his Red team had settled into acceptance that anything wrong with a human subject who had been injected was due to side-effects of the juice.

Drew adored the 13-year-old George, as Lord Byron graciously allowed Drew to call him. That was when he got his injection of butterfly juice. But Drew's favourite memory was of a night in 1822. "In some wonderfully gorgeous European city. Probably Venice. I remember there was water. No, no, it was Pisa. Is there water in Pisa? George loved water." It was a night when Drew indulged his creative urges and helped Byron with Don Juan. It was a stanza that created much indignity amongst the upper crust in London when it was published. Byron always loved to rattle the bars of pretentious cages, as did Drew.

"George read me the lines about gaming and loving – 'Dressed, voted, shone' – then he gulped down some wine and spurted out the immortal line, 'There's little left but to be bored …'. At this point George choked up with laughter and I stood and finished the line for him boldly, roaring out, '… or bore!' Oh dear, oh dear, how we laughed and then we drank even more until we fell on the floor and fell into sleep. What a wonderful night. George might have been mad … if you'd seen him in his bizarre costume inspecting his Greek troops you'd have realised. Mad, mad, mad. Well, mad he might have been, but he was such marvellous company."

Drew went on to list a few others he had visited in '22 including Alek [Pushkin] and John Clare. Clare was just 20 then and he asked for another dose of the juice, which Drew administered. Later Drew came to believe that second dose was the factor that pushed Clare into his insanity. The whole team was still struggling with the issue of the effect of the juice when other substances were in the body, especially alcohol and even harsher drugs. At one point they had serious doubts about the interaction between the juice and cabbage. This was a major talking point for some years, raising much concern about side-effects, particularly in their Russian subjects, many of whom seemed to go completely out of their minds.

[I know the cabbage situation seems rather ludicrous but I had realised quite early in my interviews with Drew that Red scientists had no concept of proper scientific method as we think of it – despite having 'created' Newton – and would never have thought to carry out laboratory experiments before injecting a drunk man, or one filled up with a cabbage meal, or an opium smoker. The experimental part for Reds was the actual 'doing of it' to a live subject. Whenever I mentioned this Drew would become quite surly and blame it all on that "bloody holy virgin Isaac [Newton]" who was blamed by Drew for infecting Tell science with all sorts of bad habits, like detailed observation, logical analysis and testing by experiment.]

Red dropped in on Gee as well. Goethe was one of his favourites, although Drew often complained about all the wretched rocks the man had collected and how you could hardly go for a walk without getting a short dissertation on several interesting stones along the pathway. Eighteen thousand rocks on display in Gee's house was the count at one stage of his life. And then there was a visit when Gee had Schiller's skull on a cushion, in a bell jar. He even wrote a poem for the skull. Drew, being quite familiar with the contours of Schiller's skull, knew the object was not the real skull. But he never told Gee. "Oh, green juice what strange effects you have wrought," was the first line of a poem Drew meant to write one day.

Drew loved speaking German. He thought it was a wonderfully muscular language. You really had to struggle physically to speak German, he would say. Gee was one of the best users of German, orally and on paper, in the history of the planet, Drew had assured me often. "Trust me on that," he would chuckle. "With a couple of millennia of experience, I'm in a position to know. Bert [Brecht] was very good, but not in the same coliseum as Gee."

This 1822 visit was special because Gee started talking about writing a play that would be a tribute to his "rot Freund", Drew, and that alerted Drew to watch for another script he would have to steal, although fortunately for the world Drew was never able to get his hands on the manuscript of Faust, so we still have it with us. Drew laughed heartily and said, "Guess which part is based on me."

"Mephistopheles, of course," I said. "You look like the devil, and you act like him too."

"Perfect casting!" Drew laughed long and heartily. "Writing that play killed him, but what a way to say farewell to this cursed veil of wells and tribulations and rented apartments."

I looked at him with a raised eyebrow which was how I had become used to letting him know that his English usage was astray. But almost always he would say something like, "I meant to use that particular terminology. If Jimmy [James Joyce] had written it you'd be applauding right now." And, almost always, I would applaud, with irony of course. It was a splendid time I spent with Drew. So much humour mixed in with the amazing stories. So much to think about. So much to care about. By now, I had stopped trying to catch him out on mistakes and stopped worrying about what sort of conman he might be and was just enjoying his company. And the crazy stories.

The stories were not only entertaining and informative but also in unlimited supply. Had I been a player of musical instruments, Drew could have told an encyclopaedia of stories about great players juiced up by Reds. Had my interests been in medicine, or invention, or philosophy, Drew could have dazzled me with a bookcaseful of stories in those fields. And any member of a team from any of the Red-visited sectors of the world would have had an equal fund of tales. The tales I recorded with Drew were very much tip-of-the-iceberg. And in this book I have, perhaps selfishly, only written about a fraction of the stories Drew told. They are the ones that fascinated me the most, for a variety of reasons. But I hope they will be sufficient to demonstrate the way the Red invasion of our planet created a race of creatures who are never going to be civilised, who will always remain mostly brutes, brutes with very clever computers.

In many ways, for a human being, the stories were enormously satisfying. Some mystery about an event in the world's history? Disappearance of the dinosaurs? The Reds did it. Apparently trying to increase their brain power was a bad mistake. You hate someone in human history, the Reds created him. [Unfortunately if you hated a woman, Catherine the Great for example, or one of the Brontes, then you were on your own. Unless you hated Joan of Arc, and that didn't seem very likely even for a non-religious person such as myself.] If you didn't like El Greco's skinny, elongated people you could blame it on the butterfly juice and the effect it had on his eyesight. Hardly anything terrible was accidental or fate or the gods; it was the Reds. But then most good things done by men, except exploring, came from the Reds and their juice too.

This last point was not entirely true. I could no longer think of anything that had, did or would happen as being 'entirely' true. The juice only enhanced qualities that already existed, magnified potentials already embedded in the subject, and did not create anything new. Drew kept telling me that anyway. Unless you count the side-effects as new issues. But even they were exaggerations of existing characteristics. The Red team was not sure about such matters as Beethoven's deafness, Milton's blindness and the eyesight problems of quite a few painters. But they stuck to the assumption that those problems already existed and had just been made prominent by the juice. So without the juice Beethoven would probably not have gone deaf, but then he certainly would not have composed music half as well. This all becomes an argument to which I keep returning in my mind and to which there seems to be no satisfying historical or moral conclusion. Would a half-as-good Beethoven be enough for us?

Drew found 1829 a saddish year and its results became less interesting as time went by. Firstly he had his marvellous triplets: three 20-year-old highly talented men. These were Tennyson, Darwin and Gogol. The first was boring, the second obsessive and then boring, the third depressive and a religious fanatic and, ultimately, a bore. "Surely, you don't want me to talk about any of them. Can't think of a single interesting story. Maybe I've made a mistake and I never even met them. As you are now aware, Darwin was totally wrong about everything. It was never natural selection that shaped the fate of the world, it was Red selection. Did you know that there used to be blue people on your Earth? They still existed in England back in the ancient days and were fierce warriors. Historians have written about them but keep insisting that the blueness was some sort of war paint. It wasn't. They were just blue-skinned people. We didn't like them at all. So we wiped them out. Not in a cruel way, of course. We just tweaked their genetic material a bit and they stopped having children."

Drew found it hard to admit that this genocide was not a good thing and he insistently asked me if I really would like to live in a world where some of the people were blue. Having admitted to his slight errors, Drew now moved on to what he called the two huge mistakes of 1829, Darwin and Wagner. Having already pointed out that Darwin was boring and wrong – and adding that he was mean to his wife and children – he went on to damn Wagner as a Nazi before the time of Nazis. I tried to suggest that he was being somewhat hypocritical but he would not accept that criticism. In fact, he rarely accepted any criticism from me. He felt that he was the only person on Earth of sufficient mental capacity to be able to offer criticism of Red behaviour and, to be honest, he was often scathing about himself and other Reds for the interference and devastation they had brought on the Tell race.

"So the 1829 batch was a major disappointment," Drew said. "Although I got Chopin at 10 and he turned out to be a fair tinkler on the piano. There was also that dreadful sentimentalist who perfected the magazine serial. What the dickens was his name again?" And Drew bellowed with laughter at his own joke. I laughed along, but I was laughing at him for being so impressed by such a slight witticism. "Who wants to read about slum dwellers and criminals and sick people? Very tedious. Karrel loved the Dickens books. Loved them. But then Karrel would, wouldn't he? So what was my score then? A few bores, a scientist who was monumentally wrong in his theories, a modestly good pianist, and a moderately decent story teller. Oh yes, and one terrible operatic Nazi."

VINCENT VAN GOGH, 1871

At this time, at Goupil's Gallery in The Hague, working as a menial assistant, Vincent van Gogh was 18 years old but already knowledgeable about the world of art. He had red hair and was ugly and unpleasantly religious so, to Drew, it seemed a good joke to impose on such an unlikely lad the ability to see the world in ways that no-one else could. It was easy to take advantage of the young man as he was an innocent. He loved to enthuse customers about the paintings and they enjoyed his eagerness.

For some years the Red team had been using absinthe as a means of getting the green juice into unknowing clients in continental Europe. The French were particularly addicted to the stuff and Rimbaud and Verlaine had been topped up many times by Drew through their absinthe, which was already green and had a vile taste, so added butterfly juice was never noticed. It was only many years after using this vehicle that the Reds came to understand that the drink tended to burn out parts of the subject's brain. So now they had another set of incomprehensible variables caused by the wormwood and other ingredients of the deadly drink.

Poor, young Vincent, although not much of a drinker of alcohol at all in his youth, was easily seduced by Drew into imbibing one 'green cordial' with his lunch as Drew questioned him about several paintings that he was proposing to buy. Lunching with a customer put Vincent in a position where he felt obliged to finish the nasty drink. Drew did buy two awful paintings – thrown in the garbage later – so that Vincent would feel good about his selling abilities.

Drew discovered seven years later that this first dose had only a minor impact and an unfortunate one for it helped push Vincent towards religion. Vincent's misadventures in London in the meantime, where he was rejected by his first great love and dismissed from his job at the gallery, also undoubtedly played a big part in driving him towards the theological college near Brussels.

Despite his personal dislike for Brussels, Drew endured a visit there so he could meet up again with Vincent. This time Vincent would drink only milk. However, by carefully selecting a dark glass, Drew was able to lace the milk with some green juice. This time the impact was greater. This left the Red team with an even more perplexing problem of trying to work out whether milk might enhance the juice more than alcohol had seemed to in the past. Suffice to say that within weeks of Drew's visit Vincent had failed his examinations and left the college.

Drew recorded that there were no further doses and only one other visit, in Antwerp, was possible as Vincent was dead 12 years later. During that visit Drew realised Vincent really did see the world as if it were made up of vivid blobs of colour and swirls of light. He painted exactly what his eyes told him was out there in the world. Drew and the team were astounded by Vincent's brilliant work and distraught at losing him. But there seemed no way under the rules of this project for there to be regular monitoring and intervention between visits. When the team applied to amend the rules their request was rejected.

[In my journal I noted that by this time in the tales I felt relieved that those rules existed and that the request for change was denied. More visits would have been even more disastrous for humanity. That might sound mean-spirited. Who would not want to have a decade or two more of van Gogh's paintings? And, apparently, fairly simple medical attention could have saved him. But the idea of how much other damage would have been perpetrated by having Reds on Earth on a full- time basis is terrifying.]

SERGEI DIAGHILEV, 1871

In the bitter winter of 1871, Drew found himself in the far-flung Russian province of Novgorod, attending the pregnant wife of an army officer. Not that the journey had taken more than a few minutes. It was only a short walk from The Hague and his adventure with Vincent, a short walk when one used the specially folded map of the universe as Drew often did to save time. One of the team had examined the bloodlines of the Diaghilev family and had pronounced it extremely likely at a high level of probability and at an almost zero chance of failure that the boy-baby Evgenia was carrying would be susceptible to the charms of the juice to a remarkable extent. The innovation the team decided upon was to inject the child while it was still in the womb. Such an exciting venture, although also fraught with dangers.

As is now a matter of history, the injection was an astonishing success, as the child produced from this daring experiment was the greatest impresario of high art the world has ever known, Sergei Pavlovitch Diaghilev. A mild sedative kept the mother unawares of the medical procedure being undertaken on her body. The needle went in through the navel leaving no detectable marks.

Drew was not to meet the results of this experiment until 1899 at the magnificent International Exhibition of art at the Stieglitz Museum. The exhibition was organised by Diaghilev and no-one else in the world could have done it, certainly no other man of 26 years of age. Drew suspected there were probably a few young women who could have undertaken the task in a less rigid society.

At the exhibition, Drew shook Sergei's hand and uttered words that drew a gasp from the accomplished young man: "I knew your mother." They spoke intimately for over an hour, Diaghilev postponing meetings with distinguished artists to listen to this strange man talk of his unknown but much beloved mother, in such glowing health and happiness, in the mid-term of her pregnancy. He did not inform Sergei that he, Drew, had probably murdered the lovely Jenia in an experiment that went rather wrong, for her. The boy was born perfect and strong and with a very large head, a head large enough to hold and protect an oversize brain caused by butterfly juice. Sergei's mother died just a few days after the birth. Sergei, all his life, carried the burden of knowing that his brilliance was also the cause of his mother's death.

Drew had already been informed that Diaghilev was widely known to be homosexual. Nevertheless, he was surprised at the open affection Sergei showed his cousin, Dima, an extremely handsome young man who had been his lover for years. "There is nothing a Red man adores more than romantic glances between two beautiful Tell men in a cavernous room filled with ravishingly stunning art," Drew said at the end of his tale. "Unless it be a man and his mistress or two women or an older woman with a breathtaking younger man who also has an older male lover, perhaps the woman's husband, or even perhaps …" Drew allowed his fantasies to dissolve into giggles.

THE GOLDEN AGE, 1878 to 1899

The North-West Red team nominated this period as golden for two reasons. The first was that there were so many tremendously influential geniuses in such a wide variety of categories juiced in this 21-year period, that is, four Red visits. Drew took delight in rattling off the biggest name-drop he had ever undertaken. It included "dear" Oscar, Strindberg, Vincent (second dose), Freud, Shaw, Yeats, Wells, Stanislavsky, the "lovely, gentle" Chekhov, Nijinsky (twice), Diaghilev (second dose), Nietzsche, Lenin, Rasputin, Einstein (twice), "Oirish" Synge, Kafka, Joyce, Pound, Le Corbusier, "Neddy" Lawrence, and Charlie Chaplin. There was a second astounding list of names which Drew brushed aside as of "second-ranking brilliance".

[Even a handful of the stories I recorded about the first ranking list would be enough to fill another volume or two, so a sprinkling of Drew's comments will be sufficient to give the flavour of the period and to highlight some of the large issues that kept arising for the team. Much of the material Drew told me about this period is also documented in human biographies.]

The second reason this period seemed such a blessing to the team was that, although more and more women were coming to prominence through their natural abilities, the period held no giant variation in the flow of the project as represented by someone such as a Jane Austen. Just prior to the Golden Age there had been those "wretched" Bronte sisters. No trace of inherited or accidental butterfly juice in their veins. Then after this period there were all the brilliant Ballets Russes women and Isadora and the "divine" Sarah Bernhardt. The Golden Age was a breathing space from having to consider the astounding achievements of uninjected women although Drew gave the impression that the team was keeping itself very, very busy so that they could legitimately avoid thinking about any women of the period who were geniuses. So the Reds ignored great women, as does much Tell history, and Drew now assumed there were many great women around in the North-West segment in the Golden Age who were unknown to the team.

Busy-ness was the whole approach in this time period. They set out to broaden the range of mentorees and the range of ages at which the chosen men were injected or dosed. There were now several different methods of administering the juice. There were also problems. Strindberg and Kafka, from different ends of the period, turned out to be depressed and gloomy and twisted. Nijinsky and Nietzsche went crazy. Shaw lived forever, Chekhov died young. No-one could work out why any of these things happened.

Fyll was the one who fostered Freud's development. Although cautious by nature Fyll was completely taken in by Freud's ideas and methods and often slammed the Freud slate on the table at meetings. Drew always remained sceptical and thought some of the ideas totally silly. As Reds could quite easily adopt female mode, all of them, including Fyll, were highly amused by the penis envy ideas of Freud. Lenin was to be the great hope for Russia, but Drew was again sceptical and added, "If I'd known he was a blasted lawyer I would have left him well alone. Wouldn't have touched him with a bosun's oar." Drew had also done Marx back in the 1830s or '40s. "I'd have to look it up. But I remember thinking that he was another novelist like

Verne, Dickens and Dostoyevsky, and those damn Bronte sisters came along at that time too. They threw quite a few spanners in the mind workings of the team and made it diamond clear there was leakage through the genes. But then when the team get some samples and tested them, there was no trace of green juice. Why can't humans be like other animal test subjects? What makes them so difficult and perverse? Certainly perversity has never been a feature of Red nature and so it could play no part in the make-up of the juice."

[I had noticed several times from Drew's comments that the juice seemed to be made to reflect all the good qualities of the Reds. So humans were an experiment in creating a race of creatures who should, eventually, be able to mix at a level of intellectual and artistic equality with the Reds. Drew confirmed that much of the universe's life was still at the creepy-crawly stage or else had evolved into highly defensive, self-protective, ruthlessly violent creatures who killed first and spoke later. Despite their wars and violent natures generally, Tells were cuddly kittens compared to most other evolved creatures. The Reds felt rather alone in the universe until they discovered moderately clever monkeys on planet Earth. Drew used to joke, "At first we called it Planet Dirt but some transpositions have occurred since." I was rapidly coming to believe that the whole Tell experiment was meant to cure Reds of a terrible type of cosmic loneliness. I think it is not dissimilar to the way many humans take domestic pets to their hearts so fiercely and almost desperately.]

There were some juice subjects in the Golden Age whom Drew did not like. Strindberg and Kafka were merchants of the dark and dire in life and so the antithesis of Reds who saw a big joke in almost anything. Drew thought Kafka's *The Trial* had a belly-laugh on every page. A pet hate of Drew's was Herbie Wells. Twice Drew stole the manuscript of *The Time Machine*. Wells used information in the book that Drew had given him in confidence. Shaw was an irritating, preacher of a person and the Reds as a whole team disliked his social hypocrisy. Drew got a bit tired of the Irish story-teller thing at this time but Dail was absolutely committed to keeping Ireland on the Red cultural map and so the period included Joyce, Yeats, Shaw, Wilde, Synge, and a few others.

Drew's particular favourites of the Age were Chekhov and Einstein. "When Chekhov died I felt that Russian civilisation had lost one of its great pillars. A kind and generous man, a sensible man. Anton Pavlovitch took me into his confidence and told me about his early life and his student days and his love affairs and I felt privileged to know him so well." Drew let out a raucous laugh. "Later I discovered that he took everyone into his confidence and told everyone everything. Because he made you feel so special all his confidants kept his secrets. And then he told the world everything in his wonderful plays. Ah, those plays. Forget Henry and Will and Bert and Henrik and Gee, Anton Pavlovitch was the real thing. And such lovely contradictions in the man. A shy man and yet an open book for everyone to read. He understood how ordinary people could have a deep need for their religion. But he was bewildered that educated people should be religious. He was an intimate of the great – Tolstoy, Diaghilev, Stanislavsky, of course – and a friend to the serf. He doctored others – served the peasants for free – but ignored his own health and died too early.

"It was Oscar [Wilde] who created the quote about putting his genius into his life and only his talent into his writing. Chekhov had enough genius to fill up both his life and his writing. I went with him on what he called his rounds on one occasion. It was in Yalta in '99.

He was supposed to be living there for the sake of his health but it was the health of the ordinary folk that benefited. He would stop by their humble cottages and tend to them. They called him a saint." Drew laughed heartily. "When you think of his opinion of religion that's quite funny, isn't it? And it's true what Tolstoy said of him. Oh, my boy, Tolstoy did love Anton Pavlovitch. Loved him. No-one less than Gorky himself testifies to it. He wrote about it but also told me in person. We got on well, Gorky and I."

"You forgot to say what was true. The thing that Tolstoy said."

"He said many fine things about my Anton. That Chekhov was magnificent and magnificently modest. But what I was remembering …" He giggled. "… I was remembering how Tolstoy said that Chekhov walked like a girl. It was so true. He had the funniest little walk." Drew got up and impersonated the Chekhov walk and we both laughed. "And golly gosh I do miss that man. He is someone we could write at the top of our list of worthy men, not too tainted or distorted by the juice. I am forced to admit that it was his human nature that made him so beautiful. He not only walked like a girl but also thought and felt and believed like a girl. Dare I say it, that he was as wonderful as my dear Jane [Austen]."

I was bursting with pride at these statements, that I could finally identify a worthy Tell male. But I could not resist asking, "What is this 'golly gosh' stuff? Where did that come from?"

"Too much American television, I'm afraid. They are so mimicable, the accents, the expressions, the nonsensical ideas. Sometimes I think I should throw this wretched screen device away, but I would miss the Chinese news broadcasts. They are so funny. And there are many serious things I enjoy from it too." He shook his fist at the giant screen in mock anger.

"What about Einstein? Was he a worthy man?"

"Probably was in Tell terms. He was an inveterate womaniser and boasted openly about his conquests. We have to put that down to the juice I suppose. And he was brilliant, even in Red terms. He came to our attention because at the age of 12 he taught himself Euclidean geometry. We injected him in '92 when he was 13. He detested schools which is a huge point in his favour. And like many great minds, he loved the violin. He often skipped out on classes from the various institutions people tried to lock his brain up in so he could really think and feel and keep in tune with the universe. Not unlike Sherlock Holmes who hated schools and played violin too."

"Holmes was a fictional character. You can't have injected him with juice. He didn't exist."

"Goodness gracious me, you're right." He laughed and twinkled his eyes at me and I realised that yet again I had been royally teased.

"As I said before, Einstein was brilliant, for a Tell. Most of his teachers never recognised this, naturally, and he was even refused a teaching job at university after his graduation. Brilliant enough to change the whole world's view of physics, but not good enough to be a teacher. I love the contrariness of your world. It's hilarious. I have to point out that Einstein's physics were not Red physics and it was difficult to have conversations with him on his special topics. As a result, I think he found me rather dull."

"What do you mean by Red physics?" I asked.

"Different dimensions require different laws of physics. The parameters of the Seventh, the Eleventh and your three-dimensional universe – in this case not counting time as a dimension – are all quite different."

"How can our universe have parameters when it's infinite?" I demanded in a rather too clever tone. [Listening to the tapes is sometimes a little embarrassing for me.]

"Infinity itself is an all-embracing parameter that is everywhere and also nowhere. Infinity wraps itself about and through every entity, cosily, bringing us each home."

"That doesn't make a lot of sense to me. Perhaps it only means something to a Red intelligence."

"No. Not so." Then, as if quoting, he continued, "Infinity's endless fingers reach into our guts and teach us that no matter how cool and cosy, no matter how calm and carefree, no matter how courageous and cowardly, we are all alone in an infinity of loneliness. I regret to inform you that god is merely the lonely echo of our whimpering prayers bouncing back from the parameters of infinity."

"Is that how it feels for Reds also?" I asked quietly. "Is that what Reds believe?"

"That was written by Sammy Beckett. I had to steal it so that no-one would ever hear it. Although most sensitive Tells know these truths in their bones, we felt it better not to put it in words. You are the only person to ever hear even a partial performance of this play. It's called Red. Infinity. Squared. Sorry that I had to omit the technical elements of the show. They were that pinpoint lights should shine on one eye, the tongue tip and the Adam's apple of the speaker. All else was to be in darkness. The play was only four minutes long. At the time, 1934, nobody would have produced it.

"Admittedly, it is in his naïve voice which is not always so convincing. He was immersing himself in his novel, Murphy, at the time so did not notice the tone of the text so much nor did he notice the loss of the script. He did something similar years later I believe with a light on someone's mouth. I helped him settle into Gertrude Street when he moved back to London. He read the script to me. It was a complex combination of data that led to this piece. He had been analysing and writing about the work of Cézanne and then he and I had spoken about Einstein and the parameters of infinity. Add to that the fact that the strange world of Murphy filled every brain cell he had and, voilà, the infinity speech.

"Not strangely, I had business with Cézanne in 1857 when he was 18. What a year that was for the French. Émile and Paul were good friends and I did them both together. I see you wonder who Émile is and I am shocked. Zola, of course. Who else? Where is your French history? That same year the team dosed Rodin and Pierre Renoir too. All of them latish teen years. Good age. Puberty over and serious life ahead. We threw in Louis Pasteur that year. Although he was mid-30s we did hope that he would change his emphasis from physics to chemistry, especially medical research, which was lagging well behind the other sciences. He did so and the rest, as somebody famous once said, is history.

"Another interesting factor in all this is that Pierre Renoir passed on the juice through his genes to his son, Jean. When I dosed Jean in 1906 I took a sample of his tissues beforehand and later discovered that he already had the juice in him. And what a coincidence because that same year I paid a visit to Nijinsky who had been dosed twice without any testing. But because we had previously dosed Nijinsky's father, Thomas, I took some samples from Vatsa in '06 and discovered that we could clearly see the difference between the juice that he inherited from his father and the juice we had given him directly.

"Unfortunately we never did discover what power the inherited juice had. In Nijinsky's case it probably was the ability to jump remarkably high. That was the only thing his father, Thomas, was famous for. Thomas never had the artistry his son came to possess. However, that one is still only a guess. You can imagine the variables. The team's knees turned to milk at the very thought of embarking on more examination of even more variables. So we didn't."

"That must be the hugest set of digressions ever produced from your fevered mind in all our discussions," I blurted out in exasperation.

"Aha! You are starting to sound like me! The pupil might actually be learning something."

"You went from Einstein to Beckett to Cézanne and Émile Zola and Rodin, side-stepping to Pasteur, then through Renoir senior and Renoir junior to end up with Nijinsky and his father. You're bloody impossible."

"And so are you!" he retorted. "Why are you so bedazzled by the intricate interweaving of history? I sometimes wonder if I might be wasting my time with you. Thank the heavens that you have it all on tape and that you might make more sense of it when you mature a little more."

"Sorry," I said abjectly. "I keep worrying that I have lost the thread or probably threads. I actually enjoy the digressions ..."

Drew interrupted crankily, "Which is why I keep making them. For your entertainment and the entertainment of your possible audience. If you ever get it on paper that is."

"But I do genuinely worry if I can grasp all this and turn it into something coherent."

"You will, my boy. I have faith in you." He said this with a hand on my shoulder and looking directly into my eyes. I knew he meant it – Reds do not lie well – and I was thrilled by such a marvellous compliment.

[Readers must remember that by this time I already had enough tapes and notes and had seen enough marvels in his museum to fill several very large books. The sheer quantity of material was daunting, let alone the sensational and fascinating nature of the revelations.]

Drew found it interesting that during this Golden Age Fyll chose to help Sigmund Freud develop his psychoanalytical theories and practice – more than he should have! – at a time when the rest of the team were turning out great depressives like Kafka, Joyce, Synge, Ned Lawrence and Nijinsky.

"I popped up to Oxford in '99 to see Ned Lawrence at the Polstead Road house. He knew I had come for him. He was barely 11. He told me that he had always known that one day somebody would deliver him his fate, for he was certain he had a destiny to fulfil." Drew told the boy he would grow up to be a great hero and probably something of an explorer too. "Not such a bad guess," Drew commented, "but given he was to become Lawrence of Arabia, you'd think I would have been able to see a camel or two in his future."

Then Drew recounted a funny story about a young cockney lad who accosted him at the station in London when he was on his way to Oxford. The boy put on the accent and the swagger anyway. Everything he did and said seemed part of a performance. But essentially he was begging. Only about ten and bright as a cuff-link. Their eyes met and for Drew it was like looking into the big brown eyes of a seal or some other knowing fish. The eyes were immensely sad while the face was being funny. The eyes knew the awful truth.

Drew bought the kid a pot of tea and a pie and a sticky bun. They sat down at a nice table in the railway café and the boy was not at all overawed. The kid told Drew that he and his brother had been in the workhouse and that his mother was mad and he asked why Drew was travelling. All of that in his energetic, matter of fact tone. The boy could see the purposefulness in Drew's bearing. He even did a bit of an imitation of Drew's walk and they laughed together. So Drew truthfully told him the reason for the trip and the boy immediately asked if he could have some of this magic juice too. He needed it so he could be clever and earn a lot of money and help his mother. Drew poured some in the boy's tea and Charlie Chaplin drank it all down.

NIJINSKY AT SCHOOL, 1906

Drew injected Vaslav Fomitch Nijinsky when he was only three years old. This was in consideration of the fact that the parents were both dancers and their children were likely to take lessons quite early in life. Leaving the juice until Vaslav was 10 might leave him out of the training race. This was also an interesting experiment because they had injected Vaslav's father, Thomas, in his early teens and Thomas had become a famous leaper and an entertaining dancer but showed no greatness. Consideration of in utero injection was no longer reasonable, given the circumstances of Diaghilev's birth, in which he could have been lost as well as his mother.

The reports about the dancing of young Vaslav from his school were so astounding that Drew ensured that the entire team was present at the Imperial School for Vaslav's graduating examinations. As predicted, Vaslav's performances were quite incredible: three tours en l'air, entrechat-dix effortlessly. He was like a bird in air. After the boys danced the allegro pas in a group, Nijinsky was asked to repeat the sequence by himself.

Mikhail Mikhailovitch Fokine, distinguished choreographer and teacher, had rushed to his classroom with the foreigners in his wake, hardly able to contain himself before he could tell all about the marvellous Nijinsky and now he was at the denouement, "And then, my dear pupils, a thing happened that never, ever happens at examinations. Never! Suddenly, everyone – all the teachers – applauded. Yes, applauded. The Director, Telyakovsky, his assistant, Krupensky, and the teachers and our distinguished foreign guests applauded Nijinsky as if we were at a full performance. All the teachers are late for class because we could not leave without talking about this marvellous dancer – Vaslav Nijinsky."

One rather plain girl in the class was blushing and giggling. Her face was almost as red as those of the foreign guests. Fokine pointed to her and spoke, "And you, Bronislava Fominitchna, are giggling that our lateness is the fault of your brother, Vaslav Fomitch."

Bronislava stood politely and said, very softly, "I am sorry, Mikhail Mikhailovitch Fokine, I was merely happy that he has not caused trouble again."

Fokine laughed. "Trouble? No. Astonishment? Yes. Bronislava Fominitchna, you have such a marvellous brother that I must congratulate you." He shook her hand in a mock-serious way. All the pupils laughed. "As you all know, my dear pupils, the boys have been taking their dancing examinations this morning. All the teachers stayed to watch Nijinsky and there were several important guests present too." He gave a flourish in the direction of the Red team and the pupils politely applauded. "Vaslav Fomitch Nijinsky is remarkable. All the examiners gave him the top mark of 12. But this was not at all fair. In other examinations students have been given 12, but there has never been anyone who danced like Nijinsky. For him we should come up with a new mark. Today I would have given him 20 or even 30, he so surpasses anything we have seen before. How lightly he jumps. How high. All the difficult pas are so easy for him. The whole school is so proud of him. He has a great future, Bronislava Fominitchna, a great future."

Fourteen years later, Drew had a private conversation with Bronislava and reminded her of that examination day. She smiled broadly, remembering a happier time for her brother and told Drew, "Never before had I known a teacher to address any student in such personal terms, especially in front of the whole class, and especially with such wonderful praise for another student. I was breathless. I could not wait to rush home and tell my mother what Fokine had said – what the whole Imperial School was saying about my brother. His future was assured! My mother wept with joy. Vaslav's future was assured! All our futures were assured."

Her mood grew darker. "From this time he was pursued by so many people – and hated by a few jealous dancers. Everyone wanted to be his friend. Even before he graduated, the premier danseuses were approaching Vaslav to be their partners. Vaslav's graduation performance made mother and me so proud. Everyone was amazed by his dancing. Almost everyone. Father came but his praise was for me in my small roles. He said little about Vaslav, only that the program had shown him as 'a jumper' and that he had to work hard to become a real dancer. Vaslav was so hurt by our father. So deeply hurt."

T.E. LAWRENCE, LORCA, DALI & Others (at wildly differing dates)

Ned Lawrence did not lose the first manuscript of The Seven Pillars of Wisdom on the train as legend would have us believe. Drew stole it. It was in his museum. The book was just too good to be allowed, too honest to be acceptable, too brutal to be believed. Drew tried to dissuade Lawrence from proceeding with another version, saying that he had so many more important matters to attend to in pressing the Arab cause, but unfortunately there were too many friends and devotees of his talents urging Ned on, so another version cropped up. Even when rewritten, usually a way to downgrade the impact of a Tell work, it was rather better than Reds would have liked.

"The original was too good by a country mile for human consumption," Drew said. "Even when he rewrote it and lost some of the original white heat passion and diamond clear clarity and ocean deep philosophy, it was certainly better than the Red team thought advisable. We developed a scheme to steal that version too, but Khryss mis-read the train timetable and we missed Ned by several hours. We all agreed that a mugging or murder or kidnapping was out of the question, although we had great fun working out the scenarios for such adventures. We laughed a lot as we imagined the headlines in the cheap newspapers: 'Lawrence of Arabia mugged in broad daylight'. And so on. I can see you're not interested."

"I'm interested in the history not the imaginary escapades of a bunch of overgrown schoolboys."

"You don't think that sort of thing might give your readers more of an insight into Red people and our good intentions in all our dealings with you Tells?"

"Humans are not idiots! Well, of course, you know that – you people made sure we weren't."

"Don't worry there are plenty of Tell idiots left in the world and some of them are in charge of entire nations. Anyway, my boy, my pupil, my mentoree, I don't like this 'you people' stuff." Drew cackled to himself over my loss of temper.

"What I mean is that people would only have to read half of one of these episodes you've told me to realise that you were playing with us, that we were toys for your amusement. Nothing more."

"'As flies to wanton boys are we to the gods. They use us for their sport' or something to that effect, as Henry wrote."

"Henry? That quote's from …"

"Yes! And Shakespeare was mostly Henry. The fine words were anyway. Did I tell you that the entire Porter speech in Macbeth was improvised by the actor in the first performance? He forgot his lines and couldn't find where he'd attached the keys to his belt and then tripped over as he made his entrance. So in a flash of inspiration he pretended to be drunk and rambled on as he tried to remember the speech and find the keys and – voilá – one of the truly great Shakespeare moments. Transcribed faithfully by Will in his own hand. And claimed as his own when sent to the publishers. Whoever said Shakespeare wasn't clever?"

"No-one as far as I know in human history has ever said Shakespeare wasn't clever."

"What's wrong with you today? Got out of the wrong side of breakfast, did you? That's an old Red saying."

I groaned because I could see what a laughing mood he was in. I knew I was going to be given the cute sayings that were just a bit different from human cute sayings, and told about English words created by Reds, and about legends created by Reds. And everything in threes. "How the hell am I ever going to get all this down and make it believable?"

"Just pick the kidneys out of it – another old Red saying – and present those on a nice platter with a slightly bland sauce. No need for augmentation in these circumstances as kidneys are very rich of themselves."

"You make fun of everything."

"I'm sorry but it's in my nature to do so."

"Well, it's in my nature to worry about my readers. No point writing a great work if no-one will read it or believe it."

"So now it's a 'great work', is it? And whose doing is that? Mine! All mine! I do narrate a lovely story, don't I? Anyway I thought we said this was a novel. People aren't actually expected to believe it, are they?"

"I thought that was our whole purpose?"

"If they do then they will truly think you're batty. By the way you know don't you that bats themselves are not at all batty. They're quite intelligent little beasts in fact. Oops, yet another side-track."

"Maybe I need a break from stories for a while." This was something I never thought I would say to this particular story-teller.

"I know how to cheer you up," Drew said with a big smile. He started searching in a large Louis XIV or XV wardrobe [Drew wasn't sure and I had no idea.] stacked with papers. "I know how sentimental you are and how much you love love stories. Here we are!"

He dragged out a bunch of papers and handed them to me. As I looked through them I could see they were in Spanish and I mentioned the fact that I couldn't read Spanish. Drew sarcastically expressed surprise at that. "Imagine meeting an Australian who cannot speak another language. Aussies are such great linguists too. It's a national strength." He always had to push everything too far.

He summoned a beautiful young woman from the tribe to read them to me in English, instantly translating them from the Spanish, although she would sometimes also say the phrase in Spanish because it sounded so beautiful. Drew also insisted I get out of the manufactured air of his hut and into the hot, real air of the outside world for a while. The tribespeople provided a nice hammock and some green tea and vanilla cream wafers [from a Viennese recipe]. I lay back and listened to the sweet voice of this perfectly gorgeous girl read the love letters of Federico Garcia Lorca to me.

The letters were so charming and filled with passion that they brought tears to my eyes. However, the situation was still disturbing for me for several reasons. Getting used to the idea that an unschooled girl was translating to me from a language I could not understand was difficult and humbling. Her beauty was a little too exciting. And the love letters were addressed to Salvador Dali. I knew, of course, that Lorca was gay but had not delved into the life enough to know that he and Dali had been lovers. What an absurd combination.

I truly wondered on that day and for many days afterwards whether it was wise to reveal the truth of our evolution or whether I should just leave the world thinking that either God did it, or Darwin explained the process, or a mix of the two. However, as the days proceeded and I learnt more and more about the total mess the Reds had made of my own century I became more hardened in my resolve to reveal the truth, no matter the consequences.

After the Lorca reading, Drew told me that he had done both Lorca and Dali with the green juice on the same day. Lorca was 15 and Dali only nine. "Lorca grew up to be a wonderful, sensitive, beautiful man and Dali became a nut-case. Salvador could never deal with the all encompassing passion of Lorca's love. Lorca was the one Tell whose life I desperately tried to save, even though we weren't supposed to do that. But I was too late. They shot him dead on the road. I held him in my arms and defied them to shoot me too. That really messed up their heads because they wanted to but couldn't. I did a trick with their brains – it's too complicated to describe – so they could not press the triggers of their guns and the next time they got into a skirmish his assassins were shot down without being able to fire to protect themselves. I regret that I couldn't think of something more horrible to do to them but I was so grief stricken. To kill Spain's greatest poet and one of the greatest human beings I had created. It was devastating for me."

"And pretty damn devastating for Lorca too."

"Oh yes, you think I am too self-centred. Well, it's true."

"I know. It's in your nature."

NIJINSKY AT DINNER, 1913

Nijinsky watched the cat. It was a young and sprightly and ginger cat but not in the same class as Nijinsky. Once Vatsa decided to become a cat he was a much better cat than the cat was. His movements, his arrogance, his purring were all more beautifully cat-like than the cat. He even leapt higher than the cat and landed more elegantly. Drew could see that the cat was feeling quite defeated by Nijinsky's superior cat-ness. But then the dancer started playing more gently with the cat, being a cat friend to the ginger. The cat-man encouraged the cat to become more of a cat, to leap higher, roll more vigorously, meow more generously. The two cat creatures urged each other on to greater heights but finally the bemused observers nodded their heads in agreement that Nijinsky had clearly out-catted the cat. The ginger could sense the verdict and curled up on the floor in surly disgrace.

Proust watched with thinly disguised disgust, his thin lips even more thinly tightened. Proust hated cats and had never taken to Nijinsky as a person, so truly hated him now he was such a superior cat. Of course, the chap could dance and do it very elegantly most of the time but, really, this pretence at being an animal was just too much to bear. Drew could read all this easily from Proust's body language and from his eyes. Proust was such a sour lemon of a man. Drew never liked him and thought his genius was greatly exaggerated.

However, Drew would go anywhere, and care not who else was present, as long as Nijinsky was there. And Diaghilev. Nijinsky was the perfect physical creature and the ideal soul. Diaghilev was the great oversized head, encasing a massive, brilliant, organisational brain.

"The little, Polish acrobat will perform even if his only audience is a ginger cat," Proust said icily.

Apart from the broad insult involved, Proust had managed to deride Nijinsky's size, ancestry and profession in the one sentence. If only his writing were so precise and brief, Drew thought to himself. Diaghilev scooped up the cat and stroked its head and looked into its eyes. "This cat's soul," he said, "is inherited from an ancestor which lay at Cleopatra's feet in her barge on the Nile when Anthony was making love to her. It is a most discerning cat."

Diaghilev then stroked Nijinsky's head and neck and Nijinsky, looking directly at Proust, purred beautifully and then let forth a fierce roar. Now he was an African lion. Proust trembled. Diaghilev smiled. The actual cat leapt from his arms and ran from the room. Meanwhile, Cocteau was doing a quick sketch of the dinner party. Later, Drew purloined it for his private collection. Cocteau was one of Drew's favourite bed-mates, in male mode. A truly eccentric personality even before the juice, Cocteau post-juice was a wild fiend, spewing out his intensely creative ideas continuously and expressing his sex-drive in marathon love-making sprees with numerous partners. Drew had also noted Cocteau's voracious appetite for genuine love. Cocteau had sex almost indiscriminately, while falling in love deeply, truly and faithfully. It was only his body that made sex-love but it was his heart, soul, mind, body, liver, kidneys, genitals, and lungs that participated in his gorgeous and admirable love-love.

Drew loved both Nijinsky and Diaghilev but never even attempted to have sex with either of them. He had once been tempted to pose as a Paris prostitute, in female mode, at a house that Nijinsky frequented but he stopped himself. That was most unusual, a Red creature stopping himself from indulging in any pleasure, any whim, any lust. Perhaps the prostitute idea was too degenerate an act even for Drew. It would have meant confronting the illness already lurking in Nijinsky's mind and soul. It might have meant taking sides with the lewdness of his imagination which even then was beginning to overwhelm all else except his dancing. Although Drew hastened to note that there were few male ballet dancers of that or any other time who choreographed a masturbation scene into one of their works as Nijinsky did at the end of Faune.

But why did Drew hesitate to seduce these two Tells, despite his obvious feelings of lust for both of them? Nijinsky was a genuine naïf, even while locked in lust with a drug-addled prostitute who knew nothing of his genius and would not have cared even if she did know. So perhaps his very simplicity and inner innocence might have been shields against Drew's appetites. But Diaghilev was sophisticated and urbane and ruthless. After all, Drew had not resisted the urge to have sex with Shakespeare, his most favoured Tell. And he would have done it with his favourite intellectual Tell, Isaac Newton, too if only the man had not been so stubbornly faithful to his chastity, so stubbornly faithful in fact that his body was able to resist Drew's olfactory powers, hypnosis and other mind-moulding techniques. However, there was something precious about the singularity of the Vatsa-Serioja partnership that Drew could not bear to disturb.

Later when Nijinsky foolishly married, Drew was probably the only living creature on the planet who could understand the emotional earthquake that occurred within Diaghilev's breast, the terrific pain he felt. And in his ghastly agony Sergei Pavlovitch could only do one thing, tear the cause of the pain from his heart, rip the canker from his breast, slice a scalpel through the leech of love that was sucking his heart dry. Diaghilev cast Nijinsky out of his life and thus accelerated Nijinsky's decline into inevitable lunacy. Without Diaghilev Vatsa's life turned to ashes. His dancing meant nothing. His world was empty. Even with fame and his children and wealth, nothing could save Vatsa once Diaghilev was lost to him. Drew knew it and determined to stay away from them, forever.

But 1913 was the year for Drew to rejoice in the genius gang the Reds had created around the Ballets Russes. On this occasion their concerted effort to create another Renaissance or Shakespeare workshop style of creative cohort had worked and worked wonderfully well. Despite the arguments and resignations and volatility, the Ballets Russes remained a recognisable, viable, creative entity for many years.

It had been disconcerting for the Red team to see so many great women surround the Diaghilev gang: Karsavina, Pavlova, Isadora, Bronislava Nijinsky, even Sarah Bernhardt from time to time, to mention but a few. However, eventually, the team came to feel considerable pride in the mix of natural genius, in the women, with the juice-created-genius in the men. The two groups were almost indistinguishable. If anything the male genius tended to be more intense, exotic and erratic, but no one would be able to guess that it was manufactured.

Picasso was not conceived as part of the Dhiag-Nij-Strav-Bakst-Benois-Fokine-Debussy-Ravel-Cocteau-etcetera cohort. He was a monumental individual project. Picasso was a special case and his involvement with Diaghilev was peripheral to the great achievements the team could see in his future. They predicted that he would eventually move away from painting and become a monumental sculptor to rival Michelangelo. As is now known, they were wrong yet again. A more serious matter was the cubist stuff Picasso started to develop. Drew thought for a while that he had destroyed Picasso's eyesight as had happened with Vincent. But the only permanent side-effects of the juice for Picasso seemed to be his insatiable lust for women and his unnatural attraction to bulls. When it came time for slamming slates on tables, Picasso was slammed down often.

But the story races ahead of the story-teller. The year 1913 was the time of the notorious, outrageous, pure Eleventh creation by Nijinsky and Stravinsky of Le Sacré du Printemps. If the truth be known – and it was known because Drew knew it – both of the Sacre's creators were rather afraid of it. There was such explosive power in every movement of it and in every note. Drew was at the premiere performance. He sat with Rodin who had been a juice-boy at quite a young age and an artist who remained close to Drew all his life. There is a likeness of Drew on The Gates of Hell. He posed for the figure of Ugolino and was proud to have done so. He had two smallish Rodins in his collection.

Drew had attended rehearsals and prepared special teas for Vatsa when he got into his tempers and even administered marrow-massages that were not supposed to be used on Tells. [These had nothing to do with bone marrow. It was somehow a stimulation of the cell marrow that exists in every molecule of our bodies.] "But this was Nijinsky!" he would declare whenever anyone in the team raised the issue, as they did quite often. "You slept with Shakespeare and you marrow-massaged Nijinsky. How unscientific, unprofessional and un-Red can you be, Drew?" some peeved team member would bellow at him. And Drew would snap back, "Never so un-Red that I can't laugh at my own mistakes. As every decent

Red should do." Then he would finish the spat with a vast burst of laughter and all the rest of the team would inevitably join in.

RITE OF SPRING, 1913

Le Sacre du printemps – The Rite of Spring. It was the rite of Nijinsky's spring, as a choreographer now in full bloom. He was only 24 years old – le dieu de la danse and Principal Choreographer of the Ballets Russes. The new dance poured out of his fevered brain. He was mad with the urgency of utterly new creation. No-one had ever done anything like this before. Not even Nijinsky. Everyone was afraid that it would fail. Even Nijinsky. Especially Nijinsky. As if Stravinsky's amazing music were not amazing enough, here was the lunatic Nijinsky with his astonishing dance steps. Only Diaghilev seemed to be without fear. He believed in his two geniuses.

It was truly the time when creativity and madness lived hand in hand. The Ballets Russes was a company of mad artists, striving to produce one of the greatest explosions of dance ever seen, led by the crazy Russian, Diaghilev, to the ridiculous and unplayable music of Stravinsky – the mad composer. And through it all, Nijinsky, beautiful and young and undoubtedly mad, roared and screamed and pushed. Drew was in the room when Nijinsky confronted his sister over an awful betrayal she had perpetrated.

Vaslav roared at her, "Bronislava, what have you done to me? You have committed this act on purpose to destroy my ballet. You are the only one who can execute my moves accurately. Everyone else turns their feet and every other part of their anatomy in the wrong directions. Only you can help me."

"They turn their bodies the way we were taught, Vaslav.

Everything you want is the opposite." Bronislava was not a pretty woman but such a great dancer. And remember, there once was an English great dame who said Nijinsky was an ugly monkey. Perhaps all a matter of taste.

Vaslav implored, "But you, my sister, who do know how to do the steps, will not."

"I cannot, Vaslav. Be reasonable. I cannot throw myself to the floor as you ask."

"It's all the fault of that stupid, boorish husband of yours. Why did you let him near you when I need you so much for my work? Why did you let him do this disgusting thing to you? How can you destroy me, your own brother?" Vaslav was almost out of control with bitterness.

Bronislava snapped at him, "It is perfectly natural for married people to have children. How can you ask me to endanger my unborn child by contorting my body into unnatural shapes? It is you who wants to destroy."

Vaslav roared again, "It is grotesque that you should be pregnant now, at this crucial time. It's unfair. It's unartistic. That husband of yours is an uncouth moujik. He should be horse-whipped for touching you. Sergei Pavlovitch is right, women are truly disgusting."

"Vatsa, sometimes you frighten me. You need to calm yourself. I will not dance in this ballet no matter how many insults you throw at me and at Sasha." And she ran from the room.

When Diaghilev heard about this outrageous brawl in front of the company, he was furious. He forced Vaslav to apologise on his knees to Bronislava. But this was just one of the many outbursts and rows and screeching arguments that went on during the rehearsals. Stravinsky and Vaslav were at loggerheads for much of the time too. And Nijinsky was confronted with an entire ballet company that opposed and hated his work. Diaghilev had to save him from them on many occasions.

Drew walked into the rehearsal room one day when only Vaslav and Stravinsky were there. They had obviously been arguing, both were distressed. Their faces were tear-stained. Suddenly Igor reached out and wrapped his arms about Nijinsky and held him close to his breast. Vaslav let out a terrible sob. Igor said, "The players in the orchestra threaten to boycott the performances. They say the music is harmful to their instruments. Your dancers say their bodies cannot perform your choreography. Are we both mad then, boy? Are we quite, quite mad then?" Drew longed to tell them the truth. He had often seen the pain his genius could cause a Tell but never had seen pain of this intensity before. However, to reveal the truth was not an option. Not then.

May 29 1913 came at last and Drew sat in his seat at the Théâtre des Champs-Elysées in Paris beside Auguste Rodin. The premiere of Le Sacre du printemps. That a ballet could provoke such a riot was incredible to Drew who laughed and laughed at the turmoil. Rodin was furious with the audience. The uproar shook the theatre. It was beyond description. Everyone was shouting. Some shouted at the music; some shouted at the choreography; some shouted at the shouters to be quiet. On stage the dancers could not hear the orchestra. Nijinsky had to stand in the wings and shout the beats to them, like some lunatic.

Diaghilev stood in his box and appealed for calm, his powerful voice, in his slightly Russian-accented French, ringing out above the turmoil. The riot did not abate even for a moment. The music could barely be heard in the auditorium. Diaghilev had the house lights brought up and this provided a few moments of peace, but then the howling and screaming and the shouts and whistles all began again. The violence was so great that Drew feared the audience would invade the stage. Nijinsky's mother was in the front row and she fainted before the affair ended. Drew noticed her slumped body as he was following Diaghilev backstage and saved her life with a few quick strokes to her face and hands.

Diaghilev rushed backstage to try to calm the company. Drew saw him and followed, pausing briefly to attend to Vaslav's mother. Backstage was pandemonium. Nijinsky was standing on a chair shouting numbers to the cast so that the dancing could continue. The numbers seemed to make no sense at all. As Drew arrived there was an irate man behind Vaslav, holding an iron bar of some kind which he was about to crash down on Vaslav's body. In such an emergency, Drew did something that was totally forbidden for Red visitors, although there was a cataclysmic clause in the team's manifesto that meant the event could be forgiven. Drew deconstructed the attacker, bar and all.

[This, Drew explained in an aside, was a matter of disconnecting all the atoms in the man's body. I could not get out of him the exact method but the effect sounded very much like the type of alien disintegration effects often seen even in early science-fiction films and television. Drew explained the coincidence by confessing that Red teams had often been so careless with their powers that many Tells had seen miraculous events occur and had then interpreted them in their own way. Some obviously saw them as miracles. Others used what they had seen in creative work and so effects such as deconstruction started to occur in science-fiction books and movies. Jules Verne was an example of someone who had been privy to many Red secrets. Far too many Red secrets, Drew told me. His Red mentor turned out to be a total show-off as almost all Reds are, but this one was an extreme case. He had become obliged to shift himself to another project.]

Nijinsky saw what Drew did and later thanked him. In typical style for Nijinsky, he never enquired as to how Drew was able to bring about the deconstruction but assured Drew his secret was safe with him. Only much later when under treatment with powerful drugs for his madness did Nijinsky ever directly mention this event. Bronislava was with him and wrote about it in a letter to her husband. But then everyone knew Nijinsky was mad so no-one took notice of his ramblings about a disintegrating body. There is also a clear reference to the event in Nijinsky's diaries – his real diaries, not the bowdlerised version published by his wife, Romola – but again this was overlooked as the words were written by a man on the brink of madness.

Diaghilev called the police and they made an appearance between the scenes. By then it was too late and the presence of police uniforms in the auditorium made very little impact. When the second scene began and the dancers adopted their poses a voice in the audience called for a doctor and then another called, no, a dentist, and then another called, no, two dentists! Rodin actually struck this second man a stout blow to the side of the head with his fist. Many people in the auditorium were struck. Blood flowed. People were spat on. Many traded insults. Some exchanged cards and several duels were fought the next day.

Vaslav was distraught, shattered. Later, friends and even strangers from the audience told him and Stravinsky and Diaghilev that the ballet was a work of surpassing genius in both music and dance. Diaghilev said to Nijinsky, "My precious Vatsa, I could not have asked for a better result. The reaction was exactly what I wanted." But there was something in his voice that led Nijinsky to believe that he had, on that night, lost Diaghilev's confidence as sole choreographer for the Ballets Russes. The trials of the rehearsals, the arguments, the tantrums, the disaffection of the company, and now the riot, all added to Diaghilev's nagging doubts about the quality and stability of Nijinsky's genius. Vaslav also felt that this night was a significant moment in their drifting, intimate relationship. They had been moving apart for some little while but suddenly Vaslav could perceive the great gap that had opened up and felt, desperately, that it could never be closed. Nijinsky felt an aching need to keep their love aflame. But when he looked across the dressing room at Sergei Pavlovitch he saw emptiness in his eyes, saw doubt, saw loss. Drew was watching and he saw it too.

As soon as the riot of Le Sacre du printemps was over and the backstage area cleared, Vaslav had to change into his pretty rose-petal costume and dance the pretty steps of Le Spectre de la rose. The rose-petals were becoming a little sparse on the costume as Nijinsky's dresser, Vassili, kept cutting them off and selling them as souvenirs to adoring fans. In the chaos of the preparations for Sacre, he had not sent the costume for "re-rosing" as one of the seamstresses called this regular activity. At first Vassili tried to sell off spare cloth roses but the fans were not so stupid. They needed to see the rose they bought being cut from the actual costume and to be able to smell the sweat of Nijinsky on the rose as the purchase was completed.

The greatest dancer in the history of the Tell kingdoms stood backstage, his mind and heart pounding from the Sacre riot, but when his musical cue announced his entrance all thought was gone and Vaslav Nijinsky became the spirit of a flower, its essence, its embodiment. And the same audience who hated and reviled his most daring creativity in Sacre, leapt to their feet to applaud his twirling and jumping, to wildly cheer his final great leap through the windows as the spirit of a rose flew away into the night, to adore le dieu de la danse: Vaslav Nijinsky.

Drew stood backstage as the crew waited to catch Nijinsky after that mighty leap to stop him from crashing into the walls. They sat him on a chair and fanned him with towels. Cocteau was nearby and sketched the scene. [This is an occasion when Drew does appear in a record of an historical event, according to his own testimony. In Cocteau's drawing he stands, with a bald head on this occasion, in between Bakst and Diaghilev and is listed in the caption as 'unknown'.] Then Vaslav went to his dressing room. Drew looked in a few minutes later and the great dancer was lying crumpled, exhausted, on the floor, still in his rose-petal costume. And Drew saw him as a wilted, dying flower. Drew could see what he was going to become, the madness and the agony. Drew responded as a Red must, he laughed to himself at the melodrama unfolding before him. But, due to the human diseases of pity and empathy that now infected his personality, he also wept several tears.

BRECHT, 1913

Drew quite liked dealing with Tell teenagers, even in the days before they were called teenagers. Those adolescent boys rapidly advancing into manhood had such an enticing smell about them and smell was very important to Reds.

He was in Augsburg secondary school in Germany talking with a tall, lean, very blond 15-year-old, Viktor Kubin. Drew always found that teens were very amenable to being injected, especially when he told them about the powers of the juice. He rarely bothered to list the side-effects because, after all, there was no way to know which might strike any particular subject. Viktor was an excellent student already, with a bent for the sciences and the team had spotted his interest in engineering and had seen some of his clever sketches for bridge supports and for cities with elevated pedestrian walkways and even elevated plazas.

Drew was chatting quietly to Viktor in a classroom. The teachers thought Drew was a scout from Munich University, on the lookout for students worthy of receiving special scholarships from the Kaiser. All the teachers loved Viktor and gave glowing reports to Drew without even being asked. There was so much an air of gunpowder in Europe at this time and the team was frantically looking for a range of near-geniuses who might push the sector back towards peaceful achievement. Viktor was intrigued by the idea of a secret medical formula which could guarantee brilliance, as almost any human would be. He was not afraid of pain, he assured Drew, but was just a bit concerned about having the needle stuck in his brain.

Suddenly a voice said, “Don’t waste it on him. Give it to me.” Another boy of 15 strode into the room. He had clearly been listening at the door. Drew gave himself a mental note to explain these things in future by telepathy to avoid such embarrassments. The new boy was almost the opposite of Viktor in every way. He was shortish, skinny and almost ugly. There was a certain intensity and confidence about the boy that was attractive. He carried a guitar and immediately sat down and strummed it as he waited for Drew to answer.

“Why should I?” Drew asked in a manner as blunt as that used by the intruder. “What talents do you have?”

“Don’t listen to him, sir,” Viktor said. “He thinks he’s some sort of bohemian artist. He can’t even play that guitar properly.”

The new boy played a collection of chords quite well to refute the accusation and kept playing them as he improvised a rough poem about seeing a very red-faced stranger in the school, leading the very pretty Viktor Kubin into a room for a private consultation. He thought he might see some sex happening, so crept in closer to hear and see all. But there was no sex, just a conspiracy, and a man looking for a genius. Well, look no further, for here was a genius in the flesh and his name was Bert Brecht. With a slight vocal twist the boy managed to rhyme the German word for flesh with Brecht.

Viktor was furious, “He’s always saying disgusting things, sir. And the only one he ever thinks of is himself.”

“There are a dozen girls in this school who know that’s not true, Viktor,” Bert sang.

“Even when he’s with a girl, sir, he only is there for his own … disgusting desires.”

"You have them too, Kubin. Don't play innocent. I know that you masturbated over a drawing of that Heidi girl, who no-one else would want anyway. Admit it. You have a friend – should I name him? – who draws sketches of girls naked. Not bad for someone who has never seen a naked woman except in art books. Oh yes, I could tell a lot of unpleasant stories about this school, Herr Red Man, if that's the sort of thing you're here for."

"He's lying, sir. That's not true. None of it. He just makes up stories all the time. Disgraceful stories."

"So tell us, Herr Red," Bert grinned, "are you here for Viktor's pretty face and sexy body, or are you really seeking a brilliant, creative mind to experiment upon?"

"I only have one dose of the green juice," Drew said, lying to test them out. "Which of you should have it?"

"Of course, you must decide yourself, sir," Viktor said. "I could not be so selfish as to request special attention."

"Only because he never does have to request it," Bert said sarcastically. "He just flutters his golden lashes and opens his big blue eyes as wide as possible and gets everything he wants. Except women, of course, who aren't so easily fooled."

"Bert, I have seen Viktor's wonderful drawings of bridges and tunnels and elevated walkways. I haven't seen anything of yours, just heard some strumming and a lot of sarcasm. It is nice to be serenaded by a suitor as devilishly handsome as yourself, but is that all there is to you?"

Bert handed him a folded sheet of paper. "Here's a poem. I did it just before school. This is what I can do in a moment. Imagine what I can do when I work at it. And with your juice my talent would be unstoppable."

Drew quickly read the poem which was certainly very good.

"These three lines here seem to be written in a different hand. Why is that?"

"That was my friend, Lutz. We write together sometimes."

"Maybe I should inject Lutz because these three lines are the best thing in the whole poem."

"I told him what to write."

"So he's your secretary, not your friend."

"When you're Bert's friend," Viktor said, "you're also his slave."

"If you give the juice to this fool," Bert said, "it will be wasted, because he won't be alive to share his genius."

"Surely, Bert, you won't kill Viktor just because he tells me the truth about you." Drew laughed at the idea.

"I would never kill anybody," Bert said very seriously. "I'm talking about the war. Hasn't anybody in Augsburg noticed that Europe is on the edge of war? And no-one can stop it now. The industrialists need it and the politicians need it. You can smell it in the air if you have a nose. And when the war comes Viktor will sign up and rush off to defend his country and never even know why he died. He's a stupid nationalist and a chocolate soldier. He might even do something brave and die a beautiful hero. That's what he would like to think. But in reality he will die like most soldiers do, afraid and with his face buried in mud. What's left of his face, that is."

"And you will not enlist?" Drew asked.

"Never! I will never fight and die for any Kaiser or Chancellor or rich man."

"Your father's rich!" Viktor blurted out in frustration.

"That's not my fault," Bert said. "And I would not fight for my father any more than I would fight for my fatherland."

"He doesn't mean that, sir," Viktor said. "He's all bluff. He will fight. Don't hold it against him. He loves his country."

"I love my country enough to stay alive and become a great artist in its service," Bert said. "I hope my life is more valuable to my country than my death. I will never die face down in a ditch."

"This is all useless talk anyway," Viktor said. "Germany's leaders are much too smart to allow a war to happen. And even if a war does begin, Germany is so powerful we will crush our opponents in a matter of weeks. Very few will need to die."

"I have decided," Drew said and kept the boys in suspense for a few moments. "I will give each of you half a dose of the green juice. When I return in seven years, I will give you both another half dose each, unless one of you is dead …" – he looked at Viktor – "or one of you has abandoned his principles …" – he looked at Bert – "in which case I will give the full dose to the survivor."

The operation of injecting the boys was carried out quickly and painlessly. Bert played a quick ditty on his guitar with bitingly cynical lyrics about the uselessness of war. Drew was impressed.

"That's the silly song he's been annoying everyone in the school with for two weeks now," Viktor said.

"Das ist kunst!" Bert declared.

After telling the story, Drew laughed for a bit. "Bert was never the most likeable person but he had a power."

"What does it mean? What he said," I asked.

"That is art," Drew whispered dramatically. "I really am shocked at your lack of languages. The modern world! Ahhh, I will miss it just the same."

Drew then sang the song in a rough English translation for me, imitating Brecht's high-pitched voice and the exaggerated rolling 'r' sound Brecht used.

"The air is full of war

It suffocates me.
My mouth is full of mud.
It drowns me.
The earth is full of body parts.
Some of them are mine.
My ghost cries out,
This is madness.
No-one listens to ghosts."

I applauded his performance and Drew took a bow. In my memory I hear a plucked guitar playing behind the song. But there was no guitar in Drew's hands and I have to admit there is no guitar sound on the tape.

"I know Brecht survived the war, of course," I said, "but I've never heard of Viktor Kubin."

"Because he died, exactly as Bert predicted. Signed up at seventeen. Blown to pieces at seventeen and a half. When they dug his body out of the mud he had no handsome face left. He had no face at all, and his enhanced brain had been blown out of his head. Bert was true to his principles which tended to be 'Me first, second, third and always.' When he was called up he enrolled in medicine at university to avoid war service. As per our agreement, in 1920 I gave him a full dose. And so we got the Brecht writing workshop and the Brecht legacy to world theatre. Not a bad achievement. Unfortunately, he was a total bastard to almost everybody he met, especially women. He abused and cheated and lied without a moment's hesitation. He was obsessed with women. He also did have a few homosexual flirtations early in his career, with men who were useful to him. Later he became unfortunately homophobic. He was obsessed with money. Kept large Swiss bank accounts all his life. Not such a bad score of side-effects really for one and a half doses."

“The juice seems to work well with playwrights. Shakespeare, Goethe, Molière, Brecht …”

Drew cut me off, excitedly adding to the list, “Marlowe, Schiller, Jonson, Wilde, Gorky, Shaw, Ibsen, Strindberg – terrible depression there – and Sammy Beckett had lots of depression too – and there was the lovely Lorca and my wonderful Chekhov. I think you might have hit upon something. The playwrights. Now all we need to do is run some more data surveys on the lives of the playwrights and their side-effects and their strengths. This could be a breakthrough.”

Drew suddenly stopped and collapsed back in his chair, realising that he was doing the usual Red thing of believing some clue could lead to a solution that would allow the Reds to correct the mighty blunders that their interference on Earth had caused. There was no fix available, no cure discoverable, no correction possible. He wept a couple of tears and withdrew into himself and I left him alone. It was the only thing I could do. There could be no solace.

NIJINSKY CONFESSIONS, 1913

Drew explained that he and Nijinsky became confidants during the 1913 visit and this delighted Drew for he had the utmost affection for Nijinsky, whom he called by his intimate name, 'Vatsa'. Drew said, "Twice in his young life Nijinsky had confronted arrogant strong men on matters of principle. It was hard when watching his almost listless manner away from dancing to imagine he could be angry or strong or anything other than pliant. He seemed to mould his mood and his thought to those around him, never considering dissent. But he was, in fact, a man of passion and principle.

"At a Paris garden party, Vatsa and I walked alone and he told me about these incidents. The first strong man he confronted was his father, Thomas. It was shortly after Vatsa's graduation and his father invited him to dine with him at a rather nice restaurant. When Vatsa got there he found that Thomas had brought his mistress with him. Vatsa's parents had separated many years before but Vatsa still saw this matter as an insulting indiscretion. He acted out the conversation between himself and his father and his performance was just as intense and riveting as all his dance performances were. Sara Bernhardt once confided to me that she thought Vaslav was the best actor she had ever seen as well as the greatest dancer. So Vatsa and I stood in a sheltered area under massive trees and he acted it out. You should present this episode in your novel as if it were a play."

And so:

THOMAS: This is a disgrace, Vaslav.

VASLAV: Have you no standards of decency?

THOMAS: Have you no manners?

VASLAV: Have you no sense of morality?

THOMAS: I am your father! You will treat me with respect.

VASLAV: I am your son! Don't I deserve respect? How dare you bring your mistress to meet me. It is a dishonour to me and to my mother.

THOMAS: You are 18. You're a boy. When you're older you'll understand these things.

VASLAV: I understand now. That's why you disgust me. I came to have dinner with my father. I came because I still felt some affection for you, even though you have treated my mother in such a shameful way. I thought you may even be able to say something kinder tonight about my dancing. You were so cruel to me at my graduation. You called me a jumper.

THOMAS: That's what you are. That's how your teachers use you. Jumper! Toad! Ugly toad!

VASLAV: You have no heart.

THOMAS: They think they taught you to jump at that grandiose dance school. But it was from me you inherited that ability. The Imperial School taught you next to nothing. Half of what you did in your graduation performance you learnt from me when you were a child.

VASLAV: You're jealous.

THOMAS: I'm jealous that they will never give me a chance to appear at the Mariinsky when I am a better dancer than all their trumped up upstarts.

VASLAV: You're jealous! And you want to hurt me. You want to hurt your son the same way you hurt your wife. My mother was devoted to you. She is a saint and you crushed her heart. Now you want to do the same to me.

THOMAS: My son! My disgrace, you mean. Look at you. You are more a daughter than a son. Did the Imperial School teach you such effeminate grace?

VASLAV: If you are an example of a real man then I would never want to become one.

THOMAS: You're a girl and a jumper.

VASLAV: You're a disgraceful villain who deserted his family for a cheap whore.

THOMAS: Effeminate frog!

VASLAV: Whore-monger!

"Throughout this exchange the embarrassed woman sat at the table, sipping water. Thomas, after the final insult, took her arm and they left the restaurant. Vatsa told me that he never saw his father again after that day. I felt proud of him, at 18 to be able to take such an ethical stance in such a delicate situation.

"The other man of authority he confronted was Krupensky, head person of the royal theatres. Nijinsky's boss. That confrontation changed Vatsa's life. And again it was ethics, sensible morality and high principle that won the day. I will tell you this story briefly. Nijinsky acted it out for me at great length but the humour depended on the overly proper way in which Russians speak and constant repetition of full Russian names and titles. For example, the words 'Alexander Dmitrievitch Krupensky, Administrator of the Imperial Theatres in St Petersburg' were spoken more than 23 times. You – and your readers – would be bored to tears. Speakers of the English language tend to bore easily.

"The long and the short and the tall of it is that the Russian aristocracy and the Imperial Theatre people assumed that Nijinsky belonged to them and that his success in Paris was almost a form of treason. It was decided he had to be taught a lesson as to who his real masters were. He presented them with an opportunity by wearing a Benois costume – designed for the Ballets Russes performances in Paris – during a performance of Giselle in front of the Russian Dowager Empress. She protested that the perfectly modest shorts were obscene. Ah, if only she had lived to see the mini-skirt era. Making matters much worse was the fact that a Grand Duke had gone backstage at interval and ordered Nijinsky to change the costume. Vatsa quite rightly ignored the order. Krupensky called the lad – Vatsa was only 19 or 20 at the time – to his office the next morning and sacked him. This, despite the fact that at Nijinsky's every appearance on stage there had been overwhelming applause. This, despite the fact that the orchestra was often forced to stop playing until the ovations for Nijinsky subsided. No, it was certainly not his artistry that was in question and the costume was a trifling thing. The boy had to be brought to heel like the well-trained dog he was supposed to be.

"The intention was not only to shake Nijinsky up but also to give the Imperial Theatres a chance to change his contract – in fact give him more money – to ensure his commitment to Russia rather than to that villain Diaghilev. It all fired back on them, of course. They had not taken into account the lovely boy's integrity. Krupensky sacked him and Nijinsky said that was fine because now he could work only for Diaghilev. Krupensky said if Vatsa would apologise and present a petition begging to be re-instated, they would give him a raise in pay and status. Vatsa said no. I am so proud of him! Krupensky offered him a contract which would carry the same conditions as those for the great artists of the Imperial Theatres – Chaliapin, Smirnov, Kusnetzova. Vatsa said no. Krupensky said the job would allow him to dance as a guest with, and tour with, other companies such as Diaghilev's. Vatsa said no. Krupensky pushed the salary offer to an incredible 12,000 roubles. Vatsa said he would consider the offer if several highly placed persons apologised to him over the incident of the shorts and if the Imperial Theatres sent him a petition begging him to return. Then he turned on his heel and left the room.

"Vatsa acted it all out for me so wonderfully. The final exit from Krupensky's office was a gem. Vatsa knew that no apologies or petition would be forthcoming. Vatsa's mother was distressed and even more distressed when Vatsa's sister, Bronia, resigned from the Imperial Theatres too. Vatsa told me that both of them had such a sense of delicious freedom, with their futures in dance safely held in the hands of the brilliant Diaghilev.

"On another occasion, Vatsa confided in me his most intimate thoughts about his love for Diaghilev. It was a true love, I can assure you. Never mind his angry words in the mad diaries. That love was true. Vatsa whispered to me – and I remember every word of it – in a Paris garden, 'It might sometimes appear that I do not care for Serioja because I am cold towards him in public and because … I cannot stop myself from going to women in brothels. It was the Prince who introduced me to that wickedness and still I am drawn there. I once became very sick from one of those women and yet … I am drawn there. I have to be a man, you see. With Serioja I am what many would call his lady. But I have to be a man. For my mother. For my sister. And it is that good desire that will destroy me. Not the bad desire for prostitutes. I must marry. I must have children. And that will cause the greatest insult to my Serioja. I don't know what might happen then. But I cannot help myself. It must come.' And I knew he was right. I wept some tears with him that night, although I did also laugh about it on my walk home."

Drew paused and sighed deeply and finished the tale, "The rest as they say in cheap novels – I hope yours will not be a cheap novel, my friend – is living drama. Nijinsky married. Diaghilev almost died from the blow. Nijinsky was dismissed from the company. Diaghilev created other brilliant dancers – with my help – Massine, Lifar, Balanchine. And my poor Nijinsky eventually went mad. A sad, sad, sad story. But not the fault of the juice, in this case."

THE GREAT WAR, 1917

For the Red team what came to be called the Great War appeared to be the Biblical apocalypse. It called into question every belief Drew and his colleagues ever held about the human race. There had been atrocities before but this was "another matter entirely. Bad planning, bad leadership, and just bloody-minded bad manners." The first time Drew tried to speak of it he could not go on.

Drew leapt into the past for salvation, quickly visiting stories from several years. He told me how he gave T.E. Lawrence his booster shot of juice when "he was about 17 or 18. It was 1906 and he was one of the brilliant minds of the time. It was an era that bred many precocious young Britishers. We used to wonder if the juice had started to permeate the national gene pool much earlier than ever predicted. I had done lovely young Rupert Brooke in '99 although he was more famed for his beauty at that time."

"He must've been a child then," I said indignantly.

"He was 12 or 13. That's not a child when you're Rupert Brooke."

"Interfering with children is …"

"Dear friend, when I say 'I had done him' I mean I gave him the juice. I have used that terminology a hundred times before. Goodness me, I think you need to have a cold shower. Or better still, a night or two with one of our beautiful ladies here. This tribe has a very open sense of hospitality. Can't keep your mind above your navel, eh?" He said all this in a terribly pompous sort of English 'old colonel' accent and laughed and laughed and laughed. I was extremely embarrassed. I became more embarrassed when he asked, "And what about the tavern boy, little Robert, in Will's story? You didn't make a fuss about him. One of the working class. Does that rule him out from your sense of indignation? Is it only beautiful young aristocrats who should not be violated? Hope not, because in Rupert's time it was happening all over the country. Oscar Wilde was not the only bugger buggering young males around that time, you know. The sheets of Eton were stained with the anal blood of many a young lord, earl and even prince. At least Oscar was a democrat, he enjoyed the street lads and the aristos equally. To be strictly truthful I have to say that Oscar didn't bugger anybody. He had altogether other preferences with his lads."

"Is all this really necessary?" I asked as curtly as I could manage, through my blushes.

Drew laughed again, raucously. "I was trying to see if I could make you blush enough to turn you into an honorary Red," he said and bellowed with laughter again. I blushed even more.

In normal tones now, he said, "Poor Rupert, it distressed me beyond pain to think of him lying in that corner of that foreign field, rotting. Of course, he could be a total bastard, but mostly not, mostly as beautiful in his heart, mind and soul as he was in body, face and hair. And just as a little aside I must tell you that 'honey for tea' was a particularly favourite activity of his. The places he would put the honey before we licked it up. Well. You can imagine, I'm sure."

At that I stormed out of his house or hut or temple, whatever you could call it, and walked in the forest. I could not fathom why I was so upset about his sexual teasing on this occasion. I had never been that much of a fan of Brooke's work, although now I would never be able to read his poems without certain unsavoury images hanging over them, especially the one to do with honey. That's the problem with gossip, it taints everything with layers of smut and sleaze and distaste. I was ill from that distaste after weeks of hearing about the weaknesses and banal lusts of so many of the best and most wonderful people in Western history. Wasn't there anyone who was just a good person, without the seedy underbelly? Someone reliable and true and modest, without an ugly subtext?

"No," was Drew's answer to this question when I apologised for my behaviour and explained my feelings. "There is no-one. There is no golden model for masculine humanity. Well, some were not so bad. Lovely Lorca. My precious Blake was certainly virtuous and true to his beloved wife. Chekhov was, indeed, a darling of a man. Perhaps he is the closest slate to ... well, not perfection but certainly worthiness. Mozart, despite his love of kicking shins, was not a terrible person. Will and Henry were both decent enough fellows. But most of the models of greatness I might quote were mad as rattlesnakes, as our American team loved saying. Certain women are the only people who can be admired for the range of qualities you list. For men it is too late. The fault of my Red people, their terrible fault, their most grievous fault. You men are mottled beings. Nasty, dark patches of evil are stuck to your souls, glued there by green juice."

"And this is what you want me to tell the men of the human race in my book?"

"Ahhh," he sighed. "The book. Of course. It must be heroically male or no-one will buy it. That wouldn't do, would it? You must make as much money as possible so that you can afford the guards you will need to keep you safe from the resentful humans who will want to kill you for telling such lies about them. You would replace God – a wonderful, life-enhancing but very worrisome concept – with green liquid, with butterfly juice. You will be crucified. No!

They did that before and it didn't work. But you might be stoned, or blown apart with a car bomb, or tortured until you recant moments before an agonising death as your liver is wrenched by the handfuls from your body."

"What are you saying?" I cried in alarm.

"Just having fun. Calm yourself. As far as you can be, you are a reasonable enough human person with mostly harmless flaws and lusts. I would not be revealing all this to you unless I felt that you were moderately worthy. Many others have come and I have told them nothing."

I realise this exchange might seem rather self-serving but I include it to reassure readers about my intentions in writing this book. Old Red's commendation of my integrity is your warranty that this book does not lie.

"Back to the war!" Drew called. Suddenly I saw that the vulgarity and unpleasantness came from his emotional attempt to side-step talking about that war. He should have been laughing about it, that was the Red way. But he was not. Apparently none of the others from the North-West team ever laughed about that war either.

Drew flung open a curtain and revealed a small archive room. He pressed a switch and photographs appeared all around the room. These were not the grainy, though poignant, black and white pictures by human photographers from the Great War, but clear and detailed, full colour, three-dimensional images. They were Red images which collected the whole moment. Every sight, sound, emotion, smell. And they were awful to behold, more than any other images of war I have ever seen.

Drew left me there for some hours to take in a record of just one day's destruction on the Western front in Europe in World War One. I wept. And I was someone who had filmed war in Vietnam, on the ground, in amongst the troops. I had seen war, seen bodies blown apart, seen the sniper bullet penetrate the brain of a friend. Seen everything! Or so I used to think. Until these pictures. There were other dimensions to them, emotional qualities. They actually reeked of the emotions of the people they were showing. Every picture smelt of fear, every one felt like death, every one looked like hell. You could see the hellfire in the eyes of dying men. The photographs by the Reds invaded all the senses not merely sight. It was awful.

I wept in Drew's arms. He gave me time to recover. I could see why so many people had allowed him to make love to them. I felt myself wrapped in the arms of pure empathy and understanding. Then we talked.

"Before humans came along, we Reds – on any planet or existence area we had visited – had never seen a million animals of one species line up and kill another million of their own kind. A million elephants killing a million other elephants from the next bend in the river. Five million sparrows from London attacking and destroying five million sparrows from Stuttgart. A million New York brown bears killing a million brown bears from Vancouver. How can a species set out to destroy itself? How can a species hate its other members so much that it would risk annihilation of the entire species? We poor Reds had never seen or imagined such things before. Oh yes, there had been wars and conquests and seizure of territory before but nothing like this. A quarter of a million men die so their army can advance a hundred metres. Insanity does not begin to describe it.

"We were astounded. We had heard from our regular probes that something catastrophic was occurring. So the North-West team came for a visit out of our proper seven year sequence. But we came as holograms – well, what you Tells could only describe as holograms

– so that our presence could not affect anything and so that we were safe. Sadly, when I appeared on top of a trench a soldier trying to drag me down to safety was shot by a hail of bullets that flew through my holographic body right into his real body. I immediately looked down at him in fear that it might be one of our juice boys, somebody important, someone brilliant. His green eyes were wide open and his neck and chest were bloody and I saw that he was nobody. Just another Tell.

"Then the strangest thing happened to me. I cried because I suddenly felt through my entire being the fact that he was, indeed, somebody, an important body, an individual someone who was loved or even was solo or was hated. It didn't matter. All of them were somebodies. I could no longer think of them as my lovely monkeys. They were lovely Tells, beautiful young men, wondrous individuals who each had so many variables in them. So many variables that we mere Reds would never be able to satisfactorily medicate them into what we thought of as perfection. Each one with all his imperfections was a work of bio-chemical artistry and psychological complexity that we Reds could never contain within our predictions and our science and our laughter.

"After our visit the entire team was comatised for a year so that our emotional, spiritual and physical trauma could heal. I assume you can guess that this is a medical process and one that is only used in cases of enormous physical breakdown and distress.

"I must tell you, my friend, that from that day I never again physically harmed a human being, except in self-defence. You people were no longer cute monkeys to me. Let's face it, monkeys do not run into a house and shoot dead a mother and her five children. They don't drop bombs on defenceless civilians. They don't gas, and blow up, and beat to death others who don't believe in some particular god. They don't pulverise cities with nuclear weapons. They don't embark on chemical warfare against whole races of other monkeys. But I am mixing up my wars again. I think you get the point."

"Did you stop using the juice, once you saw what people were capable of?"

"No."

"Why not? How could you continue?"

"The fatal Red flaw. We always believe we can fix things. We can't. We can mess things up but we are hopeless at fixing anything. We're like modern day Americans [1980s], hopeless optimists about our own selves. We always think we're the good guys, the cowboys in white hats who can run the baddies out of town and restore faith and law and order. We're not. One of the reasons I was exiled was because I came to understand and accept this truth.

"We would say idiotic things to each other like, if only we could inject the juice into leaders and politicians to make them greater. That would fix things. I read a glowing report about Stalin's humanitarian qualities in 1920. It was clear the team thought the man was a saint and that he had to be given the juice for the sake of all humanity. So we did. Yes, we did. We fixed Russia up all right. Jolly good! It never occurred to us that Stalin's propaganda machine had written the material we had gathered about his fabulous qualities.

"Or let's inject scientists so that technical advances will bring people together. We got the atom bomb. Reds are so blind. We kept trying but everything clever humans invented was adapted for weapons and killing and destruction. Jet propulsion to enhance travel and exploration also created superior weapons. Lasers. Wow, how marvellous. But how can we use them as weapons? They found a way. And so. And so. And so." He took a deep breath and looked me right in the eyes. Then he blurted out in a cry of abject despair.

"You are looking at the Red who created Hitler. He was yet another Eleventh Joke."

He rushed outside and when I got to the door he was vanishing into the forest. It was shame but also humour. Hitler was one of the funniest jokes ever perpetrated on the human race. I could hear his bellowing bursts of laughter from the forest, but there were also heart-wrenching sobs.

1920s and 1930s

In the early 1920s news was leaked out that people could be made into geniuses with special injections – like the perpetual human search for the fountain of youth. In London, there was even a paragraph in The Times. Then advertisements were placed seeking genius injections. The Reds had been so indiscreet so often that rumours were inevitable. There was even reliable information out and about that the secret injections had been created by the Irish. At a party Somerset Maugham approached Drew and asked him if he knew of the juice because Drew had been speaking with an Irish brogue. The Reds had days when they were more red than others and often used the Irish thing to cover that. Drew found Maugham a disgusting person and treated the idea of genius injections as a joke. Not a hard thing for a Red person to do, it came more natural to Drew than trying to lie. Maugham apparently was offering a finder's fee of the modern equivalent of a hundred thousand pounds and a 'medication' fee of a modern million pounds.

Later, Drew said it might have been Evelyn Waugh who approached him. "Very English, very English," Drew kept saying. "No Frenchman, or German for that matter, would ever have admitted to needing more intelligence or creativity or brilliance. The English are so … English."

Jean-Paul Sartre at just 15 years of age refused to accept an injection. Drew sarcastically pointed out that the lack of the juice enhancement can be seen clearly in Sartre's woolly thinking and his inadequate sexual abilities and his cowardice. Drew flippantly suggested that Sartre possibly was just scared of needles before admitting that the refusal was almost certainly French pride in action.

This time period for Drew and apparently for all the others in his Red team was filled with panic and confusion. They were still trying to deal with the losses of the Great War and then at the end of the 1920s there was the world-wide depression and the Reds could see another war on its way. Their vision must have been very blurred as they injected Stalin and Hitler in an attempt to create clever politicians who would prevent the war. Because the Reds themselves had always accepted the loss of life coming from failed injections it never occurred to them that Hitler's brutal tactics in establishing himself and his Nazi party were at all abnormal. New German pride and economic success would guarantee that they would not go to war again. Surely. Only a madman would risk the new status and wealth of the nation in another massive conflict that would inevitably extend Europe-wide. Surely, no-one would deliberately lead his country into such disaster.

By 1927 Drew was doing the whole outrider thing. Visiting all his people on the fringes and circling into the centres, especially the London, Paris, Berlin centres. On one of those trips he decided to pay a visit to Nijinsky, now confined in madness. "Karrel came with me to see Vaslav and on the train he spoke about his interaction with the Ballets Russes gang. Oh yes, we travelled by train at times so that we had the chance to reflect and think and confer with colleagues. And also because it was such a lovely way to move. Trains were the peak of human achievement in travel. Wretched new flying machines are not at all nice. Of course, there was the great ship, the Titanic, which was such a fabulous conception but I never got the chance to travel on it as America was not in my sector. Anyway, for journeys of that length, it would be impractical. But the occasional five or ten hours on a train could be well worth the time spent."

"What do you mean you never travelled on the Titanic?"

"As I said, I never actually went to America. All the teams had so much work in their own sectors. We couldn't flit about from quarter to quarter. And there was a lot of jealousy too. Each sector had its own favourites and heroes and methods. No-one would brook any interference in their own ways of doing things. This will also explain to you why the geniuses from each sector were so different in their natures. A lot of the impact of the juice came from the personalities of the team administering it. Ingredients were mixed to reflect those personalities too. We wanted to avoid turning out stereotype geniuses.

"You could never have had a Mozart in America or had an Abraham Lincoln in Europe. Also, I think it would be fair to say, judging from some of the global reports I glanced at, that each sector already had its own Tell personality too. Certainly by the end of the 19th century they did, despite – or perhaps because – such large proportions of the populations came from colonists and slaves and adventurers. The variables were so interesting and exciting. We didn't always curse the variables, you know."

"I'm talking about the Titanic because it sank. You must know that it sank."

"It sank? That marvellous giant vessel sank? That's incredible. Are you sure?"

"It's one of the most crushing events for human morale in the past few hundred years. Just when we were starting to believe we could control our own world and master …"

"All the variables!" Drew added in for me, triumphantly.

I continued, "It sank! The unsinkable sank!"

"Oh dear," Drew said. "I can see how that must've upset a lot of people."

"Yes. Especially the 1500-odd passengers and crew who died. And then we were into the most ugly, devastating …"

"Pointless," Drew added the third adjective.

"… war ever waged. Human stupidity came stampeding to the fore in that damn conflict."

"I'm afraid Tell stupidity is almost always at the fore, my friend. Even our golden geniuses had to struggle against their own cupidity and stupidity. I do like to rhyme occasionally. But, tell me, when was this Titanic thing? You're losing me with all these digressions. Can't we stay on the topic?"

I gritted my teeth, ignoring the provocation, and said, "1912."

"Not one of our visiting years." Drew wafted a hand in the air as if to explain totally his lack of knowledge. "And when we were here in 1913 there was a hell of a lot of other business to discuss."

"Didn't you ever check up on events that happened in the years in between?"

"Only things that had to do with our subjects. We had a complex system of alarms. We knew about the Great War, of course. Perhaps there were none of our people on the Titanic. Maybe they were all too clever to be taken in by the false claims. Unsinkable! Hah! No such thing."

"But you were taken in. You thought it was unsinkable until I told you it had sunk."

"The sinking proves it wasn't unsinkable, doesn't it? And that the builders' claims were outright lies."

This type of Red thinking had been foisted on me before. I was beginning to realise that the Red brilliance, although far superior to any Tell brilliance, was no guarantee against Drew putting forward some of the most illogical, most irrational and just plain stupidest arguments and observations ever heard on this planet.

1927 was also the year when Drew brought Sammy [Samuel Beckett] and Jimmy [James Joyce] together. Drew loved to tease my oversensitive human reverence for genius by giving some of his charges pet names. [Possibly the worst example for me was his calling Goethe "Gee". Sometimes he even would call him "the big Gee". He also used to joke that the W in "W. Shakespeare" stood for "Workshop".] As we know from human history, without any embellishment needed from Drew, Beckett became a disciple of Joyce's. It can be seen in Beckett's writings about Joyce as well as in his creative work. No need for juice explanations there, but I suppose we should be grateful that the introduction was made. Sammy and Jimmy were both fine examples of Drew's ongoing interest in fostering the tale telling abilities of the Irish.

"The juice helped their writing along admirably, of course," Drew told me. "But strangely enough it turned Jimmy into a coward who was scared of the slightest thing, while Sammy became a lion-heart. His courage in the second horrible European disaster was enormously noble."

"Probably that was just the human nature of both of them. Why does everything have to be the juice?"

"Exactly!" Drew pounded the nearest table victoriously. "I kept telling the others that but they could never see it. Except that in Jimmy's case his deteriorating eyesight was probably caused by the juice, and the eyesight was the probable background to his nervousness, and what might appear to the insensitive to be cowardice. For us Reds, everything did have to be presumed as the effect of the juice unless otherwise provable. I wish you'd been at those meetings to jolt them with your common sense, my friend."

I left that alone. My human ego at that point was a bit too fragile to allow me to investigate every comment for sarcasm or jokes. Also, I realised we were getting into the nature versus nurture argument that humans have carried on for centuries and that has so many pitfalls you would have to be far stronger mentally, physically and emotionally than I was right then to even consider embarking on that murky ocean. Was Sammy's courage in his nature or in the juice? A question for future philosophers? Or does it actually matter?

THE TURING TALE

It was also in 1927 that Drew destroyed one of the great romances of modern times. "A couple so close that Romeo and Juliet seemed strangers by comparison," he assured me. I pointed out to him that Romeo and Juliet were in fact strangers. They just saw each other and fell in love. That was the human way quite often. Or was this another juice induced quality. Did he actually juice up Romeo? Drew brought me back to earth by reminding me that Romeo was a fictional character. Even I had to laugh at myself over that one. Then Drew denounced himself for the tragic destruction of the love, never consummated but lasting beyond the grave, between Alan and Christopher. This was a love that changed the entire history of the entire world, entirely, as we now know it. In 1927.

[The 'entire' sentence was in my notes and I thought it worth repeating here because it shows how weary and cynical and even sarcastic I had become by this time about every event that Drew related to me being the most cataclysmic of all time in the unofficial history of the planet. It became rather like today's ads for TV soap-operas in which we are assured every week that next week's episode will change all the lives of all the characters totally and forever.]

"Teenage love, premature death and suicide. A true tragedy worthy of the best creation of either workshop – Bert's or Bill's. [Brecht and Shakespeare were the writing 'workshops' he was referring to.] Even Dante or Sophocles himself would have relished such a story. Not that I ever knew Sophocles, of course, but my grandparents spoke very highly of him."

As with many of his outrageous declarations, the emotion of the situation left Drew exhausted, and he rushed off into his private rooms to weep or sleep or reflect. I was left alone again to reflect myself upon the weird mix of comedy, tragedy and farce in yet another of Drew's tales. I went wandering in the museum to see if I could find a clue to who these two teenagers were who had entirely changed the entire history of the entire world. There was only that curious half apple with bites out of it which was labelled "Alan". I guessed that the next story would explain the apple as well as the romance reference.

At almost 15 Alan fell in love with Christopher without quite knowing what love was, except that one could never speak about it without great embarrassment and, in the case of being in love with another boy, without fear of tremendous harassment from his schoolmates and teachers. Even in cases of merely suspected crushes between boys, the teasing was ferocious. Alan had always been an intensely lonely boy but there was something entrancing about Christopher Morcom's face that made him want to look at it all day long. Morcom was a year older than Alan but smaller in height. Alan deduced there was some illness involved. Shortly after Alan fell in love with him, Christopher stayed away from school for some time. When he returned, he looked quite gaunt. But still beautiful in Alan's eyes.

Although it was not easy to be a friend to an older boy at their school, Alan soon had Christopher interested in his ability with mathematics and science generally. Alan had bright and surprising ideas which Christopher enjoyed. Christopher was meticulous in his work and had won many prizes, which Alan liked about him. Alan also became part of a gramophone club, although he had little interest in music, so he could be in Christopher's company. They set each other maths problems and discussed solutions. They shared chemistry experiments. Alan was not ever able to tell Christopher of his feelings but others noticed the pairing. Perhaps it was Christopher's bouts of illness that saved them from being teased. Perhaps there was a purity and innocence about this relationship which even schoolboys could perceive and respect.

The Red team knew of bright, successful boys like Christopher through scans of examination and scholarship results. Drew went to visit Christopher at his school. It was not readily possible to see Christopher alone because anywhere where Christopher could be alone, Alan was there. Drew had a fascinating afternoon tea with the two of them, discussing careers in science, dreams for their future, and so on. He noticed that Alan constantly said how marvellous Chris was at, well, everything. Drew noticed also that Alan had the kind of offbeat mind that could very possibly respond well to the juice. He decided to inject both of them, as a teamed pair. It was clear that anything Chris attempted, Alan would attempt. Drew knew that anything Chris wanted to achieve would have Alan's complete support.

He put the proposition to them that the government had developed a drug that would increase intelligence, reasoning power and scientific ability. It would help them to deal with large scientific issues and complex interactions between different fields of science. It had to be kept secret and they had to swear an oath to say nothing to anyone about this whether they decided to be part of the initial program or not. They duly swore and in those days an Englishman's word was his bond. Drew also produced an impressive set of credentials and Christopher wrote down the registration numbers carefully. Apparently, the notebook with these numbers in it is part of the collection of papers in some library that holds Turing's material. Alan kept many of Chris's books and mementos his whole life.

The injection no longer had to be given directly into the brain but could be done into the top of the shoulder close to the neck muscles. However, Christopher was wary of doing such a thing without talking to his parents about it. Alan was eager. It seemed to him like a chance for the two of them to be joined in a great adventure which would belong only to them. Drew applied a bit of Red persuasion. Chris said he would if Alan did. Alan insisted on going first so that if there was any danger, if this man was some sort of impostor, or if the injection was tainted in some way, Alan would be protecting Chris. The injections went ahead.

As he had hoped, Alan became even closer to Chris and both noticed that indeed they seemed to have become mentally stronger. Alan never spoke to Chris of his love but he knew that Chris was aware of it and did not disdain it. Alan knew this because of the crankiness that Chris showed whenever Alan was being a little too obvious about his affections. Two and a half years later, Chris was dead and Alan was embarked on a journey of painful loneliness for the rest of his life.

"So you think the injection killed the boy?" I asked.

"There's no doubt. In our usual Red way we never checked subjects for previous illnesses or gave any kind of medical examination or even believed it was necessary. We assumed that the juice could not have any medically adverse effects. Right up to the end of the Butterfly Project no team was ever provided with medical support. As you can imagine, Red medicine is quite advanced. But the organising authorities believed our medical expertise would not apply to you Tell monkeys because of various startling differences between our species. So the headaches and madnesses and deafness, all that stuff, was never checked out medically. Who knows, if we'd had a doctor with us on one of our trips we might've cured Beethoven. But the project just did not have high enough priority and no further resources could be applied. Does that process sound familiar?

"It turned out that Chris had suffered since a small child from bovine tuberculosis. He'd been given diseased milk. Why human children should be thought to benefit from milk made by another species of creature for its own young is beyond my comprehension. Nevertheless there it was. The butterfly milk I gave him hastened his death. Oh, he would've died at some early point anyway but without the juice, those two could have had 10 more years together."

"To be honest, after your build-up to this love affair, the actual story is a bit of a let-down. It's not exactly the passionate declarations and climbing up the balcony for a good night kiss sort of stuff that I expected."

"If you could have seen them together you would have known the depth of their true love. The devotion in Alan's eyes every time he glanced at Chris; the joy he showed when Chris smiled; the intensity with which he listened to every word from Chris's lips. It was true that Chris gave less away and sometimes pretended to dismiss Alan's overwhelming affection. But he did enjoy playing to his captive audience and he did enjoy watching Alan, especially when he was being physical – running especially, which Alan did often and so spontaneously. Alan would spot something ahead and dash up to it suddenly, pick up the stick or leaf or rock that had caught his attention and bring it back to Chris and their heads would come together as they scrutinised the object, discussed it and tossed it away so they could move on to the next fascinating thing. They found fascination all around them every minute of their journeys together. They were a beautiful, inspiring couple.

"Their love was far more noble and true than the stuff Henry created for Romeo. Admittedly, the Romeo story was early days and Will had not learned to trust Henry enough yet and he kept interfering. The plot was a mess. Only minutes before he sees Juliet he's dotingly in love with someone else. Then he's so desperate to have sex with Juliet that he immediately drags her off to an understanding preacher to get married. There's no depth to that love. Alan and Chris were beautiful together. And I destroyed their lives."

He paused for a sigh but before I could say a sympathetic word, he brightly added, "The human race got one of the best bargains ever out of this premature death and crushed love. I made Alan Turing's life a total misery at age 17 but … the world was saved from the Nazis and you got computers. That's not a bad deal now is it? Come on, tell me, admit it. Christopher's death was worth it, wasn't it? One nice, sick kid who would've died anyway in exchange for all that? Isn't that a good deal …?

"Of course, there was the suicide thing too. I suppose that counts. Never mind, in the long run at the end of the day the final summing up is that the world got a good deal for just three loads of juice. Yes, three because I gave Alan a later dose. I know he was rather hoping it would kill him too and he'd end up wherever it was that Chris's soul had gone to. He didn't believe in a god – Alan that is – but he did passionately believe in the human soul."

The next time that Drew saw Alan, in 1934, the scene was painful and intensely sad. He held Alan in his arms as the young man sobbed and sobbed. There had been no-one else Alan could talk to about his love for Chris even though many acquaintances were aware of it. The most important relationship, the most devastating loss, the most intense pain he would ever feel in his life and yet there was no-one for him to confide in except this weird Red alien being who, fortunately unknown by Alan, had killed his beloved.

Alan became close to Chris's mother after the death and had even gone on holidays with Chris's parents, almost as a Chris substitute. He had visited their home and stayed in the Clock House which Chris had told him so much about. Mrs Morcom gave Alan many little keepsakes of Chris, plus a small photo, and Alan cherished these all his life. He carried on a correspondence and relationship with Mrs Morcom for years. It was clear to Drew that the mother knew what Alan had felt for her son.

Alan repeated to Drew things he had written to Mrs Morcom about feeling certain that he and Chris would meet again and that they would have "some work" to do together. He kept telling Drew about how "kind" Chris had always been to him, of the "kind" things Chris would say, of the "kind" gestures. Drew found it hard to maintain his composure, the scene was so desperately sad, and he was seeing deep into Alan's soul and seeing what a beautiful and innocent man he would always remain. Alan vowed that he would work doubly hard to achieve enough success so that Drew would see that Chris's influence was palpable and worthy.

"Alan did work very hard but, ironically, his achievements are largely unknown and the significance of his presence in so many cohort situations is still undervalued. But I often think he was the best subject I ever had."

[I did wonder at that remark at the time. How many "best subjects" could Drew have? Galileo, Mozart, Shakespeare, Chekhov,

Turing? Yes, Drew did get to love his monkeys a lot.]

Drew went on, "He wasn't flashy. Hard to quantify the precise input results. Personality issues murking up brilliance overload. Frightening intelligence offset by eccentric and erratic work methods and life habits and social inadequacy. Better than Newton by light years. Newton hid everything. Turing shared everything. Newton hated rivals. Turing rejoiced in collaboration, as long as people weren't entirely stupid. Newton put his name on everything. Turing put his name on nothing. Well, 'Turing machines'. But since then the word computer has sort of taken over from all else. I know you'll think I'm making wild Red predictions again but – okay this is 1987 and we all know about computers now, we know they can be small enough to just sit there on a single desk – but I predict, and you'll find this a bit astonishing I suppose, that by the year 2010 or let's say twenty-five years from now, there will be at least one computer in every office building and in every classroom too and almost certainly in many private homes for people who can afford them. By the year 2050 people will be saying that they can't imagine what people used to do before there were computers. [With the benefit of hindsight in the computer saturated world of 2009 we can see that Drew hadn't got any better in his later life at assembling the variables accurately. I use three different machines myself, one at home, one at the office and a laptop.] I'm not sure that any race will ever get to the situation that Turing imagined where you could create a machine that could contain the mind and soul of a human being. That was his dream. In other words a machine inside which he could re-create Christopher Morcom. A kind machine. Can you imagine that?"

"From the way the computer literate whizkids where I work talk about their precious machines, I'm not sure we'll have to wait until 2010 before computers take over," I said, trying to show off my technical knowledge and also displaying the weird fear we had back then that computers would somehow, independently, seize control of our lives.

"Trust me," Drew said. "Technically, you Tells are not always as good as you think."

"I should trust the person," I said, a little too sarcastically, "who predicted that Mozart would live a long life and be rich. I should trust the guy who sent Beethoven deaf. I should trust the Red man who created Hitler in order to bring peace to Europe."

"Sometimes, my friend, I wish that you would learn a thing or two from the stories. Perhaps kindness is a quality that you might treasure a little more. I, personally, am not your enemy. I am in fact a traitor to my people. I am betraying them to try to help you and other Tells to understand."

"How can I be kind?" I blurted out furiously. "How can I understand? How can I ever forgive the stupid, horrible mess you Red creatures have perpetrated on this earth? How can I ever forgive you for turning a bunch of harmless monkeys into …" and here I broke down into deep, heaving sobs and was only just able to get out a few more hysterical words, "… into me? Into men like me? How can anyone forgive that?"

We did not speak again for three days. He organised for some of the tribespeople to take me to a riverside lodge to rest. It was a mud and sticks hut on the outside. I swam. I even slept. I realised that Drew was being gentle with me because we had reached a point in North-West Segment history which would be harder to hear than even the lot that had gone before. I appreciated, not only the kindness, but also the fact that his gesture and his story about the young Alan Turing had reminded me how under-rated kindness was. I vowed that when I returned to civilisation – a term that now made me laugh whenever I was tempted to use it – I would treat all people with more kindness. I broke the vow by writing this book.

The code-breaking cohort at Bletchley Park was, in Drew's eyes, the most successful working group of brilliant minds ever, in the North-West Sector anyway. They were of different ages – Turing was only about 27 when it began – and from various backgrounds and disciplines. Some were mathematicians, others physicists, and even champion chess players were included in the gang. There was no rank and everyone's ideas were respected. It was a true cohort working to decipher codes day by day so that the Hitler war machine could be defeated. They also had to fight the old hat British bureaucracy of civil servants and the stick-in-the-mud high officers of the British military forces and managed to beat them too.

Drew was proud to have played a part in the latter campaign. He visited Bletchley Park and Alan Turing several times in 1941. The war over-rode all other considerations for the Red team. Even the American team was co-operating with the North-Westers. Turing pointed out to Drew that the military people were not only trying to place crushing restrictions on the work on the Enigma machine codes but also were being bloody minded about necessary supplies and financing. Turing was determined to write directly to Churchill, thinking that he might be the only one who could clear the path for the code-breakers. Drew told him to hold off until Drew could get to Churchill in London and lay the ground to support Alan's letter.

Churchill became probably the oldest person Drew, or any of the other Reds for that matter, ever gave the juice to. Churchill was eager to have the injection once Drew explained who he was and why it was vital that this leader was equalised with Hitler and Stalin.

Churchill was furious about the Reds giving such power to those two. He gave Drew a roaring blast of the famous voice, "Never in the civilised history of this great planet has any one person created such chaos with as stupid an intervention as you have made." And there was more which Drew chose not to record.

He saw Churchill again two days later and was pleased to see that the juice was already giving him greater energy and insight. They talked for an hour in complete privacy. Churchill knew he could never reveal that he had been advised by an alien creature from an off-planet dimension, let alone allowed himself to be injected with a substance not known to mankind. The straight-jacket would have been applied immediately at the mere mention of such a thing.

During his hour Drew made a powerful case for Churchill's total support of the Bletchley Park gang and especially of Alan Turing. He stressed that this group alone could win the war for Britain if only the military would follow up confidently and immediately the information coming out of the place. He asked Churchill not to act until Turing wrote to him so that no suspicions would be aroused about the source of the information. Churchill insisted that he would go personally to see these great men who were saving the nation and did so. He met Turing – Drew was at the meeting – and the others and was completely impressed with their dedication and brilliance. He told Drew, "Now that I've met Turing I can perhaps forgive you for creating Stalin, but never Hitler." At the time the full horror of Stalin was not known and many of his outrageous crimes against humanity had not yet been perpetrated. Later in his life, when he did know more facts, Churchill took back his forgiveness.

Turing wrote to Churchill in October in great detail about the issues diminishing the effectiveness of the work at Bletchley Park. The three other most senior men working with him signed the letter too. Churchill acted the instant the letter reached his hand. Everything the Enigma cohort wanted was provided and nothing was ever denied them again. The military listened and learned and won battles on the basis of the information the cohort provided. The Atlantic fleet was saved from annihilation and the war would be won by the side that the Red teams thought was marginally less monstrous than the other side.

Turing was the soul in the machine, the enigma who understood the German Enigma machines but never quite understood himself. Although young he became known as 'the Prof' at Bletchley Park because his was always the mind against which ideas were checked, the brain that developed and expanded ideas that one intriguing step further, the human machine that everyone acknowledged as the ultimate approver. All this was so secret that hardly anyone ever knew it existed, even a decade after the war was over. Alan and his colleagues were never given a medal because that would have exposed the existence of the cohort. Some of them did go down to London one time to be given cash rewards for their outstanding work. Turing liked that better than a medal anyway because it meant he could buy stuff to build other stuff and develop existing stuff into things that eventually looked like and behaved like computers. Drew was thrilled by the Enigma cohort. Visiting them was one of his most exciting memories, meeting raw intellect on the hoof.

Drew said, "Turing was a catalyst for many other brains. His concepts were so advanced and yet when I met him again in 1948 he showed me a piece he had written where he explained that a highly disciplined man or woman with a notepad, a pencil and a rubber was in effect a 'universal machine' – the concept he had created which was in effect beyond even the modern computer. [As computers stood in 1987, that is.] Turing understood – as Newton never really did while Einstein certainly encompassed the idea – that a feeling for structure or shape or form was where intelligent understanding and action were created, not in the so-called meaning of words, symbols and gestures.

"His death was a tragic waste. It happened just six months before my next visit to him. Perhaps he chose that timing because he was ashamed that I might see him in his tortured state, because I was such an intimate connection to his past pride in his relationship with Christopher. He was tortured to death by the British idiocy about sex and by the general officiousness of English life.

"A couple of years before his death the police had investigated a break in and robbery he reported at his house. In his naïve, candid way he told the nice policeman that he suspected the thief was a friend of a young man who was his lover. The police acted against Alan and his lover on that information for breaking the nonsensical sex laws of the time that totally banned homosexual activity. He was dragged into court where his colleagues stood by him, but he was sentenced to two years – shades of Oscar [Wilde] fifty years on – and that was commuted to probation as long as he underwent the torture of sexual therapy. And that more or less castrated him chemically and also led to his actually growing breasts. Horrible stuff. My poor Alan. Henry was so so so right to speak often of man's inhumanity to man. And in Alan's case we all know the upshot of course."

"I don't," I said, "although you have mentioned suicide. But to be honest I've never even heard of Alan Turing."

"Ah, yes. That is probably true for most people. Not a household name. Anyway he soaked an apple in cyanide and took a bite and died. That's how the English treat their heroes. Never mind if you helped, in an enormous way, to win this ghastly war. Never mind if you are one of the great intellects of your generation. We will crush you if you desire members of your own sex and do naughty things with them."

"So that's the apple you have in the glass case?"

"Yes. I stole it from the police. They would have just thrown it away. Ironically, I suppose I will have to arrange to have it thrown away after I die. I have become very much like you monkeys. I value keepsakes and trinkets too much."

[When I was writing up this piece of the Red story in the early 2000s, it occurred to me that I often encountered a symbol of an apple with a bite out of it. In fact, it is on the computer I am using to compile this book. Surely, that symbol must be a tribute to Turing, the most imaginative conceiver of what computers might become.]

WORLD WAR II, 1941 and 1948 and OTHER MUSINGS

World War Two was the beginning of the end for Drew and for the whole Red experiment on Earth. If the first great war had stunned them, the second one turned the Red minds to mush. They were confused, in pain, and continually horrified. Some suffered more than others. Karrel had to drop out of the whole experiment immediately after he investigated Auschwitz towards the end of the war in hologramic form. The extent of the holocaust seemed totally unbelievable to the Reds, not only the numbers involved, but also the level of cruelty and suffering inflicted on the Jews and the other inmates of the dreadful camps. Karrel actually collapsed into a life-threatening coma when he tried to describe to a conference of Red teams what the Nazis had done. He had to be treated for his trauma for several years afterwards.

Shockwaves went through the entire Red race when Karrel's report was made public. That they could be directly responsible through their experiments on the human race for such atrocities was a disturbance in their existence that was ever present, Drew assured me. The next shock to them was a report from the Red American team about dropping atom bombs on two Japanese cities, as well as the preamble to that oration which detailed the atrocities committed by the Japanese military. Nothing could excuse the Japanese but nothing they had done could excuse the atom bombs.

Drew assured me that everyone in the Seventh and Eleventh

Dimensions still held the days that those atom bombs were dropped as 'blackout days'. Everyone retreats into darkness for 24 earth hours each earth year. Nowhere – in any dimension, let alone the Seventh and Eleventh – could anything like those explosions have been imagined, let alone actually perpetrated. Those blackout days represent some sort of atonement by the Reds for their part in creating the monsters who were capable of Auschwitz and Nagasaki and a million other terrors of man against man.

Drew kept reminding me that no Tell woman would ever have been able to drop those bombs or conceive of the holocaust or commit any of the terrors and tortures and massacres in our history. Religions – the inspiration, Drew asserted, for the majority of atrocities – were almost always run by men. Almost all professional politicians in the world's history had been men and the military upper echelons were still almost entirely made up of men. Could you imagine Jane Austen or Pavlova or any of the Bronte sisters dropping those bombs? Of course not. I hastened to point out that I could not imagine Blake or Nijinsky or – his latest favourite – Turing dropping the bombs either. Then I played my trump card and declared that I certainly believed that dreadful Margaret Thatcher woman – creating havoc in Britain as its Prime Minister at the time – was capable of any atrocity. Her blatant re-election ploy of starting the Falklands war was an abomination.

Just as I got fully into my anti-Thatcher, left-wing oration, betraying my feelings in a way no good journalist should, Drew stopped me and declared Thatcher was not actually a woman in any way other than physically. She was another victim of mistaken variables and more and more women were being poisoned with the green juice as passed on through the genes of their fathers and grandfathers. Yes, the juice had leaked into the full human gene pool.

In women it only acted to enhance certain characteristics that might before have been declared 'male' and mostly those characteristics blended in with their so-called 'female' characteristics reasonably comfortably. But in some cases, such as Thatcher, the juice eroded all natural Tell traits and female evolutionary development to create something akin to monsters.

The proof of his assessment, he claimed, lay in the sad mistake in the 15th century of injecting Joan of Arc. She had turned into a callous, brutal fighting machine leading an army to defeat the English. However, Drew did hold a strong hope that eventually the juice genes and the natural Tell female genes would blend and create a better race of people for the planet. Given his record in understanding variables and making predictions, this idea of hope filled me with gloom. It seemed that almost everything the Reds did over a period of the last few thousand years had turned out to be the perverse opposite of what they intended. Not much solace then in a Red prediction or hope, even when the Red was someone who was as interesting and empathetic to the Tell race as Drew was.

Drew noted the irony that just as the Enigma project and Alan Turing had created the most effective model ever for human creativity, intellect and endeavour, so other clever monkeys were creating torture and destruction unlike anything ever seen on Earth before. Just as with the writing workshops of Will and Bert, the Enigma gang had no age gap, received all ideas in a democratic fashion, and accepted without rancour the talents and wisdom of others. There was a hierarchy in the acknowledgement of a leading figure or two but it was not complex and restrictive. Just when the Red teams might have been able to report that injected humans could work alongside naturally brilliant women in free-wheeling cohorts to create art and science, so political and military cohorts showed that the power of collaboration could also create havoc.

Drew was proud to be able to say that the Americans had nothing like the Turing cohort although he acknowledged that in a negative way they did: they had the atom bomb cohort. "How completely American," Drew said sarcastically. It was clear that, like many Europeans, Drew was jealous of America as well as disdainful of their civilisation, culture and society. The dropping of the atom bombs proved they were barbarians. I tried to explain the arguments always put forward about the bombs, but Drew was not impressed or ready to listen.

"How many words will you have to use to dismiss the pain and horror of what was done to those cities full of people?" he demanded. "A certain number for each person, perhaps? Fewer for the person disintegrated in the flash of the explosion, more for the person who slowly died from radiation poisoning. Perhaps you can become an apologist for the Nazis too and give us – what? – 600 million words of explanations for the holocaust – just 100 words per person, more or less. Maybe a few less for the people who were suffocated in the railway cars on the way to the camps, a few more for those who watched their children taken from them into slave labour, or for medical experiments, or who watched as older parents were marched directly into gas chambers for 'showers'. Not so many for those who succumbed earlier, and a few more for those who held out for years. How many words for each mass grave? How many for each tear? How many for those who survived and had to live new lives, haunted by a horror beyond memory and words?

"Perhaps in this horrible century, my good friend, you could make a career out of explaining the atrocities and terrors that are occurring day by day. If we simply look at the past 50 years, there is a rich field of explanation to be offered. Perhaps you could give a cogent and positive slant to American behaviour in Vietnam, make a good argument in favour of napalm. What about giving an explanation for Chinese behaviour on numerous fronts. Tibet perhaps? Or for Japanese behaviour in China. For British behaviour throughout their colonies and in Ireland. For Irish behaviour. For all the mess of the Middle East until now we have the total turnaround of Jews treating whole races of people as non-humans as they themselves have been treated so often before. Explain to me how humans manage such a mind-whirl. Maybe a sophisticated dissertation on the French need to bomb the very life out of South Pacific islands in atomic tests. Or French eagerness to persecute Algerians. Give the world a cool explanation as to why America needed to develop a hydrogen bomb that was 750 times more powerful than the one that destroyed Hiroshima.

"And everybody hates the gypsies. My poor exotic orchids, gypsies. A race of incredible beauty and soul and blood-red-heart. They are hybrids. The only race to have some elements of Red in them. I am revealing to you something intimate to my heart and soul. There are traces of Red DNA in gypsies. If you ever meet any, please treasure them in memory of me. But all this hate against them, wherever they roam. Hatred is the stamp of humanity, I'm afraid. Ask your friends how many people they love and how many people they hate. It will horrify you. People seem only able to love individuals but they can hate whole cities and countries and races. People can easily say, I love my family – if it's a smallish family – but can they say, I love Argentineans, they are all so nice? No. But how easy to say, I hate the Turkish. I loathe Italians. Irish people drive me nuts. The English are arrogant, violent and stupid. What's wrong with saying the English are elegant, humorous and so huggable? It's true. So much hate in human hearts. So many targets for the hatred. Did we put that into you? Was that the fault of the juice? Or is the human race a hatred race? I hope, I hope it wasn't us."

Drew broke down into hysterical tears. And so did I.

I wasn't sure if I could take much more history. I was so pleased Drew had left out lots of the material he could have told me, especially things about the Inquisition, or the full horrors of the French Revolution, the gulags, the genocide attacks and seizure of lands with aboriginal people in North and South America and Australia and elsewhere, and many, many other atrocities. There were some individuals I had been yearning to know more about like Rimbaud and Dickens, but I was exhausted. That's why this is a much thinner book than could have been written even from the tapes I have. And certainly a fraction of what the Red man could have told me had I stayed several more months. But there's only so much thinking one can do about the human race – or even just the North-West Sector of Earth – before your head explodes. That's my well-considered theory anyway.

THE ENDING

"Thing is," Red said, as if summing up and about to move on and leave me with the knowledge and the responsibility, "Reds see the world's predicament as a comedy, Tells think it's a tragedy. The Shakespeare cohort and Mozart had Red senses of humour. Henry's blackest tragedies were also filled with humour. Look at the scene where Lear's Fool gets eaten by a bear. They spent months training the bear but then at the first performance he actually did kill the actor playing the Fool. Also Beethoven's deafness was funny. If Goya had gone blind instead of deaf that would have been really funny too. Tells have this thing about 'great' people – a tragedy that Goya was deaf and oh how he suffered the poor man – but he had the money to look after himself and fame and friends whereas lots of peasants and ordinary folk also had afflictions which added to their poverty and killed them, and Tells accept that as the natural order of things.

"So another reason I had to exile myself was that – since that day on the trenches in the Great War – I started seeing all this, this human life thing as a massive tragedy instead of a frustrating experiment gone wrong. All other Reds saw the tragic side of things as being their own problems in trying to get the juice right, not as the suffering and problems it caused for the Tell subjects. My team were worried that my tragic outlook might become an epidemic amongst the Red visitors to Earth, which could then be carried back into the Seventh and Eleventh and infect other Reds.

"Already over the last few hundred years there has been a worrying sense of rebellion, angst and depression amongst Red young people. Some of them would go for an hour or more without bursting into a big belly laugh. In some colonies there were long periods of deafening silence amongst the young, no laughter could be heard, some preferred to laugh in private. The situation was becoming very serious – that's just my little joke. But it's true. Reds have started to change and become a little bit like Tells. This has given rise to a new trend in medicine: laugh doctors. There was even a new theory that Red laughter was itself a disease which demonstrated a lack of genuine care, concern and empathy in our race.

"Intelligence, logic and cleverness had always been regarded as the most important and admirable qualities for a Red. This resulted in a culture of deceit, lies and double-speak throughout the Red dimensions. No-one wanted to be revealed as inadequate in his powers of reasoning. Experiments were fudged and results of projects were exaggerated to ridiculous levels. There were many prizes and fellowships for the sciences and other intellectual pursuits, but no encouragement for what might be called the arts and social sciences in other civilisations. Laughing was pretty much the only art form for Reds. Although there was chess. That was regarded by many as an art of intellectual beauty, not merely a skill. Multi-dimensional chess was the most common game played and champions aspired to be sashed with a 'lemon-eleven'. [This phrase is impossible to translate into any Earth-bound language due to its cultural context and the significance of chess within the Red multi-dimensional society. That significance, according to Drew, outdoes any Tell passion for games, or any other pursuit including television soap operas, to a mathematical power exponentially greater than earthly imagination could grasp. One of the greater disappointments in the Red experiment with humans was the mediocre level of Tell skill in chess and some of the lesser intellectual games introduced by Reds.]

"All the opposites," Old Red mused, with a tinge of anger in his voice. "All the upsidedownědness of the world. Why do the pale people love their colour so? Why hate the other colours? They don't even like red! What intelligent creature could possibly object to that most glorious of colours? Pinkish whitey skins are silly, black and brown skins are sensible, yellowish skins have colour quality, and perhaps the milky white of the Scandinavians can be admired too, but never more than black or brown. Then there are women. In so many societies treated as inferior, kept in a lowly place, subdued in domestic imprisonment. Yet they are the half of the human race that has a proper perspective on life. They are the genuine source of all that is good about this strange species. Anything good about men, except perhaps their obsession for exploring, has been injected into them by teams from the Eleventh Dimension over 3000 years. Sorry, because you are a man and you must hear this, but it is true.

"In so much of the language of you Europeans – you North-Westers – you have created upside-down confusion. I explained all this to my Alice in Wonderland friend and to George Orwell who promptly wrote his novels Animal Farm and 1984 about these very things. Some animals are more equal than other animals and big brother is watching, they were my concepts. The abuse of language and the evil, hypocrisy and cant of politicians are two of the very things George takes great issue with and that poor old Dodgson poked fun at. Poor Dodgson, such a pity in his line of work that the juice brought on an obsession with little girls. Ah well, what's an obsession and a few erotic photographs if we also get the Alice books etcetera?

"And of course my dearly beloved Henry and Will too knew of the foul evil of lawyers – 'First thing, let's kill all the lawyers', I gave them that line – and Charlie [Dickens] depicted the law as 'a ass'. I suppose my influence can be seen, can't it? But it arose from my confusion with the way you wretched humans think. It's all up-down-sideways. You boast of a justice system, but you really mean a laws-for-the-powerful system. In my dimension there are no laws except those in the fair and righteous and common-sensical hearts of each person. 'Seny', wise old Goya would call it.

"I was not compelled into exile by others. I chose it as the fitting punishment for my crimes. Didn't even choose it. The punishment and my mind and my crimes chose each other triple simultaneously. Goodness me, I really don't have the time or strength to explain our advanced sense of legalities and justice to your meagre intellect. No insult meant, but it is true. And you, my friend, seem to be one of the more pleasant and polite men I have met in my time. You certainly know how to listen, even if thinking is not one of your strong points. Eleventh Dimension justice contains the essence of fairness and wisdom. It is never a case of the best debater wins. So hard to explain.

"Look, most of your Tell judges that I have met are fools with closed minds which can only operate on the narrow-gauge railway lines laid down by their law books which were written by other legalistic parasites – usually called politicians – at a time when the laws were not needed, or were immediately out of date, or blatantly biased towards the ruling classes. Most Tell lawyers have the same mentality as criminals and are the worst sharks in the ocean of humanity. They steal! But not through the jemmied window or the picked lock. They steal through the loophole and most often through specific laws laid down for rich people to use for their advantage.

And no matter whatever happens in the court of law, the lawyer is almost always the highest paid person in the room. The whole populace goes berserk with wonder and gratitude when a lawyer does something for free, 'off the hoof', or whatever that Latin phrase is they use. Lady Justice has to be blindfolded for women cannot bear the evil of North-West justice. Their minds are too keen; their hearts too open; their souls too soft. And from all the reports I have read from our teams spread around your world, nowhere is any different from here or there. I weep for the awful Tell concept of justice."

And he did. For several minutes. I patted his heaving shoulders and tried to console him. Stupidly, I said, "You're right of course, but things are improving. We are becoming more civilised. Don't you think?"

"You idiot," Drew groaned. "I thought you were one worthy of hearing my tales. It seems my breath and precious time have been wasted. Things are getting worse and worse and worse. Awfulness and illogic are more entrenched now and the perpetrators are becoming more and more devious. Every time a person says Justice System, or Health System, or Education System, they perpetrate three of the great lies of human societies. Each system achieves the opposite effects for which it appears to be named. Can you really imagine any creature, other than horses and dogs perhaps, learning anything useful in your schools, let alone learning how to think, how to analyse, how to fuse intellect and emotion to make proper decisions?"

His mood and anger and intensity were so fierce that I did not dare to say anything. Having been born inside a hospital, treated as a disease inside my mother which had to be cured; been educated in a school, which even I had known was a time-wasting, hypocritical and even farcical experience; and, in print, been a strong advocate of the 'rule of law' idea which now seemed so preposterous to me, I hardly felt qualified to say anything. His words were impacting powerfully on me; I felt strange and faint. The impact came not only through the words but also from startling mental images he seemed to be transmitting directly to my brain and also from the overwhelming waves of emotions he exuded as he spoke. I was being bombarded with Red Truth, which could not be adequately expressed in words alone. It was like being brain- and body- and soul-washed all at the same time. I was beginning to feel a revulsion for my own kind. I mean men, not humanity. Not that there seemed to be anything much left of my usual concept of humanity, now that I knew that many women were infected too. Thank goodness for Jane Austen.

After some minutes of pausing for breath and hoping that some answer or explanation might suddenly become a living idea in our brains, Drew spoke again, more calmly, "You are human, my friend, so what do you say? Was it worth turning Beethoven into a demented, deaf, angry, lonely, tormented man so others could play and listen to his glorious music? Was it worth sending Nijinsky mad to revolutionise dance? Was it worth the blindness inflicted on the Bulgarian sculptors so others could walk in their magnificent stone garden? Was Leonardo worth the pederasty? Were Einstein's insights worth the atom bomb? Could any of it be worthwhile?"

My brain was bursting from the impossibility of answering such riddles. And bursting from the knowledge that there was only one possible answer an Anglo-Western-centric male human being could give, unfortunately. "Yes. It was worth it. That's what all Tell history … all human history teaches us. We treasure beyond all reason every individual life and yet the greatest honour is given to those who suffer or die for others."

"You treasure life and then you have the trenches of the Great War? Treasure life and have Hiroshima? Treasure life and have the Jewish holocaust? And here I restrict myself to only three horrors of this present century. The litany of horrors could go on and on and on. The number of wars seems interminable. Bombings, large and small, never seem to stop. The list of holocausts and genocidal incidents stretches forever. You humans! The word humane, which your people so self-servingly created, can only mean in my mind evil, heartless, destructive, terrifying, awful beyond belief. For me 'he is a humane person' means he is a complete monster who will commit any crime, tell any lie, destroy any other person to get what he wants.

"Anyway I must not blame others. The Council of the Eleventh Dimension realised that I had to punish myself and strongly suggested that part of the punishment should be that I never return home. As long as I truly felt I deserved to be punished. And, of course, I did. I, Drew, who had created the Shakespeare workshop, admittedly by mistake, who had first identified the Jane Austen anomaly, who had created the Renaissance, with some help, who had created the genius ring of the Ballet Russes. And I who helped create Napoleon and Hitler and Stalin. I allowed myself to be punisher, punishee and punishment out of pity for my Red friends and lovers and society. The Tell experiment was abandoned. But the impact on Red society and intellect and history of these experiments has been overwhelmingly bleak.

"We refused to accept blame and to learn the lesson that we should never have interfered. At this moment there are Red teams on twin planets in the – never mind, just know that the planets are far far from here. It's been in the planning stages for almost a century. And despite our highly alarming reports from Earth, the projects were given approval. They are repeating the butterfly juice experiments. New, improved, greener-than-green juice, of course. But with a twist. On one planet they will create geniuses and on the other the plan is to bring the bright people down to what is called a thought comfort zone. This will mean everyone will be truly equal in intellectual abilities. This should appeal to you, my friend, as a true believer in democracy and equal opportunity.

"Also these creatures will have the ability to stop thinking so that they do not exhaust themselves as many Tell minds tend to do. So many suicides on your planet are simply due to that. Desperate people who can't deal with never-ending thought, with brain chatter. They just want some brain silence and death is the only way. Although I believe some devout Buddhists have been able to achieve brain silence without ill effects. We Reds thought perpetual mind chatter was a gift. Maybe we'll get it right on one of those twin planets. You never know. Do you?"

He looked at me desperately for a moment and then laughed. And laughed. And laughed. And laughed some more. And so did I. It seemed the only possible response.

ORIGINAL SIN – The First Intervention

On yet another nerve-wracking day for Drew, he finally told me about the most terrible thing the Reds had ever done to the human race. It was known in Red mythology and history as the 'Original Tell Error' – OTE. He closely connected this idea to the Christian idea of 'original sin'. Not only was almost all male genius created, manipulated and nurtured by this weird Red race but also the entire human race itself – its intelligence, its soul, its sense of conscience, its awareness of death – was a creation of the Reds. The essence of humanity was a fabrication, an incredible fabrication by a group of meddling, giggling fools who seemed to have virtually no control whatsoever over their bizarre experiments.

When Drew's forebears found human-like creatures developing in Africa, they decide to create a perfect race of thinking, creative, aware people. The idea was to conduct a small, limited, tightly controlled experiment which was supposed to be restricted to one or two valleys in a lush, lovely, lonely part of Africa. The parameters were simple: give the creatures sophisticated language abilities and moderately high intelligence; imbue them with personal senses of morality; enrich their sensuality, including a delight in sex beyond the animal need to ensure survival of the species.

These qualities reflected Red societal attitudes and ideals. But most of these qualities brought baggage filled up with unforeseen problems, what Reds self-indulgently called variables. Those ancient Reds could see that the morality thing could lead to the creation of a multitude of gods and to diseases such as depression, so they put a good dose of mental scepticism into the mix of that juice. The sex thing and increased sensuality was bound to lead to population explosions, if unchecked, and the sustainability of the project was based on small population growth so proper monitoring could be effective. To ensure this, the clever Reds made the population 90 per cent homosexual, figuring that 10 per cent heterosexuality would allow for moderate population growth for the life of the experiment, which was supposed to be for only 500 years or so.

The mistake in the original formula permitted each person to be 10 per cent heterosexual. When the simple Tells discovered what joy it was to have children and how the pleasure of a child's love could offset much of the pain caused by constant thinking, a population explosion occurred. Next thing, natural selection principles kicked in and many people were being born 30 per cent heterosexual, then 70 per cent and so on, until eons later we have only 10 per cent of the population, or even less according to some surveys, which is exclusively homosexual. This also explains the butterfly juice effect of bringing people back to their original, mostly homosexual, genetic state as occurred with folk like Newton, Wilde and Nijinsky who were only mostly homosexual. Wilde and Nijinsky did manage to have children after all and Drew used to say he was not even sure that Newton had ever had an erection let alone actual sexual relations.

The sex thing led to Tells having a population in the late 20th century of over six billion when, according to all Red calculations, it should have been about 600,000. Quite some variable, that one. A mix of other traits in humans, such as the wanderlust and exploration obsession, kicked natural selection along further, and soon Africa was cradle to an entire world of human monkeys and every continent became polluted with the human rabbits and their abundant offspring. To add to the incompetence of Red experimentation, the delivery method of the original-sin juice was a compound error. They put that o-s juice in the water supplies and staple grain crops of our forebears. The wind and rain cycles of the valleys kept re-infecting everyone so that no useful, accurate data could be collated. They were just lucky that the formula did not work with any other animal species, although there is some doubt as to its effect on dolphins, who are known to be very intelligent and to exhibit homosexual activity quite often. And there would never be any safe method available of reversing the experiment. Earth was stuck with Tells forever more, or at least until Tell perversity got around to destroying all life on Earth.

Male and female humans should have been attracted to their own kind. That was a basic assumption made by the early Red scientists. After all, if you see someone who looks remarkably un-like you, you tend to get scared or a little wary. If you see an attractive version of yourself, isn't it 'natural' to be inclined to fall in love with that? The ridiculously high fertility rate of humans worsened the problem. Their obsessive drive to plant their seed was not natural. Why doesn't the earth have six billion lions or six billion elephants or even six billion sharks? How can it be natural for any species to procreate to the point of the destruction of its habitat? To that question Drew could only shrug his shoulders and say, "I'm not sure we Reds are as clever as we keep thinking we are. Although we don't seem to make so many idiotic mistakes, decisions and conclusions at home as we do when we're abroad, so to speak. It's probably because at home we don't feel superior to anyone, all Reds are created equal as someone famous once said. Whereas here on earth we assume we are better than our little monkey creations. If something is going wrong we just say, 'oh well it's not as if they are Reds or somehow important.' So arrogant and cruel and stupidly wrong on our part."

SOME LATE MUSINGS

In the last weeks of my stay there were musings from Drew on a whole broad range of subjects and I admit I have selected here just a few that tend to agree with my own philosophies of life. So prepare for bias. But it is good bias because it comes from an objective observer. I mean from Drew, not myself. Well, I suppose he is as objective an observer as we have had so far as is generally known on this planet to date. If there have been other extra-terrestrial visits known to anyone, they have been kept very secret.

I did ask Drew about creatures from other planets making visits and his answer was as obfuscating as any earthly politician might be. In brief, his answer was that probably there have been visits because there is so much life and intelligence out in the universe and in the various dimensions attached to 'this universe'. Yes, that sounds like there might be other universes but Drew would neither confirm nor deny such a thing as he previously would never confirm nor deny the existence of a one-only god figure, or reincarnation, or an actual physical soul, or heaven and hell, or almost any other question I asked him that vaguely touched on spirituality.

Somewhat reminiscent of the Christian Bible and other holy texts from around the world, Drew railed against the Tell lusts for wealth, fame and power. These were the three supreme betrayals of our integrity, morality and idealism that could not be forgiven. Drew admitted that he believed that the seemingly insatiable lust for those three awful things was something innate to the very monkeys the

Reds had turned into humans. I, ungraciously, laughed at this, telling him I had never seen a monkey who wanted to be a president or to own a huge yacht or to have his photo in the magazines. And hadn't the lust become more powerful and evident over the centuries since they had been injecting the green juice? Wasn't this proof that it was the fault of the Red obsession for toying with entire races of living creatures that we Tells were so imperfect?

Drew conceded that this seemed a not unreasonable conclusion but still clung stubbornly to his belief that the butterfly juice would have worked more effectively if there had not been some basic flaws in the monkey personalities to begin with. So, to paraphrase Will-Henry, the fault is not in ourselves or our visitors from the stars but in the monkeys we came from. How convenient. Sometimes, in the last days of my visit, I found myself feeling an overwhelming sense of anger against the entire Red race. How could they have dared fiddle with nature in this way? How could they treat a whole world of beings as theirs to manipulate at will and at whim? How could there be a group of people in the universe with such arrogance?

But detest the Red race though I may, I could never bring myself to dislike Drew, the Red standing before me, telling me the tales. In many ways he was a flawed god, indirectly, my creator. I had to revere him – and the other Red gods – as the engineers of this world's human existence. And I had to revile him, and them, for the many gross errors they made. Drew sometimes mused about the idea of forgiveness and how human forgiveness was so generous and kind, whereas Red forgiveness only ever extended to themselves and was egoistic and arrogant. I often had the impression that he was gaining as much from our talks as I was, that I was offering some sort of salve to his conscience.

It was strange to feel that I was acting as confessor for the sins of a creature who was my god, my creator. There was no doubt in my mind that Drew's tale-telling was not merely to let the secret out to the broader world, but was mostly an act of repentance and confession on his part. Before he died, he wanted to clear his conscience of all the crimes he had committed against humanity. I think he felt that if an ordinary human such as myself could forgive him then he might find peace. And I did forgive him, and said so several times, because I knew it was the one thing I could give him, and I knew how important it was to him.

In our rambling talks, there were many lectures from Drew about the failings and lost opportunities by both Reds and Tells. He was contrite about Red mistakes but also railed against "that dreadful human nature thing" that we Tells were afflicted by, restrained by and doomed by. And so, in my last days with him, I received some rambling "sermons from the hammock" – a note I made at the time. It seemed almost absurd that such critiques and philosophies were coming from a creature spoilt by every possible luxury, served by an entire tribe of worshippers. But he was a person of great intellect and as far as I understood his lectures there were a great many turning points when we Tells could have forged a better world for ourselves. The long, detailed philosophies are out of place in this story but it is important that people know that Drew was a thinking, planning, organising creature as well as a bumbling Red scientist and a passionate lover of the human race. One of our discussions from our last few days will give a taste of the person he was.

"The most awfully abused word of all is democracy," Drew said. "Never properly tried on this planet. Countries that call themselves democracies right across the globe have produced various tricks and laws to prevent certain types of people from voting – women, slaves, people of various colours, criminals, the mentally deranged, children. Every democracy would be much sounder, richer and more sensible if children were permitted to vote. Democracy as a concept is in such tatters that these days only the very worst people of the very lowest intellect, spirit and morals ever stand for election. I exaggerate because my team did a study which showed that eight percent of politicians do have more good intentions than evil in them. But what chance do they stand? Where kings and queens once ruled by divine right now presidents and prime ministers rule in the divine name of democracy, the people's will. And that's an absurd concept. The Americans are particularly at fault here. What president, there or anywhere else, has ever been genuinely elected by more than about 20 per cent of all the people? I include the children when I say all the people, of course.

"Every Tell economic or political system eventually comes to believe that no action that is meant to protect the system – communism, democracy, capitalism, dictatorship, socialism – nothing done to protect them can be a crime. So eventually, each and every one of these systems commits the worst crimes imaginable, usually in secrecy. People disappear, are placed in concentration camps, are turned into state slaves, are tortured, are killed. And often this happens to entire families and, in the most horrible cases, to whole racial or religious groups. Despite its pretence to high ideals, just as many crimes are committed in the holy name and cause of democracy, as were and are committed in the names of the various gods and prophets created by Tell societies, despite each religion's claims to feel love for all humanity."

"So there is no god? God is just a human construct?" I felt quite pleased with myself for once again slipping in these loaded questions.

Drew looked at me searchingly for a long moment and then

smiled. "I can't answer that," he said very cautiously. "He wouldn't like it if I told you about that."

"Who is this he? God? So God is a man?"

"It could never occur to any truly active intellect that God would have some kind of gender, let alone a human gender. That is if such a … an entity should exist."

I sank back in my seat, defeated. "What can I do now I know all this?" I asked. "How can I just announce that the entire human race, including our procreation, recreation and creativity, is all a huge mistake made by a bunch of red-coloured people from some other dimension? That this world is the result of a botched experiment? That there's only supposed to be a few hundred thousand of us, at the very most? That most of us are supposed to be black and that pinky white skin is a side-effect of a bad experiment? That 90 per cent of us should be homosexuals? The religions of the Earth will love that last bit. How do I deal with this?"

"I don't know," Old Red said, shaking his head sadly. "Who am I to make decisions anymore? It's your turn now. You Tell people have to take your destinies in hand and shape them yourselves."

"Now that you Reds have made a total mess of it."

"Isn't that what every new generation of humans is asked to do, patch up the mess their parents made of the world? You, my friend, are a writer. You're one of the almost sensible, moderately intelligent, slightly creative humans – in other words a giant amongst men – and you're capable of seeing that the world's not right. So fix it up!"

Such faint praise. What could I say? "First of all, I'm not a giant. You're just saying that because I'm the only one you've got who might be able to spread this story around." I wanted him to know that I wasn't a complete fool and that I could see through his flattery. "Many great people have seen the problems you've explained, but throughout history no-one, not even your men of genius, has been able to fix them."

"Oh yes," Old Red sighed. "Even Einstein encouraged development of an American atom bomb. He thought it was necessary for defence, for defence only. He didn't know the Americans any better than we Reds knew the Tell species. He was such a disappointment to me. At least he had the good manners to do it outside my sector. I suppose like Galileo he did recant, in a positive and human way. Poor fat Galileo did it for the most human of reasons. He was just so very afraid of the fire. And he never saw any sense in being a martyr for science. So many nice humans in my stories. Please make sure your readers understand that."

"Did you create any geniuses who might help us survive the end of the 20th century?" I asked. "Sometimes I'm afraid that we won't even get into our third millennium."

"No-one I could recommend to you. There's the painter Francis Bacon. I had many a drink with him in Soho. His sight was impaired by the juice. [I tried later to interview Bacon but he rejected all requests. Perhaps I should not have mentioned Drew the Red man in my first letter to him.] I know that the North American team, back in the early 50s boasted that they had created a genius poet who would rival the greatest ever. Even as a child he apparently had a remarkable flair for words and for imagination and for deep compassion. His name was Robert Zimmerman, but even with my excessive scanning of television programs that's not a name I've heard of again. Do you know of him?"

"Not Zimmerman. That name's not familiar." Although I had been a Bob Dylan devotee since his early songs, I decided to keep the secret to myself. Drew was in no state to hear about the impact that folk music and rock music could have on the world. And, even to me who was a believer, the significance of the so-called protest songs and the role of pop music in keeping the world sane and hale was a case still being argued.

"Perhaps your next generation, with only traces of the green stuff in their veins, will be able to work out … some cures, solutions, remedies. I've always believed more in young Tells than I should. They do have the misfortune of having to grow up."

Red looked awfully sad. I took his hand and offered the only comforting words I could. "I will write all this. I promise. And I'll transcribe the stories as closely as I can. There's a chance that some people might take notice and recognise the … issues. Maybe your words will convince people. You have a uniquely objective view."

"People will think I'm trying to avoid responsibility for all the silly mistakes I made. Why should they take notice of a dying alien creature, in exile from his own dimension and from his own people? Why should they believe someone who created Hitler?"

"You created Shakespeare too. Well, Henry and the Shakespeare workshop anyway. And Newton, who lots of humans idolise, even if you don't. And Mozart who is now loved by everybody, even the Viennese. And there was the very kind Alan Turing, even though you also killed his beloved. Da Vinci, a paedophile but still a great genius. Beethoven. Goya. Pity about the deafness in those two. Michelangelo. Blake. Goethe."

He cut me off. Now I was name-dropping. And I could see the qualifying statements were troubling him. "I don't need a catalogue of so-called successes. We've argued those. Let me tell you the story of Wu Xiang."

THE STORY OF WU XIANG

This story was as close as Drew came to giving me a moral to pass on.

"One of my colleagues from the China Sector created a genius called Wu Xiang. This was in the 19th century. Mister Wu stepped quietly one day into the Seventh Dimension and looked about. He gained so much wisdom from this experience that each year he would take a little holiday in the Seventh – a few minutes is enough – to refresh himself and imbibe more sagacity, patience and tolerance. The rest of his time was spent in giving advice to the people of his small town. He announced to them that he would give free advice but could only stay in the town as long as the people gave his family enough food, clothing and shelter to live comfortably, with occasionally a bit of a luxury thrown in: a soft cushion; a pretty fan for his wife; fireworks to amuse his children. He needed little and was not greedy. He said that if the town did not look after him he would understand that they did not want his services and he would go elsewhere. He never forced advice on anyone, only offered it when asked. He never checked to see if the advice had been heeded. He listened for however long it took for people to tell him their troubles, sometimes hours, and then gave simple advice.

"It was soon apparent that those who went to Wu and followed his advice became happy, healthy and prosperous. No-one in his town became famous and no-one became outrageously rich. But almost everyone was happy and healthy and prosperous. They enjoyed each other's company and loved their town, which they cared for so that it became a beautiful environment in which to live. As years went by so Wu's consultations were shorter as the people had fewer problems. The ones that they did have, they were often able to solve for themselves.

"They never forgot that Wu was the source of their communal ability to feel secure and happy and well. Many pieces of advice were given casually, in the market or at the fish restaurant or strolling in the magnificent park that criss-crossed the town. People who came to the town for festivals or on business always remarked on the contentment the people there gained from their lives. And this was achieved by Wu Xiang, who was the creation of my colleague. And I so wish I had been able to do that for Europe and Russia. No-one needed a Newton, or a Mozart or a da Vinci. But every town needed a Wu Xiang. The closest I ever came was Rasputin, who began as a splendid chap and ended as crazy as a loon, demented, maniacal.

"I got caught up in the white madness that still dominates the North-West Sector – the blotchy pink, half light-brown, milky white madness. The many madnesses, in fact, of that strange Euro-Anglo-Celtic-Russian-Baltic drive to confront life head-on and wrestle with it, defeat it, become its conqueror. The Indo-Chinese spirit was always more inclined to bathe in the river of life, enjoying all its pleasures, contemplating the source of the river from the many clues the waters wash up on the river banks, but content to leave the source a mystery. The North-West mentality insists that each man must battle the current in some awful steel dreadnought until he finds the river's source, catalogues, photographs and labels it, then tears out one of its roots to hold aloft as his prize, and never mind the damage. Meanwhile, the women and children must stay and play safely on the banks of the river. If I have mixed my metaphors I apologise but it reflects my passion. I so very much wish that I had created just one Wu Xiang."

LUCIFER IN STONE

The day, near the end of our time, when Drew chose to show me Lucifer was the emotional peak, or depth perhaps, of my understanding of the enormity of the Red crime against our planet. Drew had previously shown me a wondrous Michelangelo marble that he said had needed two teams of horses to kidnap. But the second team had been used to capture and transport the Lucifer statue. Michelangelo's Lucifer was much greater than Michelangelo's David. It reached a standard of greatness hardly imaginable by the ordinary human mind. When I saw it I was stunned and fell to my knees. I wept tears of sheer fright, which soon turned to wonder at the beauty of the thing, then the tears turned into torrents of pity for us, the human race, who had been forced to live with the living model of this creature in our midst for millennia and were now hopelessly tainted by its evil.

The statue was almost double life-size. It was of Lucifer, the most beautiful angel of them all, departing from heaven, striding towards hell, his wings spread wide and angry behind him. His face was exquisitely beautiful and yet also filled with the horror of hell and the pain of hell. It revealed, as no words ever could, evil and despair and cruelty, while remaining aglow with glorious beauty. And it was almost entirely red. The flowing mane of hair glowed red.

Drew told me, "As with the David, the marble Michelangelo chose for his Lucifer was presumed to be flawed, completely the wrong kind of marble for a statue and impossible to carve. When Karrel and I first saw it our reaction was much the same as yours, tears and terror. But we had more reason for horror because this is a statue of my colleague Karrel, the one who was Michelangelo's Red mentor. That is his face, transfigured by internal demons, twisted with hatred of all Tells, determined to wreak havoc on them. So it was clear that even in the mid-sixteenth century there was at least one human being who knew what the Red race was, what we personified for your humanity. We were the living embodiment, the agents, the partners of Satan. We had to steal the statue and lock it away. This is our own version of the picture of Dorian Gray. It reveals what we truly are. No creature, let alone a whole race, should be revealed so brutally. It leaves us not a shred of dignity."

"It's no less than you deserve," I said, rather cruelly.

"I know," Drew admitted.

So where could there be a solution? Should we go back to old tribal ways that have not been tampered with by the juice? Should we start listening to women? Accept the natural order: let men explore; let women rule and make laws; let gayness abound so that people become ashamed of not being in touch with their innate and natural sexuality; nurture female genius; and applaud but also pity and restrain the male genius who will pop up occasionally? Create more workshop situations? More Turing cohorts, more renaissances, more Ballets Russes gangs? Be kind? Being kind couldn't hurt.

When the day came for me to leave, Drew wept and laughed in equal amounts, hugged me for a long time, then waved me from his house. The tribespeople were ready to take me back to the edge of what I was still calling, though with a laugh in my voice, 'civilisation'. As I reached the door, I turned to Drew, trembling, hardly daring to ask but knowing I had to, knowing I owed it to myself and to my book, our book. Before I could speak, he said, "The answer to your question is no. Definitely not. Absolutely no."

He had seen into my obvious heart and mind and pinky-blotchy-white soul. But this message he had entrusted to me was too important. An apparent answer to an unasked question was not good enough. This message needed to be delivered to the world with power and vigour and even genius. I had to ask the question aloud, in words, even though I already had the answer.

"Is there any of the butterfly juice left?"

After all, I am only human.

www.ingramcontent.com/pod-product-compliance
Lightning Source LLC
LaVergne TN
LVHW030914080826
845145LV00012B/2888

* 9 7 8 1 7 6 4 5 8 4 3 1 9 *